ae Shaw

Vampires are a common subject of fantasy tales and mainstream media. But they've got it all wrong. Follow along in the recounting of one such vampire, a lady named Deirdre, born in the year of 1640, and tragically murdered — then reborn, as a pale creature of the night — at just twenty-two years young.

This book is a work of fiction. Any resemblance to persons, living or dead, actual events, locale, or organizations is entirely coincidental.

Arian Derwydd Books, LLC

https://arianderwyddbooks.com/

The Shroud Eaters
Copyright © 2024 by Alyx Jae Shaw
ISBN: 9798227690548

All Rights Are Reserved. No part of this book may be used or reproduced in any manner whatsoever without written permission.

Chapter One

It is difficult to know where to begin this tale, as it has its origins firmly entrenched in centuries past, but I shall do my best to relate my story without making it tedious. I suspect my tale shall earn me no friends, but then, being dead does tend to make one unattractive.

My name is Deirdre, and I was born in Leeds in the year 1640, two years before the royalists took the town over, and within the sound of the church bells of Briggate. My father was very much enchanted with the area, which at the time was little more than a small town, concerned with corn and cloth. However, one day it would become a great and lovely city. Of course, that was not until after the cloth market was moved into Briggate in the year 1684, and I had been dead twenty-one years by then.

Dead, and yet not dead.

Fortunately, I did live long enough to see that bastard Cromwell dug up and hung. 'Twas most fitting and a day of great joy in my home after so long having to live in joylessness, paying homage to a faith not our own and seeing dear friends dragged away to not be seen again. The day his wretched body was dragged from the earth that did not wish to be poisoned by his filth, my mother and I fell deep within our cups and ran 'bout the house and courtyard bare-breasted. My father forever referred to this as the Feminine Uprising. My brothers mentioned it not at all and forbade me from doing so as well.

I was born and raised a lady, and to that I hold true, though granted the times have changed and the meaning of the word with it. Still, there are teachings to which I adhere, even in these strange days of computers and television and cars. I behave within the parameters accorded by my station and gender. I do not swear, nor drink in excess, nor behave in an unseemly manner if I can avoid it, or unless the situation warrants such antics, as in, say, the symbolic hanging of a despotic mule's hindquarters. I am always clean and properly dressed, though I confess the latter has become something of a trial in this day of skimpy tops and low-slung jeans. I am sorry for my lack of modern fashion sense, but after more than three hundred years in hoop skirts and bodices and corsets and petticoats and bustles I simply am *not* comfortable with my navel on display for every pervert and cad I may encounter. Fashionable or not, I wear my full skirts.

It is strange to me how much is forgotten over the centuries. New knowledge seems to push out old, and while I delight in this age of science and reason, I am also troubled. Lore that was once passed from mother to child is now lost or deemed "fairy tales" and dismissed as nonsense. Let us look at the tales regarding vampires, for example, they being rather near to my heart, so to speak. These days so many believe that there is but one way to kill a vampire. Certainly, a stake through the heart would give me cause for concern, but if the stake were to come loose, I would recover. To kill me one needs must stake my heart, then cut off my head and turn it face down.

Sunlight, also, would do me considerable harm were I unable to escape it. However I am but one kind of vampire, and there are as many types of vampires as there are methods of creating them.

Being bitten is the most common method to become a vampire, according to trite childish books and films produced by fools who cannot be bothered to learn their lore. But the truth is far more gruesome. Indeed, there are as many ways to become a vampire as there are ways to kill one. Being bitten rarely results in the creation of another vampire. If such were the case then all the world would be naught but vampires, for even though we feed rarely, we do feed, and while I am no mathematician, it seems to me that one vampire becomes two becomes four becomes eight becomes sixteen becomes eventual unwanted world domination. As for this vile exchanging of blood, with the bitten tasting the blood of the vampire, this does nothing more than convince the victim that there are better ways in which to spend one's evening and leads to the perusal of websites discussing Hepatitis and AIDS. Permit me to expound upon a few of the many ways of becoming undead.

To become a vampire, one must be born on a certain day, with a caul over one's face. Such is the sign of one who will seek the blood of the living in death. An executed murderer may rise from his cursed and shallow grave to seek the blood of animals and babes in the cradle. A seventh son is especially cursed if his mother shunned salt during her time with child. One who takes his own life will surely arise to walk the night, as will those who are buried without proper funeral rites. And those who have had their lives taken unfairly will return as the walking dead. This I know from personal experience.

I was twenty-two when I was murdered by a mindless, pretty, tittering thing whose only use was to flatter my husband and give him sons. The first I did admirably. The second duty I performed with less success. By the time I was flung down the stairs I had given him three daughters, and he was not pleased with my efforts. A physician claimed that I was birthing only daughters to spite him, which was not true. Even if I possessed the ability to choose the sex of my child, I would never have done such a thing, for it would have surely disgraced my mother. Though I loved both my parents, my mother was my dearest friend, and never would I repay her years of gentle kindness with disrespect and hateful behaviour. I swore upon my knees to my husband I did not know why I bore only girl-children. To this day, still, can I see him looming over me as I wept.

"Why is it you refuse to do your duty to your husband?" he shouted, his hands in his hair, his face redder than fall apples. I knelt before him, frightened and confused by this outburst.

"I am with child again!" I cried. "Perhaps this is the son you desire!"

"It is not my son you carry, but yet another girl-child!" he shouted. "The physician attending you says thus!"

I became angry. "He knows not what I carry, for what magic has he to peer into my womb? I do not recall him peering into that opening which the child entered!"

My husband found my remark to be without humour. He threw me down the great stone staircase of his house and told my father later that I tripped upon the rug. Tripped. Oh, how I laughed at that. He dragged me forcibly by my hair as I screamed and thrashed, and the servants watched. After all, was I not his property to do with as he pleased? And was I not willfully spiting him? I was flung as the butcher does the offal to the crows, my bones crunching as I bounced. My laugh, however, was the last, for I was with child again at the time of my murder, as I had told him, and the physician showed his ignorance. It was not a daughter, but the son my husband Thomas desired, and so it was he murdered not only his wife, but his legacy as well.

After my murder, I was laid to rest in the family crypt, but eternal sleep did not come to me. As the sun sank and a great and vile storm descended over the manor in which I died, I felt a cold, ghastly will creep into my broken body. I opened my eyes to find myself in a vault of stone, laid on a marble slab in a gown of white lace, a crucifix clutched in my dead pallid hands. Slowly I sat up, feeling the cold marble beneath me, thinking it odd that I could still experience such things. I placed my hand upon my breast, and felt no heartbeat, nor did I draw breath. I knew then the horrible truth—that I was condemned to walk the night until all who had wronged me lay dead.

I reached into my mouth and felt the long, sharp fangs. They filled me with horror, yet also with wonder. However was I to use them? Did I bite the throats of my victims as I had heard tell? Killing is not knowledge with which one simply awakes possessing. One must *learn* to kill, and however difficult it is for the vampire, I suspect it is far worse for one's victim, suffering the terror of the experimental bites until one finds the correct place upon the body and begins to feed. Which leads me to another ridiculous notion I feel compelled to mention.

I can assure you the proper place to bite is *not* the throat. One does not gracefully pierce the carotid artery and daintily sip as modern folklore would portray. The blood pulsing through that mighty vessel travels with such power that I can tell you from personal experience it is not unlike placing the end of a hose into one's mouth and turning it on full strength. Assuredly blood *does* flow; it shoots down one's throat and gushes out the lips and explodes from one's nostrils like ghastly red dragon fire.

It was not my most shining moment as either a lady or a vampire.

The physician was the first to feel my ire. I did not feed upon him; rather I tore out his tongue for spreading such lies against me and left him cowering in a pool of his own water and blood. Next, I sought my husband, who had been so very concerned with producing an heir he thought nothing at all of breeding me like a bitch, then killing the unwanted whelps in creative ways so as not to draw suspicion. I bit his throat as he lay sleeping with his favourite courtesan, a foul wench with knowledge of herbs and poisons. I had little doubt that 'twas she who aided my husband in the disposal of my daughters. This, of course, was my inelegant moment of exhaling blood, but both he and his wench were so drunk neither stirred as I painted the room in my very singular manner. I drained my husband of his life's blood, managing to swallow enough for my own needs. When I departed, the wench slept still. She would awake to find herself accused of cruelly maiming one physician and drinking the blood of her lover. After all, it could hardly have been me, his poor dead wife. No, it must have been the cheap harlot, who lay all night long in his blood, like some foul witch.

Investigative methods were lacking in 1663, but sometimes justice was served regardless.

After my deeds, I fled to my mother. I cannot say why; perhaps a need to return to a place of safety overwhelmed my common sense. I know I put her in a great deal of danger doing so, and she, poor dear, did not believe my tale of being the walking dead. Rather she thought me fortunate to have escaped a premature burial. Much of the blood had washed away in the great tempest raging outside, and when my mother saw me, I was more wet and muddied than blood-soaked. She gave me money and a horse, and, after permitting me to bathe and properly attire myself, sent me on my way, unknowingly protecting a daughter dead and cursed and no longer worthy of her love. I never saw her again. I could not. Word would have spread of a mysterious woman visiting her in the night, and I would not have her harmed. Indeed, she had been harmed enough, and she need not be followed by tales of consorting with unclean monsters, lest she herself fall under the unfavourable eye of her peers.

Long I wondered why I yet exist. The only possible explanation is that one involved in my death survived my night of vengeance. I have learned to carry on and make the best of things, for peace, I fear, shall not come. Those who wronged me are long turned to dust.

* * *

I cannot say I have lived a hard life. At least I do not see it as such. I have done what one needs must to get along in vampire society, although these tales of nests and roosts and clans and houses are the silliest form of drivel. We are rare creatures; I cannot emphasize that enough. We could not remain creatures of myth if there were whole feudal dynasties of us. And wherever did this idea come from that we have a loathing of werewolves? I have known three werewolves in my lifetime; they were all quite lovely people. Indeed, the pairing of werewolf to vampire is as natural as that of squirrel to tree, or horse to hay. The werewolf changes at night. The vampire sleeps by day. Each defends the other at his most vulnerable, and each benefits the other. Whyever do people insist on spewing nonsense; is there a shortage of which I am not aware? I find it highly unlikely. However, I must repeat my earlier remark that there are many different kinds of vampire, and the tale which I am about to tell begins with my encounter with the darkest and most cursed kind: the shroud eater.

Most vampires prey upon the living—some upon babes in the cradle, some upon animals, some, such as myself, upon mankind. We take very little, and there are so few of us that we are rarely suspect in our deeds. But the shroud eater preys only upon other vampires, and feels none of their restrictions. While sunlight will turn me to ashes, the shroud eater simply rots, and collects flies and maggots as he lies stinking. His name comes from the caustic bile he vomits up as he decomposes, soaking the cloth of his burial shroud and causing it to rot away, and thus appear as if he has gnawed upon it. A brick lodged firmly between the jaws was thought to solve all, and the vile creature would be buried again, but as I said, we vampires are very rare creatures. Often, we are desperate to see one of our own kind, and shroud eaters are not without their deceits. Their favourite trick is to whisper, and to beseech for release. Many a vampire has mistaken this for one of their own, trapped cruelly by the stake, and has unearthed the monster, their error discovered too late. A wise vampire is wary of the whisper in the dark, and will ask questions, for while a shroud eater may speak, he is mindless. A vampire pinned by a stake may still converse, but a shroud eater only parrots. During the time of the Black Death there were many of these horrors accidentally unearthed, as mass graves were dug to hold the bodies of the unfortunate.

Oh, yes, the plague. Too well do I recall the plague. I was too small to really understand the full horror of it when it swept through Leeds in 1645, as my family managed by some divine plan of God to remain untouched. However, the Great Plague of 1665 that came two years after my death saw me within its blackened heart. It was burned into my mind, and all the horrors that went with it, especially the murder of dogs and cats that heralded its arrival.

Even as ignorant as I was of how such things as plague were spread, the torture and beating to death of small animals seemed like no solution to me. If it was truly miasmas causing the death, would not the people have been better served by the freshening of the air? But nay, that was not to be. The dogs died, as did the cats. Some were simply disposed of by knife or cudgel, but others were subjected to horrors that surely must have been an offense to God Himself. Dogs were starved to the point of madness, and then released into a pit to savage one another, the winner devouring the loser. Cats were hung up by their tails to tear each other asunder, and then left as sport for the ravens. Beloved beasts were murdered, ripped from the arms of the children that cherished them to meet a fate so cruel I cannot fathom how men who consider themselves decent Christians could do such a thing.

As the dogs and cats died, the rats moved in, sensing that the sentries were no longer at their posts. I had wondered at the time if the rats were not the true bringers of the plague, but common knowledge of the day dictated that it was the foul miasmas that clung to the coats of mongrels spreading illness, and I had not knowledge enough to think what else it could possibly be. Certainly, it could not be the fleas! How could something so small and foolish and insignificant bring man to his knees?

The death spread so very quickly—first from flea to man, then from man to man by coughing. There was no escape. If one person in a family showed symptoms, then all were nailed into the house together, and in nearly every instance met their fate together as well, burning mad with fever and pain as the ghastly buboes burst forth with the fetid black mire that gave the malady its name. How many children, I wonder, in this refined age of immunization and proper sanitation, understand the charming little ditty they sing to this day in the playgrounds? How many realize it came into being from the plague?

"A ring around the rosy" speaks of the red rings surrounding the bites from infected fleas upon one's body. *"A pocket full of posy"* refers to the futile clutching of fragrant herbs and flowers to one's face to ward off the miasmas, the "foul air" that seeped from the ground and clung to the coats of dogs. Granted with horses and pigs and such all about, parts of London hardly smelled as does a garden, so I can see from where the belief that the stink was bringing the plague emerged . *"Hush-a, hush-a"* is a child's mimicry of the sneezing caused as the victim's lifeblood seeped through their lungs. At times it was possible to even sneeze out small portions of one's lung tissue.

As for *"we all fall down"*, I should think that is self-explanatory.

Still the worst was yet to come, for as the people died and reputable healers fled the area, the charlatans came with vile pretences at cures; buboes were lanced painfully with burning hot pokers and left to fester. Useless cures were sold for many times their worth to folk so pathetic and desperate they would have tried anything at all to become well. I still recall seeing the charlatans, moving about in ghastly leather masks that gave them the appearance of terrible birds, through avenues of death. They were draped in strange clothing intended to ward off the bad air, but in fact warded off the fleas, the true bringers of death. They walked from fetid house to fetid house, and the screams of misery that followed their presence was like a demonic symphony rising unto the heavens.

I did not bother to hide myself from the living during this time. There was no reason. There were only two sorts of people about: the dying and the monstrous.

I did what I could for the plague victims, which in far too many cases was simply a merciful dagger to the throat. Was it not better to die quickly than to permit them to linger in agony? My mother had taught me that a lady shows humility by bringing comfort to the ill and doing God's work, though I harboured no doubts in my breast that this was not at all what she had intended. My gown became soaked in blood and plague-bile, and I became a blasphemous saint of mercy for the dying, walking from house to house in the fog-soaked darkness, slipping inside of the hovels of the impoverished dying to end their misery. How did I appear to them, I wonder? What thoughts did they have as they saw a lady with golden hair appear beside their bed, crucifix in one hand, dagger in the other? Did they think me to be angel or a witch, or did their fevered minds pay me any heed at all? Only once did any speak to me: a little girl with hair of fire, and green eyes like gems. She lay amidst the dead bodies of her family, waiting her own fate. As I bent over her, she spied the cross about my neck.

"Are you the one who rides the pale horse?" she asked.

"Nay, child, I have no horse. Whatever makes you ask such a thing?"

"You are too dirty to be an angel."

"I am not an angel, nor am I he who rides the pale horse. I am simply Deirdre."

I gave her gin enough to send her to the land of dreams and then cut her throat. There was nothing else I could do; the buboes were already growing upon her. Then, after my fell deed was done, I awaited the pretenders with their hideous masks and bloody cures that cured nothing save any last moments of peace the dying may have coming.

I feasted upon their blood openly, sometimes even felling them in the street before their morbid peers. I made no effort to hide my crimes or my presence. There was far too much death all around for the body-carters and gravediggers to take any notice, and the charlatans were missed not at all. I fed and grew powerful on the blood of monsters and freely roamed the streets, safe within my cocoon of plague.

The dead were wrapped hastily in shrouds and thrown into mass graves, there being far too many for a proper burial, and oft times they were unblessed as well, the priests rotting alongside their parishioners. In such conditions it was only to be expected that a handful of the unsanctified dead should rise from the tainted earth and seek their tormentors. However, the ones that did rise were wholly unlike myself. Too well I recall seeing them come up from the steaming earth, caked with grave mould, their burial shrouds rotted about the mouth from the bilious vomit that comes with death. I watched them with curiosity, hoping these grisly hatchlings may prove suitable companions.

They arose from their deathbed, allowing the clots of earth and their rotted shrouds to fall as they may, then stood, some in silence, some uttering a low, droning moan. Foolishly, I stepped forth and greeted them, and immediately realized I was naught but prey to these things. Screaming, they ran for me at such a pace that even I, for all my infernal powers, was hard put to out-distance them. I ran for all I was worth, scaling buildings, leaping from one rooftop to another, all the while with these creatures close upon my heel. In that time, I came to understand the terror and desperation the fox must feel as the hounds chase it to exhaustion and finally destruction.

I ran and I ran, but they were not to be shaken. They were very nearly as swift as I, and I did not doubt their intention was to feast upon my cold flesh. They were utterly single-minded in their hideous pursuit, relentless in their appetites. There would be no succour once they laid their clawed hands upon me, no negotiation, no treaty. They would tear me into pieces and leave what was left to moulder and draw maggots.

Driven to utter desperation, I dove into the cellar of a house and barred the door. My thoughts were that these beasts would be forced, as I was, to seek shelter from the murderous sun. And, indeed, as time passed, they seemed to do just that. Had someone been there to instruct me, I would have known they simply were distracted by other prey more easily captured and had left me in my crypt to sleep away the morbid day whilst they sought easier meat.

    I lingered in London until the Great Fire, begun in a Pudding Lane shop in the small hours of a September morning of 1666, seemed to toll the final days of the city. I departed and became a wanderer of the world until, centuries later, I found myself dwelling in the city of Vancouver in Canada. Here I found a place much to my liking, and this is where my tale truly begins.

Chapter Two

It was late one evening in September, and I was going home, my cloak pulled over my face and my violin in the case. It is true that even the walking dead must earn their way, and I do not understand from whence the idea comes that being a vampire guarantees one endless wealth. If only it were true! I would feast nightly upon pretty virgin boys and keep a great stable of terrible nightmares, and at day I would lie upon my bed clad in black velvet. Alas, I must instead bring nightly disgrace upon my mother by playing a violin for coins before the stone lions of the library, or on Robson Street, or other suitable places. I prefer the songs of my youth, but I catch more coin with such tunes as "Purple Haze" and "Gangster's Paradise."

I do not know where my dear mother is buried, but I swear each night I hear her doing veritable handstands within her grave.

I learned to play over a century ago, when it became quite clear that being pretty was not going to keep me housed and cemeteries had lost their meagre charm. Coffins and crypts are all well and good, but oddly enough people do seem to take notice of mysterious figures coming and going from a cemetery at night. It seemed wiser to sing for my supper, so to speak, than to sleep with the dead. Crypts are rarely private; mourners come, as well as grave robbers and body snatchers... I should like a farthing for every time I frightened the life out of some ne'er-do-well creeping about where he oughtn't. Well, since he was kind enough to offer himself as an evening meal I could hardly refuse, could I? But still, I had long ago concluded a small apartment would be far more suitable than a sarcophagus, as people rarely take fits when seeing one leaving an apartment.

It is with no small amount of pride that I say I am very good at the violin. I make enough money to have a tiny but acceptable flat in Kitsilano on Vine Street near Cornwall Avenue, a most agreeable area of the city of Vancouver. It is close to the beach and overlooks the mountains, and I have furnished it in a manner that pleases me. Much of my furniture is antique of course—and all of it purchased new. I do have one small indulgence—a pet guinea pig. She's perfectly silly, and of course my mother would have had fits over my keeping company with a rodent. But I cannot argue her charm, and it does make me smile to hear her squeak excitedly when I come in the door just before dawn. Such a simple little creature, made so happy by a handful of dandelions. I have named her Florence, and it was she who was foremost in my mind as I hurried along the street one night, when I was suddenly distracted by a soft noise above my head, a sound only a vampire would have heard.

I looked up and detected the scent of one of my own kind: blood, cold, and the grave. I could not think what he might be doing out so close to dawn, unless he, like me, was hurrying home before the sun caught him. Still, it is so rare to see another vampire that I had to let him know of my presence. I placed my fingers in my mouth and whistled shrilly. I felt my mother roll her eyes and faint. Still, it was worth it; a moment later his head popped over the rooftop edge on the building 'neath which I stood. I curtseyed as prettily as I was able and giggled as he began cautiously creeping head-first down the side of the little three-story apartment building, like some curious spider, his long curling dark hair hanging, his white cable-knit sweater nearly falling off due to his inverted position.

"Good morning, my lord!" I said. "And where are you off to at such speed?"

"Well, perhaps you could answer that. Has a maiden so fair as yourself room upon her floor for a vagrant?"

I confess I was taken aback, but then I glanced up at the sky. Time was short. "Very well. But let us make haste. And if your intentions, sir, are to take advantage—"

"Only of your hospitality, I assure you. I've spent the entire night looking for a suitable hole in which to hide. My own is destroyed."

"Then let us make haste, for the night dies quickly."

I led him to my apartment, which is in a pink, three-story building built to look like a Victorian manor, and we darted inside swiftly, away from the burning death of the sunlight. I drew the blinds and curtains, then lit a few candles before setting about making tea.

"We've not been properly introduced," I said. "I am Deirdre of Leeds."

"Your servant, dear lady. I am Stuart Cooper of London, and wholly beneath you, judging from your speech."

"Quite likely," I said primly, smiling as he gave me a sour look.

"Humility is a virtue," he chided gently.

"Humility is for the humble, sir, and after surviving on my own for over three centuries I do not much feel the need to titter and avert my eyes and play at being weak and foolish so some man need not fear for the health of his privates. Do you like sugar in your tea?"

"Just milk, please."

"Milk you shall have. How came you to lose your home?"

He seated himself at my small dining table. "My own foolishness. I've none to blame but myself. I'd been alone so very long…"

I began to have the horrible feeling I knew what he was about to say. I kept silent and let him tell his tale.

"I have been living in the Mountain View Cemetery, near Fraser Street. It's a very large one, and over a century old, so it has many old plots. I made a home in one not likely to have visitors. But you know what a cemetery is like. You know the whispers and the mutters of the dead."

"I know to be very careful of them," I said softly.

"Indeed. I thought I knew as well. But I had been alone so long I let my common sense grow dust. I was at the far end of the graveyard one night, when I heard a voice beseeching release. I began digging. But when I reached the casket, I realized my mistake."

I closed my eyes and felt my heart grow sick within me. "It was one of them."

He nodded. "Aye. And I set it loose."

"Did you not bury it again?"

"Indeed, I did, and quickly. But you know what they are like once they catch the scent of one of us. I gathered a few things and took to the rooftops with all haste. It is no short trek from there to here on foot. And now here I am, homeless. You would think after a century I would know the difference between a vampire and... one of them."

"A shroud eater," I whispered.

"Have you ever seen one?"

"Not since I was in Italy in 1813. One was unearthed by some overly enthusiastic fellow searching for Roman silver. What he found was a corpse with a brick in its mouth, and he promptly removed the brick. I departed the area with all due haste."

"This may be rather forward of me," said Stuart, "but what were you doing in a cemetery in Rome?"

"I was searching for a dark place in which to spend the day, and some mad gravedigger was seeking wealth. I was ultimately forced to seek refuge beneath a church. I spent the entire day fearing I might burst into flames at any moment." I served the tea and seated myself. "I can assure you I have not been back to Rome since. I fear that horror may be awaiting me."

"They are nothing if not persistent." Stuart peered at the cage in which Florence sat. "I beg your pardon, but is that a guinea pig?"

"It is indeed a guinea pig, and her name is Florence."

"So not for eating, then."

"Certainly not!"

I watched as he reached into the cage to pick up Florence. She is brown with a great deal of hair pointed in all directions. I confess, though it is with love, she appears as if she has repeatedly suffered a dreadful fright. I waited until I was satisfied that Stuart's intentions were only to pet, and not to feast, before I turned back to my tea.

"So did the creature find your lair, or do you not know?"

"I do not know," said Stuart, petting Florence gently. "I did not wait around long enough to find out. As I said, they are most persistent, and once they catch the scent of the undead, they do not stop until their ghastly appetite is sated." He paused and gave me a quizzical look. "My lady, why on earth are you smiling?"

"Not because I enjoy hearing about shroud eaters, I assure you," I said. "But it is so good to have one of my own kind with whom to converse."

He smiled. "It is nice, isn't it? Though I am certain Florence is very good company, too."

"I find her political insights most enthralling. Did you know there is not a single conflict happening in the world today that cannot be solved by a proper application of lettuce and carrots?"

"Ah ha! It is as I long suspected, then."

I laughed. It was almost startling to hear that sound burst forth from myself. How long had it been? I forget at times how very solitary my life is, and how very lonely. But here before me was a very handsome young man, and from near my own birthplace and century, too. Would it not be lovely if we could be friends?

"The sun will be over the horizon in but a few minutes," I said. "Let us finish our tea and make ready for bed. We can finish our conversation tomorrow night."

* * *

I was awakened in a most unseemly fashion — by having a pillow slammed down upon my head. I opened my eyes to see Stuart across the room of my tiny apartment.

"Might I ask why you felt the need to abuse me thusly?" I inquired heatedly.

He pulled open the curtains, and I sat up. Outside the sky was black as death, and the rain was slashing down. I heard a quiet rumble of thunder.

"'Tis a day fit for vampires," said Stuart. "If you've something pending, you'd best see to it."

I threw back the covers and rose to my feet. Things do indeed pile up when one is undead. It is terribly difficult to find an all-night shoe store, for one thing, as well as a fabric store, or pet store if one is partial to owning and keeping hairy, brown, squeaky rodents. Not to mention music stores and numerous *other* things one must have if one wishes to live outside of the crypt. Because I no longer partake of mortal food, I do manage to earn enough to keep my tiny one-room apartment and purchase such things as I require, but I am hardly wealthy enough to be able to afford to have all these things delivered in the dead of night. So a dark and storming day is very exciting for a vampire who dwells not in the grave.

"How long will it last?" I asked him, stepping behind a screen so that I may change.

"The Weather Channel says it is an enormous storm, expected to last for days, but that is what they said of the last storm, and it was gone and done in four hours. So we make haste. A sunny day is no place for the likes of us."

"And what of you?" I asked.

"I thought I would go back to my crypt briefly. I left behind a few things I would like to reclaim."

I did not care for the sound of that at all. "I do not think that is a very good idea. If we may move about on dark days, then a shroud eater may as well."

"Trust me, my lady, daylight is of no consequence to a shroud eater."

As this was the first time I heard of this detail, I forgot about my state of partial undress and threw aside the screen, staring in horror. Stuart gazed back at me.

"I take it my lady was unaware of this detail?"

"Yes, I most certainly was! How is it the sun does not burn them as it does us?"

"That I do not know. But they fear not the sun. Such is the way of things; each creature has its advantages. We are intelligent, and swift, but are hampered by the day. They are witless, but they may travel while we sleep."

"And you did not think to tell me this before I permitted you to sleep upon my couch?! What if it had followed us? What if it had come upon us and…?"

"I am most sorry, my lady, I thought you knew this. Forgive me."

"I will *not!*" I pulled the screen forth once more and resumed changing. "I don't suppose it would do me any good to throw you out of my home now. Not, I confess, that I wish to. Company is a rare treat. Even shockingly slow-witted company."

"My lady, for it to reach us here it would first have to pass the front door, somehow find the third floor, *after* locating the stairs because I have my doubts one could operate the elevator, and then breach your door. And it would have to manage this feat all without someone seeing a bloated walking corpse and shrieking his or her fool head off."

"I am *not* placated. If I awaken partially consumed, I shall know whom to blame."

"And I shall take my punishment like a man as you soundly thrash me with your own severed limb."

"As well you should." I finished dressing and stepped out from behind my screen. "I've just had a thought."

"I thought I smelled flash powder."

I chose to ignore his attempt at humour. "If we feed while we are out, we could spend the evening in for a change."

He laughed. "Vampires having a night in? What a perfectly perverse thought. I like it. Very well.

We shall meet back here and spend an evening in. I've a few bottles of wine in my cellar…"

"Do you not mean crypt?"

"It is dark and cold, and below ground; it is suitable to both tasks. I shall fetch the wine. I shall even share."

"Then I shall buy candles, and we will watch a moving picture together."

"Wonderful. Anything but vampires, those films frustrate me endlessly."

We left the apartment and went down the three flights of stairs to the lobby. My apartment is tiny, but it is all I require. I could have taken one larger, but I would have been obligated to take one in a less pleasant area. Here there is beauty all around; gardens and parks and pretty shops and playhouses, all within a short walk. No, I should not part with my little home, a mere few dozen feet from the beach. Not unless I was without choice.

I turned my head to look at Stuart and felt fear grasp my heart. There are so very few of us, and this man was such a gift, for he was from both my country and century. Though I had known him less than one day, I knew we shared a bond we would be most heartbroken to tear asunder. Loneliness is a dark curse the living cannot fully grasp. To be alone as we, they would need to travel far, to a distant place, and strand themselves amidst unfamiliar folk. Yet even then, they are with their own kind. The living and the dead make poor company for one another, despite what these foolish tales of romance say. Does one make love to a cow before one eats it? Does one seduce the lamb before it is lead to slaughter? They are meat and little more, and to take one into my life would be not unlike taking in a pet, though a treacherous one to be sure. The living cannot be trusted. Their fancies change, their hearts are fickle, and I have no desire to awaken screaming in the full light of the sun. I have endured one murder. It was enough.

"Do be careful, Stuart."

"And you also."

He squeezed my gloved hand, and then he was gone, moving swiftly in the direction of the old cemetery. I raised my umbrella and hastened to the fabric shop, praying the storm held out.

Chapter Three

I was terribly glad to be home. I was soaking wet right through my coat and skirts, and while I may not feel the cold as sharply as once I did, I do still feel it, and being drenched is as unpleasant as it ever was. I put away my bundles of fabric and the food I had purchased for Florence, along with the other odd bits, then placed the newly purchased golden candles upon the white lace tablecloth near the silver candle holders. I would set them up when I was done with my bath. Oh, what a blessing hot running water is! I still delight in simply turning on a tap and being gifted with clean, heated water. Too well do I recall London before the construction of a proper sewer system and the filthy Thames water that spread cholera and death. I also recall hauling water from a well to boil. Hot water within one's own home, readily available, is indeed a gift.

I bathed and changed, then peered outside to see how the storm fared. It was still in full bluster, so I decided to open the curtains, since it was too late in the day to affect me even if the weather should clear. Satisfied that all was as it should be, I decided to watch the evening news. I despise television, but it is a useful tool in keeping one current, though I refrain from watching too much of it for fear it may have an adverse affect upon my vocabulary, which is affected quite enough by the changing times. 'Tis quite bad enough I play the violin for coins before the playhouse and library; I cannot imagine what my mother would think were my speech to degrade into "Yo mama, what up?"

I was horrified by what appeared before me on the television screen. The police had discovered a body near an old crypt in the large cemetery, clad in a white cable knit sweater. The remains of this unfortunate appeared quite old — at least a century — and the police were of the opinion that youths had broken into the tomb to ransack it for what treasure they may find. Unable to locate any living relatives, they had replaced the bones in the crypt and closed the door, vowing to look into the matter. However, I knew in my heart all too well what had happened. It was not thieves or vandals responsible for the desecration; it was the shroud eater, and poor Stuart had fallen prey to its vile appetites.

Selfish beast that I am, I confess I wept as much for my own continued loneliness as I did for Stuart. I wept also in anger, clenching my fists until my fingernails cut bloodless crescents into my hands. How dare this monster slaughter a man who had seen the fall of Cromwell, and the restoration of the Monarchy? How dare this vile corpse that had no thoughts left to call its own destroy a man who had seen the Great Fire of London and the horrors of the plague? How dare this monstrous abomination kill the only friend I have had to call my own in centuries?

"Poor Stuart," I whispered in the darkness of my small apartment, the only light that of the television. "Poor, foolish Stuart. I shall miss you deeply."

* * *

I decided to go to bed. I had already fed for the night, and I was of no mind to chance an encounter in the darkened city streets with a ravenous fiend. I had to assume it caught my scent from Stuart and as such would be tracking me, though of course I had no proof. However, there was little I could do about that for the moment. Hiding seemed to be the most prudent decision, as leaving my cozy nest would most certainly leave me vulnerable to predation. I was safer in my apartment.

I changed into my night dress and lay down in my bed, taking care to shut the heavy drapes and blinds over my large windows. I have what is called in the modern vernacular a "bachelor suite,", so there is but one room, apart from the small chamber in which the sink and bath reside. However, I have drapes around my bed as well as over my windows, both as additional protection against any stray beams of light and to convey a sense of personal privacy. It is simply not proper to have one's bed on display.

I lay in the darkness, my eyes closed, trying not to think of poor Stuart. I desired only rest and was angry that sleep may not come until sunrise. I remember dreaming fondly, though it seems but a fantasy to me now, so long has it been since last I dreamt. The dead do not dream. And yet, as I lay there, it seemed to me as if I *was* dreaming. The room became uncommonly dark as the streetlights outside failed, and the soft hum of electricity ceased throughout the building, leaving me in utter silence save for the noise of the storm for the first time in many years. It was hardly to be wondered at, I supposed; the tempest outside was terribly fierce. Certainly, power lines were bound to come down.

I closed my eyes and listened to the gale as the wind rattled at my window and whistled down the narrow alleys. Is it strange, I wondered, that the sounds of darkness still frighten me, even though I am now one of the things that goes bump in the night? Perhaps not, for even I have my own monsters in the closet.

It was nearing dawn, and sleep was finally claiming me when I heard a faint sound, like that of someone trying my door. There came a quiet click, and the door opened. It was very difficult for me to respond to the noise, which was not at all a common reaction on my part. Ordinarily, I would have been up and away. But for some reason I cannot grasp, it was as if I was nailed to my very bed. I could hardly even open my eyes, and it was with great difficulty I managed to whisper a name.

"Stuart?"

I reached up weakly to pull aside one of the bed-curtains, my eyelids unwilling to stay open. Never had I been so unspeakably tired, and I wondered if I had not been afflicted with some strange spell. I saw nothing unexpected in the darkness at first. Then, as the moments dragged on, I saw a form take shape, and a stench assailed my nostrils. It was as if the very particles of night came together to form something so hideous, so horribly blasphemous, that Hell itself would not lay claim to it. How it managed to find me or even enter the building I do not know, nor do I care to speculate. What I do know is that upon seeing the creature, whatever spell I was under seemed to end abruptly.

It screamed as it threw itself upon me. I shrieked and, with strength I did not know I possessed, kicked the foul thing off the bed. Now it has been pointed out to me that when one is under duress, one behaves quite unlike themselves. Common sense dictated I should quit my apartment with all due haste. Something else, however, tacked on the addendum — not without Florence.

As the monster struck the floor, I snatched up a robe and my guinea pig. Neither of them was hardly useful, but I was not running about in only my night dress, and I certainly was not leaving my only companion behind to fend for herself. By then the shroud eater was rising to its feet, and as I was debating whether the door or the window would make a more suitable egress, the monster shrieked and lunged for me. I would dearly enjoy stating that I rose to the challenge, met the beast, and thrashed it soundly, as appears to be the fashion for ladies in the movies to do. However, women of my time and station were simply not taught how to slow bullets with the mind and deliver lethal strikes to the head as part of their upbringing. I fear my battle tactics lean far more to shrieking like a fool and running about in circles.

However, lacking as my fighting skills may be, I was keenly aware that I had one very real and serious problem. There was less than an hour before the sun came up, and while the shroud eater would not be in any way affected by this, I most certainly would be. Time was not on my side, and I could not stay in my apartment. I was in dire need of asylum, and there was only one place of which I could think that may be suitable – the small room in the basement in which the building's caretaker stored his tools. The walls were of cinder block, and the door was steel to keep out thieves. It was my only chance at salvation.

I fled my apartment, racing down the hall to the stairs. I was hardly going to await the lift in this situation. I hurried down the stairs as quickly as I was able, hearing the fetid beast rapidly pursuing me. While it is true vampires are very swift indeed, shroud eaters are no less swift, and I was hard put to stay ahead of it.

I reached the basement, slamming the door behind myself. I searched briefly for a way to secure it, but seeing none, I fled for the tool room and thanked whatever power that cares for the vampire that the door was opened. I ran inside and slammed it shut, turning the lock, and then cowered on the floor, holding poor Florence close to my breast. Moments later, the shrieking, rotting horror was pounding at the door. Outside in the mortal world, the sun was rising, and day was beginning. For me, it was time to die once more. I lay on my side on the dirty floor and closed my eyes. At least if I was to be consumed alive, I would not have to endure it whilst conscious.

Chapter Four

I awoke to silence.

I sat up, my curiosity aroused. Clearly, it was evening, or I would not be awake, and clearly also, the door had held, or I would doubtlessly be in Hell. Gathering up Florence, I rose to my feet and listened for the sound of the monster sensing my movement. I heard nothing. Gathering such courage as I had, I opened the door and peered into the room beyond my sanctuary. I saw no monster; only the things one would expect to find in the basement of an apartment building.

Something was very, very wrong here.

I decided that the best thing to do was pack a small bag and leave with all due haste. Careful as mice, Florence and I returned to my third floor flat. Then while she fed, I gathered up such things I felt I may need for a trip into exile, still unable to shake that terrible feeling of something being very, very wrong. Outside, life went on as usual; the working class came home from the day's toil as the pleasure-seekers emerged to find amusement for the evening. Inside my little home hung silence, and death, and an overwhelming sense that time was growing very short.

I paused in my packing to attend to the sounds around me, familiar by now with the routines of my neighbours. Across the hall, the woman who dwelled there with her two small children should be cooking supper, but I heard neither she nor her daughters. Below me was a young man with dreams of becoming a musician, but I did not hear the muted sound of his bass through my floorboards. It was as if the entire building slept uneasily. I had never known a shroud-eater to kill the living, but I feared this was indeed what had happened. It seemed very unlikely all the building's inhabitants would be out for the evening at once.

     I dressed in my green velvet gown and black cloak with the matching gloves. With my satchel in one hand and Florence in the other, I hurried downstairs and departed the building. I found myself wishing I had acquired a car, but the law deems it necessary for one to have a license. It also deems it necessary for the office that distributes such things to conduct its affairs during daylight hours. As such, although I know how to operate a vehicle, I do not have a license.

     By sheer luck I managed to hail a taxi, they not being in the habit of driving about this area seeking fares. I was in no mind to take the bus at the best of times, and certainly not with an undead monster on my heels. Having not seen the foul thing was no reason to believe it had given up; all I knew about the vile horror told me it would not. I could not shake the feeling that it had lashed out at those living in my building and slaughtered many, if not all. I would have liked to have learned if this was true, for if it was, then this was indeed aberrant behaviour for a shroud eater. Their prey was other vampires, and I could not think why one would do such a thing. But I had no time to learn why one would do so now.

     I was taken to Horseshoe Bay, where the ferry would take me to Departure Bay on Vancouver Island.

The taxi ride from my home in Kitsilano, or Kits as the locals refer to it, had been long and very costly, but haste was required, and I was in no position to quibble about funds when my life was at stake. I paid the driver his fare, then hurried to board the ferry and purchase my pass. I was kindly permitted to take Florence above-deck, as small creatures are not generally granted this privilege. However, in this instance, as I was on foot and she was very small, they made the exception. As such, Florence and I stood at the stern of the ferry, watching as we pulled away from the dock. We had been most fortunate; it was to be the last ferry of the evening.

    I was about to congratulate myself on my escape when I saw something, moving very quickly, run to the end of the pier and leap into the water, vanishing beneath the surface. I was not yet safe, it seemed, as clearly the horror had every intention of following me across the water. I could only hope the dogfish made short work of it, if they are inclined to eat dead, rotted meat.

    We crossed the Georgia Strait, arriving in Nanaimo. I managed to secure transportation to the small city of Courtenay, as there was a bus on board the ferry and I was able to purchase a ticket. After a ninety-minute ride which I spent on the bow of the ship, I boarded the bus and was driven the rest of the way to Courtenay, a large town bordering on becoming a city, and one which I had no time to explore. I was then on my own, as there would be no busses to the places I wished to go at this late hour. Another cab was hailed, more funds spent in the name of securing my own safety, and at last I was dropped off in the darkness past the tiny town of Cumberland on Lake Road.

The cab driver seemed very reluctant to leave me in such a place. There are no lights on Lake Road. It is paved, but it is very sparsely inhabited, and the place where I had asked to be left was utterly devoid of human habitation. The tall pine trees creaked and swayed in a light wind, and there were odd sparse splashes of rain, and once the cab driver left, I would be alone, save for Florence. I assured the driver that I had friends waiting and all was well. I do not think he believed me, but it was not his business to argue with mad young women who wish to travel to the middle of nowhere.

He left me by a near-invisible and overgrown little gravel path with the pretentious name of White's Bay Road, and I followed it through the dark, autumn woods beneath the lichen-covered trees. I did not know the area well, but I knew the history. I knew Cumberland had once been a coal mining town, and as such, the area was still dotted with mine shafts and caves, and from the ground one can hear the whispers of those who died toiling in the earth. My feet made no sound as I walked, listening intently in the darkness for the sound of anything that may be following me, but heard nothing. Finally, just as the sky began to turn light, I was secure in an old mine shaft behind Comox Lake in the Cumberland hills. It was filthy and dark and damp and far too reminiscent of the tombs I had shunned, but it was safe enough for now.

I hastily made a little enclosure for Florence from stones and piled it with grass and dandelions to keep her content. Then, using the infernal powers of strength granted me by my curse, I collapsed the entrance to the mine. I knew not how strong the shroud eater was but reasoned if it could not batter its way past the steel door in the basement of my flat in Kits, it likely could not pass the wall of great stones, earth and old timbers now sealing my sanctuary.

"We're safe for now, Florence," I said, though I wondered at the truthfulness of my words. Shroud eaters were relentless adversaries, but more than that, old mines were wont to harbour any number of foul denizens. There is evil in the darkness, and far worse things than vampires. I could but hope something truly dark and foul was not lurking in the bowels of my fetid keep, watching me with dead, hungry eyes.

Dawn was swiftly approaching. I lay down upon the dirt and closed my eyes. There was nothing else I could do.

* * *

When I awoke, I knew I had failed in my attempts to elude the monster. Even dear, simple, brainless Florence was huddled down in her bed, silent and motionless, aware of the thing that lurked outside, seeking entry. I could hear it whispering through the stone and dirt, trying to lure me out.

"Let me in…"

I did not reply. There was no reason to, as the thing was simply repeating a phrase mindlessly, with no real understanding of the words. Lacking anything better to do, I began rearranging the inside of my cave, attempting to make it something a little homier. My time would have been better spent teaching Florence to sing *Ave Maria*.

"Let me in…"

"Not by the hair of my chinny-chin-chin," I muttered, making my way to the back of the cave. I found no exit, merely the beginnings of a tunnel that ended abruptly in a pile of discarded mining equipment. So there was no escape through the back of the cave, nor entrance for that matter. I was safe for the moment but was still faced with the question of how long would my incarceration be. I did not wish to spend all eternity in an old cave, and I was quite certain that Florence was in full agreement, especially since, of the two of us, she was the mortal. Days without food would be uncomfortable to be sure, but I would not starve to death regardless of how long I was trapped. Florence did not have that luxury.

Could I fight the beastly thing? Was I strong enough? I rarely used my strength on the grounds that it simply was not lady-like behaviour, but it seemed I had not the luxury of waiting for someone to tend to the creature for me. To be perfectly honest, the only real use I ever found for a man is they are utterly convinced that a vagina is the opening through which a woman's brain drops as soon as she learns to walk, and as such males leave themselves open for easy manipulation by a gender they consider inferior to their own. It is far less effort to whimper prettily for some fool who fancies himself a white knight than take on a distasteful task one'self, but there simply was no one on hand to assist me. And for all my arrogance, I did not know if I dared face the thing. It had killed Stuart easily enough; it seemed unlikely I would fare much better.

"Let me in…"

How I wished the filthy thing would cease its ghastly imploring! Was it not bad enough I was trapped in a cave with no safe place to flee? How far and long would it chase me? Was this indeed the same wretched monster that had killed Stuart, or was I merely assuming? It seemed more likely than not; shroud eaters were no more plentiful than vampires. But had it murdered all the people dwelling in my little apartment building? And if so, why do such a thing? It made no sense at all to me. Still, it hardly made sense to ponder aberrant behaviour in a creature that is, by its very nature, aberrant.

The night slowly passed, and dawn would bring no peace from the whispering. While I would be forced to sleep the day away, the shroud-eater was under no such obligation. Would it choose then to begin digging its way into my chamber? Was it capable of rational thought? I had no reason to believe them to be anything other than mindless. Of course, I had also believed them to be without interest in harming the living. Clearly, I could make no further assumptions about this creature.

"Let me in…"

"I will not," I said. "I will not lie down and be prey for a mindless shambling slab of rotting meat more cursed than myself."

"Let me in…"

"Have you reason? Have you thoughts? Why do you feast upon the undead?"

"Let me in…"

I sighed. "Well, I can say with all honesty I have enjoyed more stimulating conversation." I decided then to attempt an insult, and see if I could provoke some reaction other than its usual rhetoric. "You are naught but the sickening remnants sloughed from a leper's bandages."

"Let me in…"

I sighed once more. "Well, you are either utterly without a mind to call your own or a master of restraint. For my part I choose to believe the former rather than the latter."

"Let me in…"

There was nothing for it. I simply had no other choice than to discover some means by which I may defend myself. I was alone. There were none riding to my rescue, and indeed, even had I a stalwart champion, how would he find me in so isolated a place?

My thoughts turned to the discarded mining equipment near the back of the chamber. I hurried over to the pile of rusting machinery and began searching through it for something I might use as a weapon, since it was quite clear this creature was not going to simply grow bored with the game and wander away. It had somehow managed to pursue me at great speed across a channel of water and follow two cabs and a bus to corner me here. Then the horrid thought crossed my mind that perhaps this was a second shroud-eater, and that I now had two hunting me. Surely if my heart still beat, it would be pounding in my breast. However, I momentarily forgot my fear when I realized there was a small hole behind the pile of mining debris. Curious and daring to hope I had found a means of escape, I pulled aside the rusted metal and rotting wood to further expose the opening. I then drew back in fright as something came out to stand before me.

The creature was tall and thin as a corpse, the flesh dead white and the lips drawn back from the horrible, stained, and darkened teeth. It had fangs and hissed a warning to me that I was encroaching on its den. Knowing this was no mere beast, but a vampire so old as to have seen many more centuries than I, I did the only thing I could and dropped down in a curtsey, averting my eyes.

"Father of all horrors, forgive my intrusion. I knew not you were there."

It hissed once more, outraged at my impromptu invasion. This was a Nosferatu, a creature that came from the land of Walachia, now called Romania, an ancient country that was unlucky enough to be home to many dark beasts, but none so dark as the one before me. How horrified, I wondered, would all the young girls of this day and age be to learn that the creature that crawls through the window at night is not tall and boyish and enchanting, but rather a dead white nightmare with dried leather skin, long black claws, and a lusting desire for not only their blood but their bodies as well? For the Nosferatu craved physical pleasures as well as blood, and would take both repeatedly until his victim died. I had no doubt he would have visited his disgusting wants upon me as well, had he not clearly sensed that I, like he, was dead.

"What brings you here? Who are you?"

"I am Deirdre of Leeds. I came seeking refuge from one pursuing me."

The creature made a sound of utter disdain. "Mortals with stakes and crosses, no doubt. Be gone!"

"I do not flee mortals."

"Then what chases you?"

"A shroud-eater."

The thing laughed—a disgusting sound like that of sandpaper on meat—and I would swear that I saw dust leave its mouth.

"Fool of a girl. There is no such thing!"

"Let me in…"

The Nosferatu seemed surprised.

"You were saying, my lord?" I inquired.

The creature seemed indignant, like an old man with troublesome children upon his lawn. "A shroud-eater? What game is this? They do not exist!"

"Many say the same of us," I said. "But those who feast upon the dead do indeed live."

"Then you speak of a *sin*-eater, foolish child."

I rose to my feet, angered. "I do not speak of some penniless mortal, compelled by the beliefs of his faith to devour bread laid upon the unblessed dead! I speak of that which preys upon those who walk the night! It is a shroud-eater, oh, slayer of virgins! And if you step outside this sanctuary, it shall consume you as the wolf does the sheep."

"Watch your words, girl. I am no sheep."

"No. You are a fool grown arrogant with age."

"Cowardly wench. Hide, then, in my sanctuary. I will tear open the entrance and deal with this monster."

As you can well imagine, I was only too delighted to let monster do battle with monster, and leave me out of the matter altogether. Taking my bag and Florence, I hastened into the creature's lair and blocked the door. Perhaps the shroud eater would be content with what jerky it may gnaw from the Nosferatu's skinny bones and leave me in peace.

I had no sooner blocked the way than I heard a small squeak of fright. I turned from the heap of rusting metal I had erected and beheld six very filthy young girls, none much older than sixteen years of age. Three were still alive; two were clearly not and had been thrown into a corner like so much trash. The last girl was tied naked to the bed, and her eyes were glazed as if her soul had fled already. Clearly, I had interrupted a demonic feast.

"Did he catch you, too?" one girl inquired, her dark eyes large with fright. She was chained naked to a wall, her hands over her head.

"I am not so easily caught as foolish little mortal girls who are out playing the harlot when they should be at home attending to their lore," I said.

A second girl with blonde hair immediately set up a great wailing. "She's like him! Don't you get it? She's going to help him catch more of us then she's going help him rape us and drink our blood until we're all like Chelsea!"

I struck her hard across the face, silencing her. "You will shut up, or I shall leave you here. Little is more despised than a coward and with reason."

"She's just scared!" said the girl with the dark eyes.

"She is *not* scared," I corrected. "She is hysterical. She is shrieking and making erroneous assumptions about my intent, and I'll not have it. That little tantrum will see the Nosferatu in here to determine what the fuss is about, and what is following him is far more dire than either he *or* I. And if perchance he decides to finish you all off rather than risk having his supper escape to warn others, you will have no one to thank while you are being violated and drained of blood other Lady Vapours. So she may shut up and let me help, or I will be quite content to break her foolish little neck so the rest of us may have a chance of surviving this night."

The girl with the dark eyes sniffed. "But... you're a vampire."

"There are many types of vampires in the world, child," I said as I walked over to the wall to examine her shackles. "Some of us commit murder and some do not. I do not. If I kill, it is only to save myself. The Nosferatu, on the other hand, is an eater of souls. He takes not merely blood but your very spirit."

"Is that what he did to the other girls?"

"Yes, child. I fear your friend who lies now upon the bed is well beyond any succour we may give her. But you are not. If you but give me time to work, it is likely that the arrogance of the withered old satyr who holds you captive will see he is well distracted when we make our escape."

"You talk funny."

I raised an eyebrow. "I assure you I was thinking the very same thing about you. Have you any garb?"

"Huh?"

"Clothing."

"He took it. I don't know what he did with it." She gazed at me with large eyes, so very like those of my dear deceased mother. "I'm Lisa. The blonde girl you yelled at is Valerie, and the girl who hasn't said anything at all is Melissa."

"I am Deirdre of Leeds, and if you are at all interested, I died in 1663."

"Cool!"

I was openly affronted. "I can assure you it was many things, and not one of them was 'cool.' It was all rather ghastly and painful."

"No, not that you died—that you've seen so much history."

"Oh, yes, I have seen a great deal of history. I have seen Cromwell single-handedly destroy some of my dearest friends. I have seen the black plague sweep throughout my homeland, as did cholera. I have seen World Wars One *and* Two, and many other stomach-turning events, all from the comfort of a rotted casket on a slab of cold marble. On the whole, I prefer a large bottle of wine and a book of Lord Byron's poetry. Failing that, I am rather partial to horror movies." I managed to pull the shackle free from the timber in which it was secured. "There. You are free. See if there is any clothing to be found whilst I free Melissa."

"But what about... him?"

Yes, that was a valid question, was it not? Was I perhaps presumptuous in promising these children freedom? I listened hard and caught the sound of a violent battle, as if two great lions were tearing at one another.

"I think he has other concerns. Make haste, child; they shall not fight for as long as Sisyphus rolls his great stone in Hades."

"Huh?"

I drew a steadying breath. "Move thy ass."

"Oh. Okay."

At last, we were ready to make our escape 'neath the cover of darkness. I led the way, creeping out of the Nosferatu's lair, into my cave and out into the forested night, forced to sneak past the two monsters as quietly as we could. We could see that the shroud-eater had bested the Nosferatu and dined now on his withered flesh and old bones as one might dried meat and breadsticks. Best to make haste before the monster realized his next meal had escaped.

Valerie emerged from the cave, took one look at the ghastly feast, and would have screamed had I not raised a hand. I would have struck her with force enough to crush her skull rather than see us all dead, but fortunately, though she was a coward, she was no fool. She closed her mouth, and we made our quiet way down the hill to a logging road, and began following it to the lake. Here Melissa chose to speak.

"Aren't you going to eat us?"

"After a bath, perhaps."

"Don't you eat people?"

"I do not eat people. I drink their blood."

"So are you going to drink our blood?"

Valerie now spoke. "She's just taking us to another place where she can have us to herself. She's not saving us. She's gonna do to us what he did."

"Valerie, shut up," said Lisa. "Like, seriously. Shut up. We wouldn't have been in this mess in the first place if you hadn't thought it would be an awesome idea to go drink in Dracula's Castle."

"What is this Dracula's Castle?" I inquired.

"It's an old mine shaft in this area. Teenagers have been going there to party for years. This whole area used to be a thriving coal mine. You wouldn't know it to look, but there used to be thousands of people here and the largest China Town in North America, except I think for San Francisco. There's mines and abandoned shacks and all sorts of stuff all over the place."

"And so you went to drink in Dracula's Castle... and were caught by a vampire." I confess I giggled.

"At least we escaped," said Melissa. "Those other girls that were there before us weren't so lucky."

"Did you know them?" I asked.

"A little," said Lisa. "We'd seen them around, but we never really hung out or anything. The other two girls were dead when we got there, and then he... killed... Chelsea. He hadn't started to hurt us yet."

"You've had a very narrow escape," I said. "There was a time when all folk knew better than to play in the woods at night. This century has made men too bold. You are never more than a single power outage away from your ancestors, and the night houses more horrors than you can imagine. This area would be a haven for fell beings and creatures. You have many places for dark things to hide, and the hills seem to be untouched for the most part."

"But no one has ever vanished before," said Lisa.

"No one of whom you have heard tell," I responded. "Your foul host has likely been in his little hole for as long as it has been forgotten by mortal men. A Nosferatu is no fool. He will take that which will not be missed. In my time, it would have been the impoverished and unimportant. In the time these mines were dug, likely he preyed upon the hapless daughters of the Chinese workers, they also being seen as lacking in worth and consideration at that time. In this day, he seeks silly girls drinking in a whimsically named cave — girls who are likely to have become intoxicated and wandered off, only to be met by a bear. Do you think your parents would have found your place of merriment and immediately concluded you were taken away by a vampire? Hardly. So he would have had his fill of you, while more likely than not some poor bear or wolf paid for his crime."

"And what do you do with your victims?" asked Lisa.

"Confuse them with my superior linguistics."

"You said you don't kill them."

"Indeed I do not. It is easy enough to prey upon the unwary. There is always some poor fool who has thrown caution to the wind and become so deep in his cups as to remember my visit as little more than a drunken fancy, and upon waking not wish to have it be known he has not the faintest idea what bit him."

"So… you just take what you need."

"Precisely. There is no need to take too much. Even in this day of disbelief, I would not last very long if I left a trail of bloodless bodies. I do not kill unless needs must."

"You were ready to kill me," said Valerie reproachfully.

"Because you were ready to kill us all with your mindless screeching. Had you begun to shriek and wail then you may rest assured I would have broken your neck. As it is, we have escaped, and are, for the moment, safe. But we know not what other things may be tracking us. Let us save further conversation for when you are safely home. Then I shall have to seek refuge from the sun."

* * *

I was surprised to learn that the girls did not actually live within the town proper, but rather in a small house on the shores of Comox Lake, in blessed isolation among the trees of pine and yew. For reasons I do not understand, the waters of that lake grow rough at night, and they were fairly pounding by the time we reached the house clad in cedar shingles. The night was not yet so old that I had to vanish, though I could not think why I cared to see these children arrive at home. Did I not have enough to manage on my own? The shroud eater still lived, though the Nosferatu had doubtlessly provided it with an ample feast. Likely when it was done it would resume its relentless hunt. If I had any wisdom at all, I would have fled, not stood in the darkness and watched as a frantic father rushed out of the rustic, pretty house to weep on his daughter and her friends and demand to know what had become of them. I gathered from what he said that he had been on the verge of summoning the police, which indicated to me the girls had not been held long by the Nosferatu. This was most fortunate for them, as it meant the horror of the night would surely fade in time. No century would be long enough to wipe away the revulsion of being raped by the dead.

It was time to fade back into darkness, yet I did not do so immediately. I stood on the stony beach and stared as Lisa and her father reunited, wondering how my own father would have seen me that dread night years ago when I came out of the rain, dead and yet not. What story did my mother give him? How did they fare after my murder? I had heard no tales of them and chose to believe they had lived long in peace. Certainly had any tales of their harbouring a murderer or having a vampire for a daughter been spoken around the taverns and roadhouses, I would have heard about them.

I once had been human, and known love and warmth as did these children, but no more. That time was well past. Slowly I turned away from the reunion and walked into the darkness once more. When I could no longer see the house, I drew Florence close and wept into her fur.

* * *

I was awakened by a voice whispering my name.

"Deirdre! Are you awake?"

A hand shook my shoulder gently, and I uttered a sigh of vexation.

"Did your situation of the previous evening teach you nothing, girl?"

"We need help!"

"More true words were never uttered. And who am I, your fairy godmother?" I sat up. "How did you find me?"

Lisa shrugged. "I just asked myself where I would hide if I was a vampire, and I came here."

"Touché," I grumbled.

Here was a tiny cabin on the lake shore that had been partially burned and then boarded up. It was certainly suitable for my needs, though I longed for my tiny home, and my bath, and my violin. Sleeping on first the dirt floor of the mine shaft and then the flat surface of an abandoned table hardly made for a cheerful disposition. Also, I was growing hungry — very hungry indeed. Soon this little chicken would cease to be charming and simply become fare for my table.

"Deirdre, you have to help us.

"Lisa, you may not realize this, but I am hardly your saviour. In fact it shall only be a matter of but a brief time before your blood nourishes my dead flesh."

"I don't care."

I confess this was not the response I had anticipated. I looked toward her, seeing dark brown eyes that softened the hard crust around my dead heart.

"I beg your pardon?"

"You said you don't kill unless you have to. Well, that... *thing* that ate the other vampire does. It killed a cop! We saw it!"

This was shocking enough that I briefly forgot my grumbling belly. "Tell me what you saw."

She was weeping as she spoke. "I told Dad it was some pervert who grabbed us. He wasn't gonna believe it was a vampire. He called the cops, and when they came out, they asked me and my friends to show them where we were taken. It was daytime so I thought the monster would be gone but it wasn't! It was standing there... howling!"

"Howling? What do you mean by howling, child?"

She wiped at her face with one small hand, a tiny gold ring on her middle finger glinting briefly. "It was just making this... long, drawn-out moaning noise! It was horrible! It was dead and bloated and grey, and all this... disgusting stuff was leaking out of its mouth. The eyes were all filmed over, and it just stood there and moaned. And the policeman told it to put his hands behind his head, and it didn't do anything, so the cop walked up to it, and... and it tore him to pieces! It just ripped him to shreds and... and he was alive, and he was screaming, and we could hear the joints pop and it was..."

I rose to my feet and drew her close to my breast, trying to comfort her as best as I was able.

"Surely, that is a dreadful experience, but what is it that I can do?"

"Well… it began to eat the policeman, and we ran. We ran all the way home. The second policeman told us to go inside and lock the doors, and he called for help. But no one came! I don't know why, but no one came! He went to see why no one was coming and never came back. Then… then it appeared out of the woods and stood in front of the house and began to moan… It was covered in flies! They were running in and out of its mouth!"

So my deepest and darkest suspicions were confirmed; the shroud eater had begun to feast upon the living. Had they always done so, and my belief that they troubled only the walking dead been false? Or was this behaviour new? How I wished I knew more about this walking plague!

"How did you escape?"

"I slid out the bathroom window, where it couldn't see me. It was still just standing there and moaning when I sneaked off to find you."

"Lisa, I do not know if I can be of any assistance to you at all."

"Please, you have to help! You know more than we do, at least!"

"Well, that goes without saying." I sighed heavily. "Very well. I will do what I may to help."

* * *

We skulked our way to Lisa's house. She crept in through the bathroom window first, and I handed up to her my satchel and then poor Florence, who likewise was wishing for a bath and a cup of tea. She prefers chamomile, so long as it is cooled, and if you were to accuse me of pampering her without equal then I should have to plead guilty. She, as I, had been days without a comb and a wash, so her normal appearance of having been dealt a severe shock had degraded into absolute hysteria.

"What is this thing?" Lisa asked, her tone dubious as she regarded poor Florence.

"My demon familiar," I replied dryly.

Lisa did not appear to believe me, as she rolled her eyes. I slipped in through the window and looked down at myself. I was a complete mess; filthy from toe to brow, my gown covered in grime, and my hair in absolute disarray. Truly I looked as if I had arisen from the dead. I greatly desired a bath, but I could hear the moaning of the shroud-eater, and as such, stepped out of the bathroom and into the kitchen. All of the lights were dimmed, though there was light enough to see Lisa's two companions of the previous night, her father, and a fourth girl with whom I had not yet been made acquainted. I could only assume that Lisa had told her father of her intentions to fetch me, as he did not seem surprised at my presence.

I walked over to the window and peered into the night. As Lisa had said, it stood in the yard, blind eyes seeing nothing, mouth hung agape and running with vile ichors. Lisa came to stand by my side.

"What do we do?"

"I confess I do not know. Never to my knowledge has a shroud eater pursued the living."

"What is it?" asked Lisa's father.

I turned my head to look at him. "A shroud eater. So named because, as they lay stinking in the ground, the vile fluid that flows from their mouths decays the burial shroud around their mouths. Those unfortunate enough to dig one up oft thought the creature had gnawed the linen away. Never have I heard of one troubling those who still draw breath, yet this creature has done so."

"How do we kill it?"

"You cannot kill it," I informed him. "All we may do is shove a brick into his jaws, throw him into a pit and pile stones upon him, then hope that some fool does not dig him back up. Thus we have a similar situation to that of the mice, the cat, and the bell. Who among us cares to insert the brick? Then there is the added dilemma of this shroud eater behaving not at all as my learning led me to believe. A brick may serve only to enrage the beast."

"So what do we do?" he demanded, suddenly impatient. I reacted not well at all.

"I do not know! I never claimed to know! My lore is limited, and if you care to shout then I shall leave. I am not bound to you or your spawn in any manner! I came at the beseeching of your daughter. Clearly, she has no *man* that may help her. Again, it falls to the women of the house to put things to rights whilst that which was born with a limp flap of flesh betwixt its thighs convinces itself it is lord of the manor. Make thyself useful, man. Board windows and lock doors. The weaker sex shall save you."

"Don't talk to my dad that way!" said Lisa.

"Even if it was pretty fucking funny," said the fourth girl.

"Will boarding up the doors and windows help?" asked Valerie, always seeking a chance to save her own hide.

"It will provide more security than thin glass," I said.

"What if we slipped out the window and ran away?" said Melissa. "We ran away before!"

"And it followed us," Lisa reminded her.

"It can track by scent," I said. "It will follow you. It will never stop. This one has already taken my friend Stuart. It has tracked me relentlessly from Kitsilano, across the Georgia Strait, and from Nanaimo to here. How it achieved this I do not know. I saw it dive into the water. I… do not wish to think how it crossed the water. I sought to hide in the mine shafts, and that is where we met. Yet I have one question in my mind more vexing than how this boated horror crossed the strait."

"What's that?" asked Lisa.

I gazed at the shroud eater as it stood moaning outside the window. "Why did the police not come? Surely even if they believed not the manner of their comrade's death, they would at least rally to avenge it."

Lisa's father rose to his feet. "If we can all pretend to be civil to one another, I would like to ask a few questions. By the way, my name is Peter."

I gave him a brief, polite curtsy. "I am Deirdre of Leeds. If I can help in any manner I shall, as I confess this mess is my doing, however unintentionally. But you have my word, sir, I did not think this monster would trouble you or your family."

"What is it after?" he asked.

"Until two days ago I would have assured you it was after myself alone. They are the undead that feed upon the undead. Now, I do not know what it desires."

"Sooooo..." said the girl to whom I had not yet been introduced. "Do you like... go hang out and party and junk with other vampiiiiiires? In like... old warehouses and juuuuuunk?"

She had a lazy manner of speaking; drawing out the last word into what I suspected would be naught but an endless series of questions. I regarded her with annoyance.

"Who owns this daughter of a village idiot?"

"That's my sister, Tanya," said Lisa. "You can yell at her all you want."

"Delightful. I suppose now I shall change my name to Maria and teach you all to sing. Now, if I may be perfectly dull and take our minds to the situation at hand, I suggest the following. Secure all doors and windows. Start a fire in a fireplace or stove if you have one. We may have need of it."

"There are some old bricks in the basement," said Lisa. "It... couldn't hurt to bring a few up."

"It will be a braver soul than I who uses them," I said.

Melissa and Lisa went off to fetch the bricks. Valerie followed Peter into another part of the house in search of boards. Tanya made a sound of derision. "You're pretty lame for a vampire."

At least I knew now upon whom I would feed when at last I could stand my hunger no more. Peter returned to search noisily through drawers for some missed item.

"I suppose you are familiar with a great many vampires," I said to Tanya.

"Well, no. But you're nothing like the ones in the books and the movies. They're all like... scaaaaaarrry? An' juuuuuuunk? And sexy? You dress like an old lady, and you're a total bitch."

"Heavens, I must go do myself an injury, a barely articulate snot disapproves of me."

Tanya was not daunted and curled her lip into a sneer. "Watch it, bitch, or I'll get a cross and fry your ass."

"Is it as lovely as mine? The cross, I mean." I drew forth the cross my mother had given me upon my wedding day. It was purest gold and set with tiny pearls. The look upon Tanya's face as she spied it was one of utter disbelief.

"You're wearing a cross! And it's not burning you!"

"Please, child," I said as I tucked my cross back into the collar of my gown. "I am a Catholic and survived Cromwell's reformation. The only religious artefact that frightens me is a Protestant."

Peter snorted in laughter, covering his mouth in an attempt to conceal his mirth. I confess I smiled.

"I'm going to start boarding up the windows," he said. "Tanya, try to call the police again."

She rolled her eyes and sighed at being saddled with this great task. Within moments, she and I were alone in the kitchen. She made no move to do as instructed, so I picked up the phone and held the receiver to my ear. I was greeted by silence.

"Have you a cellular phone?" I asked.

She sighed loudly, rolling her eyes and slamming her hand upon the table. As she rose from her seat to perform this great act of benevolence, I felled her like an animal. I am exceedingly fast when I wish to be, and silent. Before she could draw a breath to scream, she was on the floor, my weight upon her, and I drove my fangs into her arm. The blood flows quickly here, if one but knows where to bite, yet not too quickly. Within but a brief time I had taken enough to satisfy myself, and released her, the unholy marks of my feed quickly closing over to leave only two scabbed dents. She stared at me in utter horror, her eyes large with terror.

"I will find the phone," I said to her. "You have clearly been imposed upon enough for one night."

I located the cell phone and was pleased to see it was functioning. My elation was short lived, however, when my call failed to elicit a response. The police were not answering. This was indeed a very, very bad sign. Tanya stumbled into the room in which I stood, holding her arm and still staring at me.

"You're evil," she whispered.

"I am not evil," I said as I attempted to call out once more. "I am cursed. There is a difference."

"What did you do to me?"

"I took some blood to sustain myself. You need not fear. You are not harmed. Frightened, perhaps, but your life will go on as it always has."

"You threw me to the floor and stole my blood!"

I sighed. "Teen girls always cause such a fuss over pointless things. You are well and largely unhurt. Be thankful. Your sister encountered something far more hideous last night and weeps not."

She continued to gape at me as if I were some sort of nightmare entity from the bowels of Hell. "You bit me."

I gave her the cell phone. "Try to reach the police. Make yourself useful."

I left her standing in her room in tears and holding her arm, and went in search of Peter. I found him in the living room.

"The police are not answering," I informed him.

He paused in his hammering to regard me from over his shoulder. "That can't possibly be good."

"I stand in agreement of your statement, sir."

"And I want you to know the only reason I didn't throw you out of the house after what you said to me in the kitchen is because you saved Lisa."

"I suspected as much. You may wish to reconsider your kindness, however, as I did just bite Tanya."

He gaped like a fish in a net. "You what?!"

"I said I bit her."

"I heard you!" He set aside his hammer and ran to check on his daughter's condition. I picked up the hammer and resumed his work, though I confess my hammering would win no awards, save perhaps for comedy. He returned after a few minutes to reclaim his hammer from me.

"Should I leave now?" I inquired politely.

He was clearly angry. "If that thing wasn't standing out there, and if I knew where the cops were, and if you hadn't saved Lisa, believe me I would throw you out on your ass in the middle of a bright day in August then roast marshmallows while you burned." He shook his head. "That's all I ever fucking meet—crazy women!"

"To what do I owe my reprieve?" I said. "No matter the reasoning, I *did* just bite your daughter."

He seemed to wilt slightly. "In Tanya's case, I'm not so sure having the crap scared out of her is a bad thing. She's nothing but anger, and she's been plenty violent herself more than a few times."

"Well, as her father, you do have the right to correct her."

He glanced at me. "She's not my daughter. She is Lisa's blood sister, but Lisa and Tanya are not my children. I was in love with their mother. Stupidly in love. She lost her job, so I told her she and her daughters could come live here with me. Three weeks after she moved in, she said she found a job in Quebec and was going to go out there to get things ready for the whole family to move out and be with her. Instead, she shacked up with a new man and abandoned us completely. So here I am raising two very angry teen girls by myself that I can barely control because, as they are all too happy to point out, I am not their father, while their mother parties it up in Montreal. And now I'm spewing my troubles to the vampire who bit the oldest girl while a zombie moans in my yard."

"Your daughter will be fine, I assure you," I said softly. "And before you correct me, she is indeed your daughter. More so than that of the woman who bore her."

"Thanks, but at this point your opinion and praise don't really mean shit."

"Da-ad!" said Lisa in surprise, having just arrived from the basement. "Don't be mean to Deirdre!"

"She bit your sister."

Lisa piled the bricks before the fireplace hearth. "Oh, boo-hoo for Tanya. She once threw *me* down the basement stairs and locked me in. Think I have enough bricks? I grabbed all I could find. Did anybody get through to the cops?"

"I called. There was no answer," I said.

"You don't think there are more of those things, do you?" said Lisa, her tone one of great concern. "I mean, one's way bad enough."

I sighed. "I cannot say. This creature acts not as I have been led to believe. All the truths I held dear were not truths at all. It slays the living and now calls out in the yard, but to what? What horror does this monster call upon?"

"This is gonna sound like, totally stupid, maybe?" said Lisa. "But maybe we can look on the computer."

"I have heard far less rational ideas," I said as I peered out the window. "Let us see if we may find wisdom greater than mine own."

"Huh?"

"Let's go look at the computer."

"I wish you would just *say* that."

"I would, but I fear the spectre of my tutors and their rods of discipline may rise to have words with me, and we have dead enough with which to contend."

* * *

Several hours later, we were far wiser and no nearer a solution. Indeed, poor Lisa was in tears.

"There are so many kinds of vampire! And so many kinds of shroud eater! What do we do?"

"Have courage, child," I said gently. "There seems to be but a few ways to kill them. Let us make use of them all."

"But this says just the breath or the shadow can kill us!" said Lisa, weeping in fear and frustration. "It can spread plague everywhere and kill thousands by just ringing a church bell! I thought vampires were afraid of hallowed ground!"

"Much of the modern lore comes from the Victorians, who were far more concerned with charm than accuracy," I said. "Let us take the advice of the learned men and monks who wrote these pages. We must strip it of the remains of the burial shroud and stake its vile heart. Then we shall force the brick betwixt its jaws before we cut off the head with an axe. Then we bury it in a pit and cover it with stones. If that does not see the end of it, then I have no ideas left." I sighed heavily. "If I do not return, please look after Florence for me."

Lisa gazed at me in horror. "Deirdre, you can't!"

"Do not be foolish, child. There are none here better suited to the task, though I confess I do not want it. If it should but breathe upon you then you will face a lingering death more horrible than you can possibly comprehend. I have speed and strength to my advantage. It is but two in the morning. There is darkness aplenty, and if I am but careful I may survive the battle unscathed. Now be a good child and fetch me a long wooden pole, an axe, and a hammer. I shall select a brick from the pile you so thoughtfully provided."

I had but one advantage I could see; a shroud eater is mindless, whereas I am certainly not. Once I had the monster's full attention, it would doubtless run toward me, and with luck I could spear it. Thusly armed, with my hammer and hatchet in my belt, a brick in my pocket, and a broken wooden garden rake handle in my hand, I crept forth from the bathroom window to do battle with the very demon that had slain Stuart.

It was standing before the house in the darkness, moaning. Somewhere in the distance, I could hear great hounds screaming, as if being flayed alive. I could hear nothing aside from the dogs and the monster, and again I was struck with terror, though now I knew what vexed me. These creatures spread the plague with their breath, and there was every chance the police were neglecting their calls because of illness and madness spreading over the land.

What horror had I led to this peaceful little lake in trying to save my own unworthy hide?

I stepped around the corner of the house and braced myself. Oh, I was a foolish, foolish woman. Why had I shunned my warm place by the fire to do battle with death incarnate for mortals who were at best geese in a yard, meant to fill my belly?

"Spreader of filth!" I called. "Meet your end."

It shrieked and ran straight toward me. I shrieked myself for reasons altogether different from those of the monster and thrust forward. There was a gruesome, wet, crunching sound as my spear struck its mark, and I managed to fling the horror to the ground, where it lay, flailing its arms and screaming like some vile bloated infant. Grasping my hammer, I raised it over my head and brought it down with what force I could muster upon the pole, striking again and again until I had secured my quarry to the ground. Next, I brought forth my brick and forced it into the creature's mouth, portions of clotted liquid and chunks of rotted bone and teeth falling away as does dried earth as I secured the brick into place. Next, I used the hatchet to remove the hideous head and turn the face down into the earth.

"I am in need of assistance!" I called.

Peter ran out, clutching a shovel as one might who intends to use it as a weapon. "What do I do?" he asked, his dark eyes enormous.

"Dig a pit as deep as you are able. I and the children shall gather stones. We shall have this wicked thing conquered 'ere the sun rises."

Peter dug, working hard and fast as he was able in the gravelly earth of the lake shore. Lisa, Melissa, Valerie, and I gathered the largest stones we could find, and when the pit was dug, I pulled the pole carefully from the ground, ensuring I did not remove it from the body, lest the monster awaken. Once the creature had slid down into its grave, I once again pounded the stake into the ground, ensuring it was deep and secure. I placed the head with the brick in its jaws into the grave as well, then we piled the stones over it before burying it. The shroud eater, it seemed, was finished.

I was granted use of the shower, and while Florence and I lingered in its sacred cleansing warmth, my garb was washed and dried. Blessed cleanliness — how I had missed thee!

I would have slipped away to rest in the burned shack, but Peter insisted that I stay, perhaps fearing the beast would awake and claw its way out of its stony grave. I had a bed made up for me inside the pantry, which had no windows and possessed a door that shut. With the proper application of duct tape to the cracks around the door, I had a warm, dark, and secure place in which to pass the day.

I slept as the dead are wont, whilst Florence nibbled lettuce in a paper-lined box.

Chapter Five

I awoke to a discussion regarding myself occurring in the living room. I could hear the voices, and as I rose to dress, I attended keenly to that which was being said.

"Dad, we can't let her go," said Lisa. "Deirdre is the only help we have!"

"Stop calling him Dad!" snapped Tanya. "He's not our dad! He's just the guy Mom dumped us on. And I don't want that bitch here!"

I assumed that I was the bitch in question.

"You just hate her because she bit you," said Lisa. "You get your ass in a knot any time anyone kicks your fat butt. You get all pissed off when anyone treats you the way you treat them."

"We need her here," said Valerie, and I confess I could not have been more startled had Florence changed color. I had not expected her to rise as my champion.

"I don't want her here!" Tanya emphasized her point by stamping her foot. "And shut up, Valerie, you don't live here! Nobody cares how I feel! I'm scared! She bit me!"

Tanya began crying loudly in the most forced and obnoxious manner to which I have ever been subjected. Then Peter spoke up

"I think Lisa is right—it's better to have Deirdre here. There are still too many unanswered questions. We don't know why the police aren't answering or where Valerie's parents are or…"

"Well, who cares about Valerie? Why doesn't anyone give a shit that the bitch *bit me*?!"

"Gee, I don't know," said Melissa, her voice fairly dripping with sarcasm. "Maybe because you're a nasty little bitch who likes hurting small animals? Because you fuck anything that moves? Because you're seventeen and you've already had three arrests and two venereal diseases?"

"None of that was my fault, bitch, you shut up!"

Peter's voice could suddenly be heard above the screeching. "Enough! I'm still the adult, and this is still my house. We will ask Deirdre to stay. We're completely out of our league here. We need her help."

Tanya raised the hysteria level, complete with insults and threats to leave.

"So go already!" Lisa screamed. "Nobody wants you here!"

I finished dressing and stepped out of my tiny chamber and into the living room.

"This noise could raise the dead," I said.

"Shut up and get lost," said Tanya, upper lip curled into her perpetual snarling sulk. My palm itched to meet her cheek.

"We have a problem," said Peter quietly. "We can't reach Valerie's parents by phone. And we can hear moaning outside."

"Where do her parents live?" I asked.

"In the red house, just down the shore, heading towards White's Bay," said Peter.

"I shall look," I said. "And I shall stay, for the time being, providing you keep Miss Tanya away from me whilst I sleep. One so concerned with her own wants above the needs of her fellows is not one who lulls those about her into an easy sleep."

"Tell me about it," said Lisa.

"Oh, fuck all of you!" Tanya stormed upstairs to her room, slamming the door to ensure we were all well aware of how deeply she was hurt before sobbing in that same loud, obnoxious manner.

"The child is disturbed and dangerous," I said to Peter.

"She's seventeen, and her mother dumped her off on some man she barely knew," said Peter. "She's bound to be a little messed up."

"I do not disagree," I said. "But she is angry in a way that brings danger to those around her. She will think naught at all of dooming you to save herself."

"I'll put a lock on your door," he said. "And… thanks for staying. I don't know what's going on, but I'm getting scared. The cops still are not answering, we haven't seen any of our neighbours, and we can hear moaning."

"I will look to see if Valerie's parents are well," I said. "We shall deal with this one matter at a time. I have not survived for over three hundred years to be slain by mindless undead."

"I want to go with you," said Valerie.

"There is naught you may do in this situation," I said softly. "If by cruel fate your parents have met their end, then the best way in which you may honour their lives is to survive whatever evil crawls forth from the fetid pits of Hell."

She clearly wished to disagree but at last nodded and fell silent. I stepped into the darkness, and listened. The moon was not yet risen, and all was quiet. The waters of the lake were still, and I heard no sound at all. No night birds, no insects, not even so much as a slight breeze disturbed the profound night, save for a vague moaning in the distance and the telltale smell of the profane as it walked from the crypt. There was more than one shroud eater, and their fell shadow was spreading across this tiny community. I wondered if it was true, that their mere shadow was enough to spread the plague, and if so, how would the folk of this lake fare? Too well I recalled my time in London during the plague, and I prayed silently that dire malady would not come here.

Does God hear the prayers of the dead and the infernal, I wondered?

I approached the red house with its bright white trim and felt my stomach grow ill in my belly as I heard the now-familiar, droning moan of the shroud-eater. I peered through a window and spied Valerie's mother and father. Together they sat on a sofa of garish gold and green, festooned with daisies.

Dear tender grace of Heaven, were all folk struck blind in the nineteen-seventies?

The child's parents sat cold and upright upon the hideous couch, eyes glazed blue in death, staring ahead at nothing or perhaps some infernal sight only their dead eyes perceived. Their mouths were agape, and they droned in unison the single-note dirge of their kind. Great, festering, black buboes leaked fetid matter, and they were blotched with the tell-tale rosy spots. Blood was dried upon their faces and throats from bloody sneezes, and the floor was well covered in vomited blood. There was no doubt in my mind as to what had killed these folk.

I drew quietly away from the window and hastened back to my small cedar keep, where Valerie met me at the door, weeping openly.

"They're not okay, are they?"

"No, child, they are not. I am truly sorry."

Valerie fled to another room, her sobs quieter and far more genuine than those of Tanya, who was still wailing, shrieking, and throwing things about her room. I turned to face Peter as he approached.

"They are more of those things now, aren't they?" he asked.

"It is far worse than that," I said. "The rumour that the shadow and breath of a shroud eater spreads the Black Death appears to be true. Valerie's mother and father had both clearly succumbed to this most vile of ills. It is not safe to venture outside. I strongly suggest blocking any windows and sealing any keyholes, so that no shadow may fall in here."

Peter sighed in what may have been exasperation. "This is all so ludicrous! Evil shadows and moaning vampires and breath killing through a keyhole. What is this, the Middle Ages?"

"The Middle Ages are not as far away as one may think," I said. "They are never further away than an empty fuel tank, a power outage, and a hungry belly. The year matters not. It has been my experience that people do not change."

Tanya threw something, then screamed at the top of her lungs as if she were a small babe. Peter sighed.

"And what would people in your time have done with her?"

"Firstly, I can assure you that at seventeen, if she were not properly married off with babes of her own and a man to keep her in line, then her own parents would be on hand to see to her behaviour. If they could not control her then she would be sold to someone who *could* manage her. Or if she were of noble blood, she would be sealed into a wall to perish, or perhaps locked into her room until starvation took her or she learned her place."

Peter raised an eyebrow. "I'm not big on locking kids into their room and starving them."

"Peter, she is angry because she has been abandoned. That is most understandable. But you let her get away with much in the name of sympathy — too much, perhaps. And now we have a situation wherein we are most bound to one another in order to survive. That child is bound to none. She screams, she throws tantrums, she insults her sister and the man who has been kind enough to feed, clothe, house, and raise her. She is dangerous. Do you truly think that she will hesitate to harm any of us on a whim?"

"I can't nail a little girl into her room. It's wrong!"

"You had best do something, Peter. She is raising noise enough to draw each and every shroud eater in the area. Valerie's parents make two. They may be two of a dozen or more."

"All right. I'll talk to her when I get back. I'm going to drive to Courtenay and see if I can't find out what happened to the police."

"Be very careful," I said. "The road is dark. There could be much that is sinister and fell lurking along the way.

He nodded. "There's no need to tell me twice. I'll just go straight up the trail to the car and right to the cop-shop. You and Lisa start drawing the curtains and plugging up cracks and keyholes. We'll discuss the situation further after I get back."

I curtseyed, then turned to the task at hand, Lisa and I working to seal up any and all cracks we may find, whilst Melissa tried to lend comfort to Valerie. Peter took up his keys and coat and departed.

"Peter's wrong about Tanya," said Lisa quietly to me as we taped the gap 'neath the back door.

"What do you mean?" I asked.

"He thinks she's mad because Mom left. But she's always been like that. She killed my grandma's cat when she was six because Grandma said she couldn't go to the park by herself. When she was eight, she killed the budgie I got for my birthday because it was green and *she* wanted a green budgie, so I couldn't have it. I sometimes think Mom left to get away from Tanya. I mean, I'm not pure and perfect either. I know sometimes I'm pretty mean to Peter because I am mad at Mom for what she did. But I'm trying, y'know? I'm trying to be good because I see how hard he tries to be our dad. I know it makes him happy when I call him that. It's a rotten situation for everybody, but Tanya was broken long before Peter ever met her. He doesn't believe me, but... I think she could kill someone and not even think about it afterwards."

"I think you are right. I think it would be a very wise idea for you, Melissa, Valerie, Peter, and I to all swear an oath to watch out for one another, and from more things than shroud eaters."

"Totally agree with you there." Lisa cast a glance my way. "Were you ever a mom?"

"I was, three times," I replied. "Three pretty daughters."

"What happened to them?"

I drew a steadying breath, though it was merely a reflex, or perhaps a memory of life. I do not need to breathe.

"They were murdered by their father for having the impudence to be born female. Then a charlatan masking as a doctor told my husband I was bearing daughters to spite him, and he flung me down the stairs. I was murdered. That was how I came to arise from the crypt. Murder victims oft arise from the dead to seek vengeance on those who caused them harm."

"What happens when you get all the people who hurt you?"

"I return to the grave."

"Then why are you still here? Those people have to all be dead by now."

I finished taping the underside of the door. "I do not know. Perhaps I did not find all responsible. Perhaps I allowed one to live who was guilty. Perhaps I am being punished for killing one who was innocent. I know not. I should be at rest by now, but yet I wander."

"Deirdre?"

"Yes, child?"

"I'm glad you still wander."

I found that I was smiling. "We shall see how long your gladness lasts when I come to you for a pint of blood."

She made a face. "What's that taste like?"

"Not unlike licking a small battery."

"I think I'd rather have apple pie."

"On the whole, so would I, but that is not my fate. Tea would be lovely, however."

Lisa leapt to her feet. "I'll make you some."

The front door opened, and Peter stepped inside, bringing the scent of the rain with him. He closed the door and locked it, then removed his coat to hang it upon the rack. His expression was dark. I sat back on my heels and regarded him.

"You've been gone but a few minutes!"

"Yeah, well, as you may have gathered, I didn't make it to Courtenay," he said. "I didn't even make it as far as Cumberland. I found the car of the cop that left to get help the day before yesterday lying on its side in the middle of the road, and the cop standing there with blood running out of his mouth, his eyes glazed blue, and he was moaning."

"He had become a shroud eater," I said.

Peter nodded. "I think we are in very deep trouble here, and I have no idea what to do. We can't impale and behead every shroud eater."

"Then we must fortify and set plans in motion. Let us not forget they have a distinct advantage. They do not sleep, or feel cold, or fear. They live only to eat, and they will not stop until they have us."

"What unleashed them?" he asked, clearly greatly agitated. "Why are they here? I mean why are they here in these numbers spreading death? We have to assume they've always been here, but why are they out in such force now?"

"I lived in London at the time of the Black Death," I said. "I saw the great pits dug and the unblessed dead flung onto them, wrapped in their burial cloths, or not, as often the families had neither time nor means for one, assuming any were left alive to provide one. A great many of these horrors arose from the pits. Perhaps... perhaps their numbers have dwindled to such an extent they are in need of more of their kind."

Peter looked positively ill. "They're breeding?"

"It is but a thought. The Black Death has broken out since that fell time but never to so great an extent. We know now what causes it, and we take care to never let such conditions of filth and crowding happen."

"Are you telling me those mindless horrors can think?"

"No. I suggest no such thing. They are, as you said, mindless. But even mindless things will do what they must to spread their own kind."

He sighed heavily. "We need a television. We need to see if there is any more information about all this."

"There's a TV at Valerie's house," said Lisa, returning just then with the tea.

"Yes, but it appeared to still be in use by her parents," I said, accepting a cup. It was black and hot, with lemon enough to satisfy even my citric lust.

"Hazel Murphy has one in her cabin," said Peter. "I'll go get it."

"Dad, that's up the hill in the dark through the trees!" said Lisa.

"Yes, well, so was the parking area for the cars," he replied. "But we need a TV."

"We have a computer, we don't need a TV," said Lisa, exasperated. "I'm sure I can find some local news."

"All right. Let's go look."

Lisa, Peter, and I made our way to Lisa's bedroom and paused in shock and horror at the sight that greeted us upon our entry. The computer had been taken apart. Not smashed or shattered, but taken apart, as if by one who wished to not be heard whilst she worked. The hard drive was gone entirely. I looked to Peter.

"I would like to restate my case for sealing Tanya into her room," I said.

Peter's jaw muscles clenched, and I could see his rage as his face slowly became red and a vein began to pulse in his brow. Pushing past Lisa and I, he hastened upstairs and pounded on Tanya's door. Lisa and I listened from the bottom of the stairs.

"Tanya!"

"What?" she demanded, her tone angry and defensive.

"What did you do to the computer?"

"None of your fucking business, that's what!"

"We need that computer! Where's the hard drive?"

"I threw it in the wood stove, which is where that stupid guinea pig is going next so tell that fucking bitch to *watch* it."

"I'll get the wood screws and glue," said Lisa.

"I shall fetch the boards," I said.

Lisa and I sealed the door. It opened outwardly, so three boards were ample to keep it securely locked. Tanya was provided a plastic pail to serve as a chamber pot, a hole was cut as to serve as a window of communication and a place through which to provide nourishment, and she was locked in until such time as we might safely release her. Peter was not at all in favour of Tanya's caging.

"Guys, this is not proper parenting technique!" he said as Tanya frothed and raged and screamed. I held the boards in place whilst Lisa operated the cordless drill in order to secure the screws deep into the wood.

"It's proper survival technique, Dad," said Lisa.

"I could go to jail for this!"

"That's just great, Dad., When the undead Mounties show up along with the undead social workers, we can all sit down and explain we had to lock her up to save us from the undead vampires."

"The child makes a valid statement," I said.

"Look, call me crazy, but I happen to take a very dim view of locking teenagers in their room."

"Dad!" said Lisa. "Wake up and smell the bat shit! She kills small animals. She trashed the computer because she was feeling pissy. This is not about not wanting her to have a social life! A time out isn't gonna work in this case! We're not hurting her; we're just making sure she doesn't hurt *us*!"

"Fine," he said. "But when the undead social workers show up, I'm making *you* explain this. Do we know for a fact that she threw the hard drive into the wood stove?"

Melissa appeared just then, holding the scorched and melted hard drive at the end of fireplace tongs. Peter sighed heavily.

"So we're back at square one. We have to get the TV from Hazel Murphy's cabin. I'll be back as fast as I can."

"Peter, be very careful," I said. "Move as quietly as you may."

He nodded. "I didn't see any shroud eaters the last time I was out there. I did see a pig, though."

If my heart still beat it would have thumped heavily within my breast. "A pig?"

"Huge, monster pig, biggest I ever saw. It stared at me from the edge of the parking area. I would have sworn no one around here has a pig."

"Is there a church nearby?" I inquired. Peter laughed.

"Deirdre, this is a collection of cottages and houses along a lake, not a town. Most of these places are only occupied during the summer. It's late September. There probably aren't even any campers left at the Point."

"The Point?" I inquired.

"There are two places on the lake where people regularly go," said Peter. "The Point and the Bottom.

The Point is that far sandy area across the lake, and it's used by campers. This area where we are, with the little cottages and wharfs and boats and such, is called the Bottom. Only three or four families live down here all year round. None of them keep pigs, and there are no churches. Why? The pig's not a shroud eater, too, is it?"

"I do not know, but a pig where no pig should be is a troubling omen, and there are monsters that take such a form."

"Terrific." Peter sighed heavily. "Right. I'm off to get Hazel's TV and Hazel, too, if she hasn't gone back to Courtenay for the winter."

"And if she's not a vampire," said Melissa, regarding the smouldering hard drive. I watched Peter as he departed down the stairs.

"How is Valerie?" I inquired of Melissa.

"She's really upset," said Melissa. "I gave her a beer. I know she's not supposed to have one because she's sixteen but it's sorta like what they call unusual circumstances."

"It is precisely what one may call unusual circumstances," I said. I inspected the door containing Tanya for soundness. "There, we may rest easy now that Lady Tanya is secure. I shall take this moment to give Florence a bath."

"Deirdre?" said Lisa. "Are there pig-vampires?"

"Not as such," I said, descending the stairs with the girls following. Melissa disposed of the hard drive in the dust bin.

"But what are they?" Lisa asked. Clearly, she was not a girl who cared for unanswered questions. I fetched Florence from her box and set her in the kitchen sink, then rolled up my sleeves in order to bathe her.

"There is a vampire of which I have heard rumours; one that dwells in Bavaria and the surrounding area. It lays in its coffin with only the left eye open and holds one thumb in the opposite hand. It gnaws upon its shroud until it is devoured, and when the shroud is consumed, it begins to devour its own flesh. It is said in order to find the beast, one must stand in the cemetery at night and listen for the sound of bones being crunched and devoured." I began gently rubbing shampoo into Florence's fur, smiling as she complained. "When it has devoured as much of itself as it may, it rises and seeks the blood and flesh of its own kin, those to whom it is related. It appears in the form of a pig, and when it is done feeding upon its kin, it takes itself to the church to ring the bells. Those who hear the bells rung will die."

"But it would need a grave nearby," said Melissa. "The closest graveyard around here is the Cumberland cemetery, but that's up on the old Island Highway heading towards Courtenay. It would take hours to walk from there to here, at least."

"Maybe it's not a proper grave," said Lisa. "They used to mine along this lake. You can still see old railroad tracks going into the water. The shore of White's Bay is almost nothing but coal. There could be dead miners anywhere in this area."

"This creature usually comes into being as a result of an accident," I said.

"There were a lot of accidents," said Lisa.

"Will it hurt us, or Peter?" asked Melissa.

"If he is not a relative, and if there are no church bells handy, then no, unless it, too, spreads the plague through breath or shadow," I said.

I rinsed Florence clean of soap and then bundled her up in a towel that I had purchased solely for her. Indeed, it was even monogrammed. She grumbled as she huddled within the blue cloth, baths not being one of her favourite pastimes. The front door opened, and Peter walked in, carrying the small television.

"I saw that pig again."

"How's Hazel?" asked Lisa.

"According to the note she left under the phone for Valerie's mother, she's gone to the Okanagan. Wish I was there."

He set up the television on the kitchen table, plugging it in and turning it on, searching for a local channel. He soon found one, and we gathered close to watch.

"Our top story tonight – ferry service to and from Vancouver Island is still cancelled, as the entire island has come under quarantine due to an outbreak of what appears to be an exceptionally virulent form of bubonic plague. So far it seems contained to the island, and doctors and rescue workers are doing their best to reach the more out-of-the-way communities. The main area affected is the town of Courtenay, and now Cumberland, and roads leading away from there have been blocked in an attempt to keep the plague from spreading. It is not clear yet if anyone has managed to ascertain the cause or the extent of the epidemic. Those who are alive and uninfected are urged to stay within their homes and to call the number at the bottom of their television screens to let rescue workers know of your location and condition."

Peter hastily scribbled down the number, then went into the living room to call. I continued to dry Florence, my thoughts on the pig Peter had spied. Was it merely a pig? Had someone living in this area been raising one for meat? It was possible also that it was a pet; some were in the habit of keeping pot-bellied pigs as companions. The animal could simply be wandering in search of company and food. There was no reason to assume it was a Bavarian monster risen from the waters of Comox Lake to feed upon those unfortunate enough to be kin.

In the back of the house, Valerie began to scream.

* * *

We ran into the back room where Valerie had been resting, only to find her being torn to shreds by a gigantic swine. The animal was black, with a dense coat of coarse hair and great curving tusks. It stank of the grave, and its rotted carcass showed enormous holes in the flesh whereupon it had been gnawed by rats and maggots. The eyes lit up the room with a glow like Hell fire. Peter ran in first, and, with a cold swiftness seldom seen in a man not trained in the arts of war, snatched up a great standing lamp and, wielding it as one may a pike, stabbed the monster. The pig shrieked, and Peter stabbed at it again.

"Somebody grab the fucking axe!" he screamed.

Lisa ran for the axe. I dug through my coin purse for the largest coin currently in circulation in Canada: the twonie. I found one and drew it out.

"What are you doing with that?!" asked Peter, leaning his full weight down on the pig.

"The coin must go into the mouth ere we may slay the vampire!" I cried.

"What?!"

I fell upon the monster and grabbed the snapping snout. Forcing the jaws apart and keeping one hand upon the upper jaw, I used my foot in a most inelegant manner to hold open the lower in order to throw the coin down the hellish maw. I managed to leap out of the way in time for Lisa to arrive with the axe. She was not greatly proficient with the weapon, but she accomplished the deed with three strokes, the sound of metal cutting meat and bone causing my stomach to turn. At last the head of the unholy thing lay on the ground, and we stepped back. We had slain the pig, but not in time to save poor Valerie. She had bled to death from her many violent wounds, whilst on the floor the pig that had killed her slowly transformed into a young man, long dead, his hands and arms partially devoured.

"That's Valerie's cousin Douglas," said Lisa quietly. "He died last year."

"What the hell is going on?" asked Peter. "Why the fuck is this happening? I have lived my entire fucking life believing vampires are not real and now I'm up to my fucking ball-sack in them!"

"What do we do with Valerie?" asked Lisa quietly. I thought her far too composed for this situation, and wondered perhaps if she was in shock. I placed my hand on her shoulder.

"I shall take her to the small, burned cabin close by and lay her there."

"Is she going to turn into a pig, too?" asked Peter.

"I cannot say. She was murdered, but not all murdered dead rise. I will lay her soul to rest as best I may and pray she stays dead. I shall take her cousin as well."

Peter shook his head and sat down heavily in a chair, tears clouding his eyes as he gazed upon Valerie's torn and lifeless body.

"She was just a little girl! What the fuck did she ever do to anyone? She's just a little girl!!"

Lisa rushed to his side, and the two held each other, weeping, as I began slowly wrapping Valerie's body in a flowered sheet in order to move her. Melissa stood close by, clutching a brick in one hand and trembling, her eyes gleaming with unspilled rain.

"Can I help?" she asked softly.

"Burn the sheets," I instructed her. "The blood will call attention we do not need."

Peter gently moved Lisa aside. "I'll drag the mattress out and put it in the shallows."

He rose to his feet, and then paused, as if he had seen something that we had not. With a puzzled expression upon his face, he walked over to the window and pulled it open, then leaned out, his hands braced on the ledge. For a long moment he simply stared and left us to wonder what he may be pondering. At last he spoke.

"Lisa, was Valerie having her period?"

The child went positively rigid, and her eyes grew wide. "Da-ad!"

"Was she?"

"Yes, but that's not the kinda thing you tell people!"

Peter looked from the ground skywards, pondering once more. "Did she ever use the small trash can in Tanya's room to put them in?"

Lisa was flustered and flapping. "Maybe, but Gawd, why are you asking this stuff?!"

"Because someone has flung used tampons down onto the ground from Tanya's window, and I'm thinking they did it to lure ~~the pig~~ something here."

I was riveted to the ground in horror. Not even the most vile and wanton harlot flung such things about where others may find them, and yet ~~that child~~ Tanya had done so in a fit of pique in order to bring death upon the innocent. It was true I had not cared for Valerie and thought her a coward, and I would indeed have slain her in the Nosferatu's lair had her fits placed us in danger. But there is a difference between killing to save one's own life and what this disgusting slattern had done. I did not like Valerie. But she had deserved better. Lisa just stared at her father in horror.

"Tanya killed Valerie?"

"We don't know that she did it on purpose," said Peter weakly.

"No, of course not," I said. "There is absolutely no reason in the world to assume that Tanya had the first idea that tossing down wads of cotton soaked with the most intimate and richest of blood from Valerie would in any way draw creatures that prey upon it. And in the event I did not make myself perfectly clear, *that* was sarcasm."

He sighed heavily. "Well what would you have me do with her? I can't kill a child. We've already locked her up, I'm assuming she's now out of ammo."

"Unless she's having her period, too," said Lisa.

Peter sighed loudly and heavily. "Fine. Deirdre, take Valerie to the shack. Lisa, you and Melissa burn the sheets. I'll take the mattress to the lake. In the morning we'll move my stuff out of the upstairs bedroom, board up the windows, and move Crazy McBatshit in there. She can have her own bathroom, and she won't be able to set any more traps or throw any more disgusting things out the window. Agreed?"

"Fine," said Lisa. "If you're not gonna beat her to death like she deserves. Hey, I got an idea: let's put Valerie's dead body in the room; Tanya can eat that when she gets hungry enough."

"I'm not even gonna argue with you," Peter grumbled. "Let's just get this dealt with."

"Agreed," I said. "Did you manage to call the rescue workers? Are they aware of our presence?"

He nodded. "They know we're here, but they don't know when they can get to us. So all we can do is stay put until they get here. Assuming they do."

We cleaned the room as well as we were able, scrubbing the stink of death from the walls and floors.

We were not finished with our task until the night was old, and the sun would rise from the crypt of night within the hour. I took myself to my small room, and there I slept, as the dead are wont to do.

* * *

When I awoke there was much screaming and raging, and I knew without yet laying eyes upon the creator of the great din that Tanya was being moved to her new quarters. Florence was sniffing the air, unused to such carryings-on, and I lifted her from her box to hold her close to my breast.

"There, there, little one, it is only a madwoman who seeks to doom us all. I shall venture forth in a while to seek out some of the very choicest of dandelions for you."

Florence clucked to herself, clearly not appeased at all by my promise. Nor indeed should she be; a box in a pantry was hardly an acceptable substitute for her large cage with a bed of timothy hay and nice places in which to hide. I set her down once more and dressed, then left the safety of my pantry for the insanity of the household.

I made my way upstairs and found that the situation was more dire than I had believed it to be. Tanya had managed to acquire a large shard of broken mirror, and was using it to ward off those who would rightfully contain her. She was shrieking at a volume that I am certain could cut glass and flesh alike.

"Leave me alone! You have no right to lock me up!"

"You killed Valerie!" Lisa retorted.

"I did not, you stupid bitch!"

"Oh, well then, who threw down the fucking tampons from the upper floor? Santa Claus?"

I shall now and henceforth unto my dying day be haunted by that most singular and unwanted of visions.

"I was just cleaning my room!"

"Oh, bullshit," said Lisa. "Just get in the bedroom, you fucking murderer."

Tanya began shrieking and weeping about being so unjustly accused. In no mood for her histrionics, I strode forth and shoved her and her shard of glass into the bedroom, then pushed the door shut before stepping aside to allow Peter to secure the boards. It was not until I turned to face Lisa that it was brought to my attention I had been struck an injury.

"Deirdre, you've been stabbed!"

I gazed down at myself and saw indeed Miss Tanya had been most sincere in her threats. The weapon had not made it past the boning of my bodice, but had it done so, the shard of glass would have certainly done grave injury. Indeed, were I still alive I would have not long remained that way. I fingered the cut in the fabric, then turned my attention to Peter.

"I will not demand you perform a deed for which you have no stomach. But we cannot permit her any more liberties."

He nodded his agreement. In a moment of weakness I permitted myself to find him handsome.

"I must depart for a brief time," I said. "I have needs I can no longer ignore. I will be back as soon as I am able."

"Don't be daft," he said wearily. "There's nothing out there for you to hunt and plenty of other things that will hunt you."

"Are you proposing that I bite you?"

"You can if you don't drain me dry or turn me into something."

I hesitated. It would be so easy, would it not? I could stay, warm and dry and safe, and feed here and be done with the chore without needlessly trudging through unfamiliar lands and risking detection. I could let Peter provide for me and make myself comfortable, and stay.

"I cannot accept your offer," I said quietly. "In my world one may be friend or food, but never both. I will hunt. Perhaps someone is still alive."

"And perhaps you will walk right into a nest of monsters," said Peter. "Deirdre, we need you."

"I will not discuss this matter," I said. "I will not be gone long."

I left the house, but my senses were in turmoil, and hunting did not come easily. I was breaking my first and strongest rule; one did not befriend the cattle. The farmer could not slay the beast that had become dear to him, and I could not feed upon men who called me friend. Nor could I feed now upon Tanya. As reprehensible as I found her, I could not use her to my convenience as she lay locked in a chamber. She was not a carton of milk within a refrigerator, and I knew too well the feeling of being trapped and helpless within a room, awaiting the whims of my keeper, to force that upon another.

I wandered along the lake shore in the early evening darkness, alert for the scent and the sound of my prey. Yet, as Peter had predicted, there was nothing alive that I may feed upon. What folk had dwelled in this tiny Eden had since fled or been consumed by the evil in some manner; whether body or soul, I knew not. There was naught I could eat. I can prey upon beasts if needs must, but I did not care to use a simple creature in such a manner. It seemed ghastly to me, to clutch something frightened and helpless with not wit enough to comprehend what manner of torment it was being forced to endure. However my feelings in the matter were moot. There was nothing upon which I may have fed, neither man *nor* beast. Frustrated, I returned to the house, and to chaos as Tanya screamed and kicked doors and smashed the glass in her boarded window. She filled the air with vile words and insults, and ended her tantrum by defecating upon the floor and poking as much of it as she could beneath the door.

"She wants out," Peter said wearily. He was seated in a chair before the fireplace, the flicker of fire upon his brow drawing my mind back to time and people passed.

"Yes, of course she does, but I sincerely hope you are not considering doing so," I said.

"I don't know *what* to do. She's crapping and pissing on the floor like an animal. How long until she's made such a mess we have no choice but to let her out?"

"She has a bathroom," I said. "She has the means with which she may care for her personal tidiness. It is not our concern if she elects to wallow in filth."

"I don't like having a little girl locked in her room."

"Peter," I said softly. "She is not a little girl. In my day she would have been wed and with babes by now. She is a young woman, and she is having a tantrum worse than any I have seen by even the most spoiled child. She will realize soon enough we are of no mind to cater to her whims. If she chooses to soil her room thusly then what business is it of ours? I for one will not clean up after a shrieking doxy."

"What if she doesn't stop screaming? She can keep this up for hours."

Yes, the screaming was certainly unbearable, and nerves within the house were raw enough. Valerie had been dead but a brief while, and Lisa and Melissa had not yet recovered from their imprisonment within the lair of the Nosferatu before they had been forced to face a siege in their own home by the legions of the undead. Tanya's antics were not welcome. However, being of English birth, I knew the solution to any problem.

"Tea?" I suggested.

"Yes," said Peter, rising from his chair. "I'll make cream scones."

I smiled. "Be still my already still heart."

"Can you eat?" he asked as we walked to the kitchen. I began preparing the tea as he took a large bowl from a cupboard.

"I can," I replied. "But only very little. It takes a great deal more effort to digest solid food than once it did, and it slakes not my infernal thirst. However, after all that has befallen us in these recent days, a warm scone running with butter and jam is simply too lovely to resist. Where are Lisa and Melissa?"

"Watching TV," said Peter. "I think they find it comforting to know life is going on somewhere in the world. I would give anything to know what the hell is going on. Where are these creatures coming from? Why are they rising now? I mean they must have been there for years, why start coming out of the woodwork now?"

"I have no answer for that," I said. "We have never been plentiful in number. This rising tide makes no sense to me. It was remarkable enough that I encountered a second vampire like myself."

"Just now?" said Peter.

"No. A few days ago. His name was Stuart. He and I became friends very quickly; vampires are few in number, and finding a second member of one's particular species is much like finding a diamond ring on the sidewalk. He was murdered by the very shroud eater that I was fleeing when I met Lisa and her friends. At least Stuart's loss was not futile. Had I not fled the monster, I should not have found them."

"I'm glad you did," said Peter. "They've all been through enough. Valerie's parents were nice enough, but they couldn't really be bothered with her. You'd think a mother and father would want to know why a teenaged girl was hanging around a grown man, but they never said a word. She liked to watch the birds that were nesting in my yew tree and help me make jam. Then, when Lisa and Tanya arrived, she had an excuse to hang around more often."

"And Melissa? What is her story?"

"Her mother drinks like a fish, and her father likes to pretend all the family problems would magically go away if Melissa was a boy."

"So tell me, Peter, have you noticed that your life is magically problem-free as a result of having a penis?"

"Nope," he said dryly. "As my brother used to say—same shit, different toilet."

We both paused in our conversation to look up as Tanya began pounding on the floor in her room, shrieking as she threw things about. Peter sighed quietly and turned his attention back to the scones.

"I can't keep her anymore," he said quietly. "I keep trying to tell myself she's just angry because her mother walked out on her, but that's not anger. I don't know what that is. I don't want to walk out on her because I think she's had enough people do that to her already, but this is out of my league. She needs help that I just can't give her."

"She needs to be in a hospital," I said.

"Yeah, I think so, too. At the very least she needs to be locked up where she can't hurt anyone anymore. I can't believe she… killed Valerie. She did, didn't she? It was murder. She lured the pig. Maybe not the pig specifically but she was trying to lure *something*."

"Yes," I said quietly, "it was murder. Valerie did die by Tanya's hand. The pig was merely the weapon."

He nodded. "As soon as this mess is over, I have to call her mother and let her know what's going on, assuming she cares. You know, I could lose these girls at any time. I have no legal standing. I'm their babysitter. If their mother shows up out of the blue and wants them back, there's nothing I can say."

"I wouldn't go," said a voice. I looked up to see Lisa standing in the kitchen doorway.

"I wouldn't go," she repeated. "And she's not coming back anyway. She phones at Christmas and on birthdays, but she doesn't want us. She never did. She only had us because she thought it would make Dad stay."

"Where is your father?" I asked.

"Who knows? He vanished five years ago. At least Mom calls. Funny how a lot of women think getting pregnant is a great way to make a boyfriend stay. I was reading about it on the 'net. You know what the number one cause of death among young pregnant women is? Murder, at the hands of the man who didn't want the baby. I'm never getting married, and I'm never having a baby. I don't want a kid of mine to have to grow up on a planet this stupid."

"You're such a little ray of sunshine," said Peter.

"Statistically speaking, you should be molesting us, you know," said Lisa.

"Well, I'm a very rare breed of pedophile—I like women my own age. Which makes me the world's most unsuccessful child molester. How's Melissa?"

"She fell asleep. Wish I could. Between the screaming and the stomping and the stink and the monsters I can't relax. Oh, yeah, Tanya's pissed on the floor again, and now she's stomping on it."

"After this is over, we're gonna find a hospital for her," said Peter.

"Finally," said Lisa. "Took you long enough to see the light."

"If I'd thought, for one minute, she could kill someone… Look, let's just forget it. As soon as this mess is over, we'll hospitalize her and be done with it. Let's just eat our scones and try to survive."

"*Are* we gonna survive?" asked Lisa.

"We will be just fine so long as we are careful," I said.

"We'll survive better than your pretty bodice," said Peter. "That's a shame, that was a nice piece of yellow and green brocade."

"Better the brocade than my liver," I said.

"Did you eat?" he asked.

I felt myself become somewhat flustered. "No. There was nothing to eat. I shall look again tomorrow. But you raise a point of concern for yourself as well; what fare have you in the house?"

"We're pretty well set for winter. I've laid in a lot of canned food, and I've got beef, deer, and bear meat in the freezer. I've got beans, lentils, rice… the humans are just fine. The one we have to worry about is the lady vampire."

"I cannot bite my friends.

"So we just wait until you're so hungry that you go into a killing frenzy?" said Lisa. "Explain to me how *that's* a nice thing to do to your friends."

It irks me so very deeply when a child is right.

"Fine," I said curtly. "I will eat later. After tea. Seems perfectly unacceptable to do it *during* tea."

"If you eat Tanya, can I watch?" said Lisa.

"Assuming that I was in the habit of feasting upon things soaked with their own water and filth."

"I could force her to take a shower," said Lisa.

"Lisa!" Peter chided.

* * *

We had our tea in the living room, gathered around the golden warmth of the fire. Tanya had ceased her rant, and it sounded as if she was grudgingly cleaning up the filth she had left upon the floor, which she had been so certain we would scrub for her. I had removed my bodice and was carefully mending it whilst Florence sat upon my lap and helped not at all. In fact, she rather hindered the entire process by repeatedly biting my thread and nibbling upon my garb until I was forced at last to find her a carrot so that we might both busy ourselves in peace. Melissa remained asleep, whilst Peter and Lisa played chess, badly. We paused in our pastimes as a moan began to rise from outside in the darkness.

"Sounds like we have a visitor," said Peter. "Is the back door secure?"

"It is," I said. "I made certain it was latched and locked."

"Just think," said Lisa, her tone morose, "there are all these idiots running around squealing about how sexy vampires are and how cool it would be to turn into one. And chances are they would end up a fat, bloated, dripping, moaning… thing."

"Reality blows," said Peter.

"I would at least want to be an interesting vampire," said Lisa. "Those moaning things are glorified zombies."

"And what do you consider an interesting vampire?" I inquired.

"One that can do things, like turn into a bat or a wolf. Can you turn into a bat?"

"No, but my husband assured me repeatedly that I did a singularly remarkable impression of a harpy."

"That's not nice," said Lisa. "Did they have tales of vampires when you were alive?"

"Considering cosmetics were crafted of white lead, mercury, and arsenic, we had a great many tales about a great many things, some of which were occasionally lucid. But I do recall the story of the Dog Priest. The tale was documented by a Canon at Augustine Priory, I believe his name was William of… Newcastle? Newark? Newburgh! Whether this tale is true or not I have no idea. William of Newburgh died well over four hundred years ere I drew breath, and ergot poisoning was a common thing, which could account for a great deal of the goings-on back then."

Peter grinned. "And they say history is dry."

"History is *not* dry. It is a wanton, ridiculous affair. I know — I have been observing it for centuries. Much of what modern scholars and theologians ponder and deem grave and weighty matters can best be summed as a belly full of rotten bread and bad whiskey. But on to the tale. It seems this priest, whose name is lost to the ages, would spend far more time out hunting with his dogs than tending to his rightful duties and to the mistress upon whose lands he lived. They called him the Dog Priest, and when he died, he was laid to rest in Melrose Abbey in Scotland. That should have been the end of him, but it was not. Because his life was spent in worldly pleasures rather than his priestly duties, he rose from his crypt and stumbled forth into the night to groan and scratch at the windows of his mistress. After several nights of this she went to her new chaplain, who apparently took his duties a little more seriously than the former, and pleaded with him to make an end of her tormentor. Taking with him three companions, the chaplain went to stand guard at the grave and waited well into the night. At last they were so cold and weary that three of the men, the chaplain and two of his companions, took themselves to a nearby house to warm their bodies. Quite likely the process of warming involved good Scottish whiskey, but while they were warming, and the fourth man stood alone, the grave opened."

Outside in the night, the shroud eater moaned sorrowfully to the moon above. I fought to ignore the horror.

"What happened?" asked Peter.

"According to William of Newburgh, the grave split open, and the Dog Priest leapt out, shrieking and moaning, and made straight for the man, who struck him with an axe. Retreating with all due haste, the monster returned to its grave, pursued by he who would have been the evening meal. The noise drew forth the chaplain and his companions, and the four proceeded to unearth the corpse and spied the axe-wound which it had been dealt. They carried it forth to burn upon a pyre and scattered the remains to the four winds."

"Well, that fixed him," said Peter.

"According to some, it did. But a few of those with whom I was familiar in the days when yet I drew breath said that in times of pox or plague the Dog Priest may yet be seen, and he screams as he is hunted by demonic deerhounds, his pleasure turned now to pain. Their paws churn up the flaming earth and bring desolation to the land, and the screams of the priest spreads plague to all who hear it."

The shroud eater moaned again, while Florence munched her carrot and cared not for the dead, so long as they were well away and locked outside. I finished my mending and put away the needle and thread.

"The night grows old," I said quietly. "As does the tea. Let us make a fresh pot and add some whiskey, so we may rest a little before we must face that which lurks in the night."

* * *

I found Lisa standing in the upstairs hall, gazing out the window. The house was dark and silent, and it was quite late. She was wearing a blue flannel nightie, her long brown hair tangled from tossing and turning in her bed, trying to find rest. I could not blame her for not being able to sleep. Three shroud eaters stood moaning in the yard, while a fourth roamed slowly over the shore, appearing to seek something.

"This whole place is cursed," she said quietly. "It's soaked in blood. No wonder all these monsters are here."

"A few shroud eaters are hardly indication of a curse," I said softly.

"It's not that. There is evil here going back centuries. See that area right there?" Lisa indicated a low mountain far across the lake, topped with a glacier. "The Comox First Nations named it Forbidden Plateau. I don't know the whole story—no one here really talks about it. But apparently the Comox who used to live here caught word that another tribe was coming to make war. The Comox First Nations sent their women and children and elderly up to the glacier to hide until the war was over, and got ready to defend themselves. But the war never happened. Turns out it was a mistake, and the other tribe was coming to trade, not fight. They decided to have a potluck and feast to celebrate, and they sent messengers up the glacier to get the women and children. But when the messengers arrived, they found nothing. No women. No kids. No tents, food, clothing… nothing. All they found was blood splashed across the snow. The Comox First Nations believed evil spirits ate their loved ones. To this day they regard that glacier with suspicion, and a strange red lichen still grows there, marking the area where the blood touched the snow."

"How horrible," I whispered, gazing across the lake. Though the weather was still, the waves of the lake rose and pounded as if a great storm was raging. "Why does the water do that, I wonder?"

"Don't know," said Lisa quietly. "Maybe something to do with the moon? I don't know. It's eerie. This whole valley is evil."

We froze in place as we heard a knock at the back door. Lisa made a small sound of terror, looking to me with eyes wide in fear.

"Is it one of them? Do they knock?"

"I shall see. Do not tremble, child."

I walked down the wooden stairs to the lower level, Lisa following me closely as I crossed the floor to the kitchen door, from whence the knocking came.

"Who is there?" I asked.

"Let me in," whispered a familiar voice. Lisa gasped in horror.

"That's Valerie!"

"We must be certain," I said. "It may well be Valerie's voice, but it may not be Valerie's will controlling it. Valerie! Is your mind whole, or are you but the parroting ghoul?"

"It's me. I have information."

I opened the door, and moved back as Valerie stepped inside, shrouded in the bloodied sheet upon which she had died. All that was visible of her person was her white hands, a small ring with a pink crystal heart upon it glittering on her finger. Lisa wept openly.

"Oh, Valerie…"

"Don't come any closer. I don't want you to see what I look like."

"I don't care what you look like! I'm just so glad you're alive!"

"I'm not alive," said Valerie quietly. "I was murdered. I can't rest until my murderer is dead."

"You came for vengeance," I said softly.

"No," whispered the shrouded and bloodied figure. "Even if I want to kill her so badly, I could vomit. There is nothing I would like better than to claw the meat from her face and eat it. But the dead chatter mindlessly about every single thing, and before I rose this evening, I found out why this is happening. I came to warn you."

"What is it?" asked Lisa. "What's going on?"

"The shroud eaters have been coming here for years, making their way from other parts of the world. They've chosen this valley, and this lake, because of the old mine shafts, and because there are so few people. It's much easier to hide. And now that they're here, they're spreading the plague. They're going to spread it all over the island. And once the people are dead, more shroud eaters will be born. And they'll go to the mainland. And they will start a plague bigger than any of the others. They're going to kill, and kill, and kill, and there's nothing anyone will be able to do because this is like not the Black Death doctors know. This one's fast. Even if they stop it, hundreds of thousands will have still died."

"So they are breeding," I said.

The figure nodded. "Yeah. They're breeding. It's been too long since the last plague."

"So what's going to happen to you?" asked Lisa. "Are you going to kill Tanya?"

"No. At least not yet. I just came to tell you that you need to leave here, find a place that's isolated. You're not safe. More and more shroud eaters are arriving, and the things that used to be your neighbours know you're here."

"Then come with us!"

"I can't," said Valerie. "I'm becoming like them. I can feel it. I've already begun eating my funeral cloth."

Lisa shook her head. "It's a bed sheet, Val, not a funeral cloth."

"But it was used as a shroud."

"I don't want you to go!" Lisa was weeping openly, tears dripping from her cheeks.

"You can't help me, Lisa. I'm dead. I only came to tell you to leave. Take a boat across the lake and find a place to hide. And leave Tanya to take her punishment."

"I'm not sure Dad will leave Tanya," said Lisa. "I mean, crazy and evil as she is…"

"I can't make him leave her, and I'm not gonna try," said Valerie. "He's always been nice to me. I'll try to remember that for as long as I can. But in a few days, I'll be standing on the beach and moaning with the others, and she's the one who put me there. I want him to remember *that*."

One white hand reached for another, and I watched as Valerie took the little gold ring from her finger and offered it to Lisa.

"And this is so you will remember me."

Lisa took the ring, sobbing openly as she threw her arms around the stinking neck of that which had been a dear friend.

"I won't ever forget you Val. We'll leave in the morning. I'll make Dad understand."

Valerie returned the embrace, then slowly pulled away. Turning silently, she left the kitchen and walked forth into the darkness. I wondered if she would lie upon the shore and await the sun, choosing to end her own life rather than wait for the transformation to claim her. I hoped she did.

I closed the door and sealed it once more, while Lisa had placed the ring upon her finger and was already scribbling a list of what to take. I knew I would not be joining them.

"I shall stay," I said.

Lisa abruptly raised her head and looked to me. "You can't stay, you're in as much trouble as we are!"

"Be that as it may, I shall hardly survive a nice sunny boat ride."

"Deirdre, you must come with us! We can't leave you here to die!"

"Lisa, I must feed soon, and I cannot prey upon animals! You, Melissa, and Peter are the only humans in the area."

"So you can take a little from each of us!"

"Lisa, that is very kind and generous, but I will require more than you can replenish. Eventually I will—"

"Eventually you will need to move on, I get it. But not now, please not now!"

"Lisa, you are a kind and dear child. But I cannot come with you. And I know you understand this."

She swallowed her hurt, and then nodded. "I understand," she whispered.

Chapter Six

I awoke early the next eve to silence. They had departed, and I was alone in the house, save for one furious presence, raging against her door. Had they truly left Tanya behind? It seemed almost too much to believe, but as I listened, I perceived this to be true; Tanya was in her room, screaming, throwing violent tantrums, and, if my nose served my rightly, defecating upon her floor once more. I felt something smooth and hard within my hand, and as I raised the object to see what it might be, I found I grasped a hammer. There was a note taped to the shaft.

Don't give this to Tanya until you're ready to leave the house. – Lisa.

"Why on earth would I leave the house?" I mused aloud. Sighing, I rose into a seated position and then froze as I spied Florence's box — but not Florence. Within the depths of the little carton was naught but a note. I picked it up and read it.

Help help! I've been kidnapped! Come save me! They are forcing me to live in a cabbage box and eat beet greens! – Florence.

"I know a certain little girl who is going to get a very stern talking-to," I grumbled.

I packed a few things I thought Lisa and her father might need, then gathered up my own belongings. Hammer in hand, I marched up the stairs to where Tanya raged and pounded my fist upon her door.

"If you clean up your filth and stop this shrieking, I shall grant you release!"

"And what if I don't wanna?"

"Then I shall leave you to starve. Walling a lady into her chamber was a perfectly acceptable means of punishment in my day, child. I shall think no more of leaving you in here to rot than I would of flogging a servant."

In all truthfulness I have never held the belief that it is acceptable to either flog one's servants or starve young ladies in their rooms, but I was hardly about to inform Tanya of this. And now that I think about it, I did once indeed have a servant flogged for showing me his... Well, it was not anything I wished to see, and I ensured he would never feel the need to show me such things again.

Tanya cleaned her room and bathed, and dressed herself in clean garments. I had no idea what I would do with her. Although by now I was starving from having only a very small amount of blood over the span of days, I did not wish to prey upon one who had no means by which to escape. I would find nourishment where I may without resorting to feeding upon the helpless.

"Okay, the room is clean. You can let me out."

I began to pull forth the nails, carefully removing the boards. I was delighted to find this was not at all difficult. Too often do I forget that I possess unholy strength, for it is simply not acceptable behaviour for one to be twirling pianos above one's head. I try to conduct myself in a manner which my mother would find acceptable. I cannot think for a moment she would be charmed in the least to see her daughter hurling furnishings as Zeus doth lightning bolts.

I opened the door and was struck brutally on the head with what I would later learn was a rather large and heavy plaster piggy bank. I was more astonished than harmed, though my astonishment quickly became outrage. Tanya simply blinked stupidly, surprised that her assault had done little more than cover myself and my garments in dust that had once been a perfectly charming piggy bank imported from Mexico.

I was starving, and I was angry. In a moment I had Tanya by her hair, and I was feasting as I had not feasted in many years, not since the night I sought vengeance upon my murderers. I drank until I was not merely sated, but gluttonously full with her blood, and she was white as milk, staring upwards at nothing.

I became aware of a presence behind myself and turned to see whom it may be. I saw the shrouded form of poor Valerie in the doorway. Her shroud was badly gnawed and tattered, and I could see she had been biting at her arms. She would not become one of the moaning undead. Her fate was to become like the pig that had slaughtered her. I wondered if that was a blessing or a curse.

"What have you done? She'll rise now!" There was vexation in her whispered voice.

"She will not rise," I assured Valerie gently. "We shall lay her untended upon the shore. Sunlight will end her ere she rises in the eve, and you will be avenged."

We carried Tanya to the lake shore and placed her near the water. It was growing late, and the water stormed though there was no wind, and the moon shone full and clear. Valerie and I walked along the narrow strip of sand and gravel until we found a small boat.

"Peter has a cabin across the lake," Valerie said. "You can't see it from here, but the lake curves around that hill there. Follow the curve until you see a single light. That'll be his hunting cabin. That's where they'll be."

Valerie showed me how to use the little boat's outboard motor, and I set off across the lake in darkness. The final image I had of Valerie was as she sat alone upon the wharf, shrouded in a bed sheet, devouring the meat from her own limbs. When she could at last devour no more of herself, and the shroud was consumed, she would become the night pig, as had her cousin. I still wonder if it was a blessing or a curse. Is it better to be mindless when one is a monster? It is true I have lost much of what one may call compassion over the years, and it is not easy for me to converse with the living. And yet I hope that my mind may one day bring me redemption, and I may yet find a way to end this curse. Does my mother await me in Heaven, or has she long forgotten me? And why do I still wander the night? Is it untrue that vengeance will set my spirit free? Or does one still walk the land who is yet unpunished? I hoped this was not true, for I could not find this man or woman. Where indeed would I search? I had not so much as a name, for I had slain all those I knew had wronged me. If he still lived, the centuries would have hidden him well.

Had my vengeance caused my own doom?

I arrived at the hidden cabin two hours before sunrise. I moored my little boat and then, my bag clutched firmly in my fist, marched down the length of the wharf to the cabin and banged loudly upon the door. Moments later it was answered by Lisa.

"Deirdre! How nice to see you!"

"They *hanged* thieves in my day," I informed her.

"Yeah, Florence was just telling me that."

I strode into the house and found Florence within a small wooden crate upon the table, eating cabbage. Someone had gone through the effort of dressing her in a pink princess gown. I gazed sourly at the small beast and then turned to Lisa.

"Had I known you had gone through such effort I would have dressed up as ~~Link~~ a knight."

"Cool! We can do that for Halloween. Assuming there will be a Halloween."

"Every day is Halloween now," said Melissa in a weary voice.

Peter stepped into the kitchen then and paused as he spied me. "Hi."

I gave him a quick curtsey in acknowledgement. "Good evening, Peter."

"I wasn't sure you were coming."

"Your charming daughter gave me little choice."

He turned his eyes away from me, gazing down at the floor as he spoke. "And where's Tanya?"

I spoke the truth, although I uttered not as much of the truth as perhaps I should. "I saw her last upon the beach."

He nodded. "Was that before or after she put that dent in your forehead?"

I closed my eyes and sighed. "Peter, I am very sorry. I told her to clean her room as well as herself and I would release her. I kept my word. But when I opened the door, she struck me with a large, white plaster piggy bank with a blue flower upon the side. I was as furious as I was ravenous, and I devoured her. I had not intended to harm her. I will not say she gave me no choice I *will* say my nature overpowered my will. I am sorry, Peter."

He nodded. "So how long until you kill all of us?"

"I will kill no others. I came only for Florence."

Lisa gasped. "No, you can't go! You have to stay!"

Oh, what fell curse is this that dangles all I desire before me when I may not have it? A home and a daughter—I ask naught for more. Here it stands before me. But the dead are not suitable parents.

"Lisa, your father is right. I cannot be trusted. As time passes, my hunger will grow until I cannot control myself, and though I will surely weep for harming you, I will just as surely devour you."

"Then go later! Just don't go now!"

"Child, you are no fool. You must realize this situation cannot go on."

"Fine!" she shouted. "Then go! Everybody else does!"

She fled the kitchen and into the depths of the house. A door slammed, and Peter sighed loudly.

"She just really wants a mom," he said quietly.

"And I would like nothing more than a home and a daughter," I said. "But you and I both see that my staying can only lead to harm."

"I know. But, well… you may as well stay a few more days."

"It will only make it harder to leave," I said.

"Deirdre," said Peter. "Where do you have to go to anyway?"

"Nowhere," I said softly. "I have nowhere to go and no one to await my arrival."

"Then a few more days with us won't matter. And it would be a shame to make Florence give back the gown."

I cast a glance towards Florence in her pretty pink gown with the ruffled, white lace hem.

"Somewhere a doll is under-clad and very cold," I observed.

* * *

And so I stayed in the little hidden cabin by the lake, at least for the time. I knew the hunger would come upon me and that my time with Lisa, Melissa, and Peter would pass, but for now I could indulge my fancies that I was but a normal woman, 'though one who could not face the sun. Still, I could not help but wonder how all this was affecting poor Lisa; she so very much wished for me to stay and went to bed each night uneasy that I would take to the highway whist she slept. I swore to her I would not creep off like a thief in the night, and she seemed to take solace in that.

It was the third night in the cabin that we were frightened by the sound of boots upon the shingled roof. I was distracted from my needlework by the slow measured stride of what sounded to me like a large man and could not think from whence he had come, nor how he had come to be on the roof, save for unholy methods.

"Is it one of them?" Lisa whispered.

"No," I said. "Shroud eaters lack such grace. This one came to be on the roof without our knowledge, and I suspect we only hear him now because he chooses to allow us."

"So what could it be?" asked Peter.

"Not the simple undead," I said. "This is a higher form of devil."

Melissa suddenly screamed as if Death himself had come for her. When we ran to see what terror she had spied, we saw a white face looming in the window, upside-down as the creature dangled from the roof. Peter, Lisa, and Melissa stood rapt with horror. I ran to the window and flung it open.

"Stuart!"

"Is this a private party, or may any rogue join?"

"You… monster!"

"Well, I'm hardly *that* repulsive."

Repulsive he was not. He was indeed very handsome, with his long dark hair and eyes the same shade of grey as a winter sea. He was also a knave to his very core. I dragged him inside forcibly with what strength the powers of darkness had granted me, then slapped him soundly.

"*That* is for making me weep over your demise you… you… Peeping Thomas!"

His features softened, and he reached out to take my hand. "I am deeply sorry, my lady. I dressed a corpse in my clothes in the hopes the shroud eater would lose my scent, but my ruse failed. I could not return to you, and when at last the opportunity came, you had fled. I tracked you here with no small effort on my part…"

As he spoke, his voice was growing ever softer, as his gaze slipped farther down, finally settling upon my bosom.

"My lady, may I just say this is by far the most appealing gown I have seen you in."

I confess to being both amused and vexed. "My lord, what colour are my eyes?"

"Porcelain, my lady, utterly porcelain."

Lisa giggled. I cast her a glance.

"Learn this lesson well, child, for as you see, speech may change, fashion may change, and custom may change. Men do *not*."

Peter stepped forward, wary of Stuart, and with just cause. No man in his right mind cares to see two vampires standing with his children.

"I take it you are a friend of Deirdre's. My name is Peter."

"Stuart Cooper at your service, good sir. I thank you for caring for my lady."

"Actually she's sorta been looking after us," said Lisa.

"And not succeeding at my task as well as I would like," I said. "Lisa, Melissa, I would like you to meet Stuart. He is a rogue and a knave, so do not turn your backs to him for a moment."

"My lady, you cut me to the quick!"

"Tempt me not! I wept a river for your loss, and now here you pop up like a knave in a box to frighten children!"

Stuart glanced to Lisa. "Poor woman is mad about me."

"I see that," said Lisa. "Are you a vampire, too?"

"I am, though at the moment I am a well-fed vampire, so you need not fear."

"She need not fear, regardless," I said sharply as I marched into the kitchen to make tea. Why do I always go in search of tea in order to better withstand life's vexations? An unanswerable question, I fear. "These are my friends, not your lunch. And where did you find any living beings to bite?"

"There was a goodly crowd of them at the Nanaimo ferry terminal. Alas, their wait for a ship to bear them from these cursed shores shall be long; none are permitted to cross without quarantine, to ensure the plague has not struck them."

"Then there are still living people on the island," said Peter.

"The plague is moving very fast, but so far, Nanaimo and all areas beneath her through to Victoria are clear. That shall not last long. Roadblocks have been established to ensure the infected do not reach the uninfected. Those who seem well are taken into quarantine. The undead... they are dealing with as well as they are able. However, the Canadian military, for some reason, seems untrained in the matter of zombie attack and vampire invasion."

"Can we get out?" asked Melissa hopefully.

Stuart shook his head. "I would not risk it, child. The roads are a nightmare. If you had good horses and a trail through the mountains you might make it, but all swift paths are clotted with the dead and undead. You would be lucky to make it as far as Cumberland without being devoured or infected."

"What about the slow roads?" asked Peter. "What if we got on one of the old logging roads around here? We could get on a logging road and hike down to Port Alberni."

"Dad, do you have any idea how long that would take?" said Lisa.

"But it's possible," said Peter. "There's an unmarked logging road that goes all the way down to the pack trails and eventually joins up with some of the roads leading to Port Alberni."

"Port Alberni is no longer there," said Stuart. "It is a flaming hell of burning buildings and undead. You are safer here, my lord. Heed my words. You do not wish to take your children into the wild and lead them blindly to safe havens that are no longer safe."

"We're going to need food," said Peter. "We had to leave a lot of supplies at the other house."

"I can bring you food," said Stuart.

"Some means of communication would be nice, too," said Melissa.

"Is there anyone at the Comox Air Base?" asked Lisa.

"None alive," said Stuart. "You are in the center of the storm of death. If you wish to live, you would be wise to stay where you are. Return to your former home to claim supplies when yours run low, if it is close enough. But you are far safer here than if you leave."

"I just wish we could call out," said Peter. "Let the rescue workers know where we are. They'll be looking for us at the cedar house."

"I have a cell phone," said Stuart. "You are welcome to try."

Stuart gave Peter the phone. Peter activated the device and called a number, but was greeted only with an automated voice informing him the system was overloaded, and it was uncertain when service would be resumed. Peter gave the phone back to Stuart.

"Well, who's up for a game of cards?"

The kettle began to whistle, and I went to attend to the tea. I was aware of Stuart following after me.

"And what is it you wish, you rogue?" I inquired.

"Your mortal friends are in very grave danger," said Stuart.

"I know this well;, you need not tell me. Are they indeed safe here?"

"They are by far safer here than if they are to give in to some madness and attempt to strike out for Nanaimo or Port Alberni or any other destination," said Stuart.

"How fares my apartment?"

"Locked and undisturbed when last I looked. I was there but two days ago. The police have been through the building, though I suspect they had enough to deal with and felt no need to disturb your little home."

"So my fears were correct—the shroud eater slew those who lived in the building."

"It was no shroud eater, my lady fair," said Stuart, helping himself to a cookie. "This was a monster with a mind, and a rage. This thing slid into the homes of all who dwelled there and ensured they lived not to see another sunrise. No vampire did this. No vampire has such a blood lust."

I turned my head to look at him, fear in my cold heart. "What did this beast do?"

"The police are saying naught—there is too much to fear already without the public learning of this horror. They fear the city shall erupt into madness. They are tending to the dead and alerting kin of the fallen as quietly as they may. A gas leak is the official word—unfortunate, but an accident. But I was in that building. 'Twas no gas leak that drags the entrails from the living and carves the flesh from the bone of a woman's thigh, and leaves half-devoured babes upon the floor. I saw men split as the Vikings did their enemies, with the ribs broken and pulled outwards like the wings of some demonic bird. This was a monster of malice, delighting in the carnage, as it has done for many, many centuries. This, fair maid, is something far beyond the grasp of thee and me, and, if one cares for the opinion of a simple neck-biter, the father of this horror."

I gazed at him, speechless. The kettle began to whistle shrilly, but I could not force myself to move to attend to it. Stuart removed it from the stove and turned off the burner, filling the tea pot on my behalf.

"What monster could this be?" I was surprised to finally find my voice.

"Something of age. I know not what it may be. But I am dear friends with one who long ago rowed his longboat to the shores of faraway lands, and he confirmed much of the mayhem was of the sort committed by his folk."

"A Nordic Viking, perhaps?" I queried. "An aged vampire driven mad by the centuries?"

"I suggested such myself, but my friend said he thought not. There were other forms of sacrifice as well—not only those performed by the sons of Odin. It was he who indicated to me that the small children were gnawed upon by great jaws that left flakes of fine rust. The vampires of Russia have jaws of iron, do they not?"

"So legend says. I have never had the dubious pleasure of meeting one. Perhaps we are dealing with a small group of horrors, all of very great age, taking advantage of the carnage spread by the shroud eaters in order to fulfill their ancient bloodlust."

"That I find a likely suggestion," said Stuart. "But let us not speak of this not before your young ladies. Let us have tea and pretend to be civilized folk, playing dull parlour games for the sake of appearances. Speaking of dull parlour games, need I challenge this Peter for your hand?"

I smiled. "I fail to see why," I said, placing the pot upon a tray along with biscuits and sandwiches. "After all, I do have *two* hands."

Stuart raised a brow. "I shall have to have a word with your mother, young lady. I do believe that was not proper drawing-room talk at all."

"I shall but fall to my knees and pray for her forgiveness, which she shall surely grant, for I was her only dear daughter."

"And what shall your father say?"

"He will ask you your faith, and if he likes not your answer then he will show his dogs to you… and you to them."

"And then tie antlers to my head I suppose."

"If he has no other place to put them that he deems more suitable."

"You are a most wicked young lady."

"Why thank you, my lord."

We returned to the living room. Stuart seated himself whilst I laid out the tea.

"Wanna watch a movie?" Lisa asked.

"Please, nothing with vampires," said Stuart. "I grow so weary of ranting at the screen."

"*Nightmare on Elm Street*?" she said hopefully.

"Lisa," I said, "why on earth would you wish to watch a scary movie, given our current situation?"

She shrugged. "I just like it better when the scary things are an actor in make-up."

"Well, I can't say I mind," said Stuart. "Though I should perhaps go in search of a dark place to sleep ere the night grows too late. Ah, mine is a sad fate. I shall be alone and helpless, bound in a casket made of flimsy rotted wood, fodder for the beasts…"

"Wow," said Lisa. "Emo much?"

"Well, the attic is pretty secure," said Peter.

"Oh, no, I could never evict poor Deirdre from her sanctuary."

"I have my own room," I informed him. "And it is not in the attic."

"And so I am to be hidden away, a secret lover lying still and silent, awaiting love's indiscreet kiss."

"An attic is where one commonly stores ridiculous things for which one has no use, yes," I said. I picked up my needlework, determined to enjoy my time as a lady of the house.

"How did you become a vampire, Stuart?" asked Melissa.

I smiled at Melissa's question, for I had no doubt in my heart that the tale would be grand and dramatic and utterly false. I confess to being surprised by his response.

"Oh, that is a tale for another night. I've no desire to make myself unwelcome by the sharing of dull and trivial tales."

"I cannot for one moment believe that anything about you was dull and trivial in life," I said.

"Well it's hardly the sort of tale with which one regales young ladies."

Lisa rolled her eyes. "Yeah, because we totally don't know about like sex and penises and booze and stuff."

"In my case it's more of a matter of having utterly disgraced one's family," said Stuart.

"I cannot imagine you doing any such thing," I said.

"And yet I did. I was the very worst sort of shiftless youth, far too wealthy and entitled for my own good. I had land and riches to spare, and none to tell me how I might use it or guide me along a righteous path. That is a foul combination — to be gifted with opulence and to be beholden to none. I grew bored and discontent. And as such… I began associating with brigands, thieves, highwaymen… anyone I thought would provide amusement for glutted sensibilities. I robbed from the innocent, threw women into the ditches, and took my pleasures where I could. I was a monster. And one night, I harmed the wrong person. Her brothers came for me, and… I was hanged at a crossroads."

I was silent in horror, for despite my teasing accusations, I could not believe the charming man before me had been such a rogue. Stuart smiled faintly.

"I was a seventh son and a murderer, buried at a crossroads in an unmarked and unhallowed grave. I rose to bedevil the living and have been walking the night alone ever since."

"I cannot believe you were ever such a man," I said.

"Alas, it is true," said Stuart. "I lived in a time when wealth granted one endless privilege, and I allowed myself to become the sort of disgusting lout I could never permit myself to be today. I have paid for my lack of responsibility to my fellow man with my soul. And I have none to blame but myself. If you ask me, my lady, I have naught to complain about."

"I am very sorry for you, Stuart," I said. "I wish you could have seen the error of your ways before you came to such a bad end."

"Oh, I do not consider myself so badly used," he said. "Who but I could boast to having seen both the Victorian age as well as The Beatles on Ed Sullivan?"

I rolled my eyes. "Oh, well, yes, I can certainly see how The Beatles are worth eternal damnation. Lisa, be a dear and put the movie in, lest Stuart resume speaking."

We watched the movie, though I cannot say I enjoyed it. Stuart's news that we were living in the eye of a storm of death was not comforting, and I cared not for the feeling that crept over me. I could find no ease, and my mind was filled with images of bobbing dead, making their slow and ponderous way through the depths of the lake, coming to the small wharf to drag their leaden weight out of the water, heading silently toward the cabin…

I nearly jumped out of my very skin when I heard the sound of a horse making quiet sounds outside the door. My needlepoint took flight, and my hand clutched my heart. Stuart took my hand.

"My dear, the movie is not that frightening."

"The movie be damned., I heard a horse."

"A horse?" said Peter. "Where would a horse come from?"

"Maybe it was just a noise on the movie," said Lisa.

"I'll go look," said Melissa.

"No!" said Stuart sharply, halting her in her tracks. "Do no such thing, child. There are many creatures of darkness that take the form of that noble beast. Keep the door shut tight. We know not what made that sound."

Melissa gazed at him, as if she could not comprehend such a thing. Peter rose from his chair and walked over to the window, peering into the darkness.

"There is something standing on the wharf. It looks like a horse. But that's ridiculous, where the hell would it have come from?"

"Hell would be my guess," said Stuart. "Draw the shades."

Peter did so, with needless violence and sighing loudly. He seemed to be very swiftly reaching the end of what his senses could bear as he ranted quietly so not to draw the attention of the creature on the dock.

"So it's not bad enough we're up to our ass in vampires, now we have demon-horses as well? What's it doing here?"

"It seems likely it has come for your daughters," I said. "Many such spectral horses prey upon unwary ladies. They bear them into deep water or to Hell. I have heard tell of the Horses of St. Toader, who are said to take the form of young men, sometimes with the heads of horses, and if they find a woman alone, they shall force her to dance with them until she dies."

"Why do I have the feeling that by *dance with them*, you actually mean they rape these girls to death," said Lisa.

"That would be my assumption," I said. "Some other tales say the horses will trample them and pull out their entrails. But the Horses of St. Toader are a rarely-told tale, and I find it unlikely they would have come all the way from Romania to trouble us."

"One of my neighbours is Romanian," said Peter. "Is there a chance they're here because of her?"

I walked to the window and peered into the night at the scrawny, shaggy beast, its rough black coat dull and tangled with burrs. I flung the door open and stepped outside, snatching up a stone.

"Begone, nightmare!" I flung the rock, striking it in the head. "Take your disgusting visage back to Hell, or I'll send thee in pieces for the hounds of Hades! Satan may boil your bones for glue, or I shall do it if you wish! I fear thee not."

"My lady, I am not so certain this is the wisest choice," said Stuart.

"I care not!" I said, and truly I meant it.

My disgust at this monster, waiting only to force its vile intentions on Lisa and Melissa, made me angry and fearless. The horse of Hell turned, but had no place to go other than the lake, and clearly it wished not to go there. So that was where I intended to drive it. I snatched up a shovel and marched down the dock, striking the foul beast across the skull. It turned and leapt into the water with a great explosive boiling of water, and a stench of brimstone. Slowly it sank, becoming a dead thing of slime, eyes rolling over white and steaming blood bubbled from the nose and mouth. I turned and hurried back to the cabin, hastening inside and closing the door.

"Dude!" said Melissa. "You kicked ass!"

"I did what I needs must, nothing more," I said. "Let us lock this door and draw the curtains."

"Will it be back?" asked Peter.

"I think not," I said. "It came only because it sensed the evil that is roaming free. It is not part of whatever foulness is taking place—rather, it is a scavenger of filth. Whatever reason brings it forth, we may all expect unsettling dreams."

"It's not going to lead anything back here, is it?" asked Lisa.

"No, child," I assured her. "He was here only for his own desires. He travels with none. His appearance signals only that the gates of Hell are indeed open, and we are very much alone.

"Not as alone as we would like," said Peter. "Listen."

We became still and listened to the night. In the distance came the low, droning moan of a shroud eater.

* * *

We spent the last of the evening boarding doors and windows, sealing our little cabin so nothing could enter without our knowing. Then as dawn came, mortal and vampire alike took to their beds. I allowed Stuart to share my room, seeing no reason not to trust him. However, I suspected he had rather hoped to sleep alongside me in the bed rather than upon a cot nearby.

"Your friends are in a most unenviable position," said Stuart, slipping beneath the covers.

"They know," I said. "They have lost two of their number already, and now their haven is encroached upon once more."

"They are safer here than they are trying to reach Nanaimo," said Stuart. "But… only if we are not here."

"I agree," I said quietly, "though it shall break my heart to leave them. What do you propose?"

"I say we strike out for Nanaimo ourselves and alert any we may to the situation, and send help. Then I suggest we seek others of our kind and try to find a way to end this madness. Mortal-kind will not endure this horror, Deirdre. They shall try to end it. They shall send soldiers with weapons, and damn the young men who arrive to fight. The numbers of the shroud eaters shall swell as does the tick upon the dog. And they are not our only concern. Other fools shall arrive too; fools who call themselves vampires and Satan worshippers, who believe they have some command over this situation. They will arrive by the busload, walking into the realm of the undead, and becoming them. When did mankind become so thick?"

"We have always been thick, Stuart. The fact that some see apocalypse as their personal shining moment is hardly the most stupid thing any man has done."

"We have quite enough monsters on hand," said Stuart. "We hardly require any more."

"Are you certain Nanaimo is the right decision?" I asked.

"It is if we wish to reach the mainland. When last I was at my crypt, I discovered something, but I had no time to investigate further. The dead whisper there of something having arrived and dug itself a lair."

"A shroud eater?"

"They did not say. But something of great age and malice, something that could well be powerful enough to draw to it all the evil we are seeing. It is likely it has made contact with other creatures of the dead realm; certainly, there are enough grudging dead in Vancouver to draw forth much evil."

"You speak of the Great Vancouver Fire of 1886."

"And of the way those who were brought here to work were treated. There is darkness here, but this is a young country, in a modern age, with jaded youth who believe not in the undead. They believe vampires are tinkling fairies come to save little girls, and the son of the devil wishes only to be understood, and that fairies and elves make toys. Age-old evil could take a place such as this so very, very easily. Respect for the darkness is not taught."

"As I have said myself so many times," I said.

We were silent with our thoughts, hearing the distant moan of a shroud eater. Slowly the morning crept up on us, and the sleep of the dead claimed us both.

* * *

Never had a departure grieved me as much as this one. I did not wish to go, and I cursed myself for having broken my own law regarding making friends with the living. We do not belong with one another; nothing healthy can come of such an arrangement.

Still, I wept bloody tears as I packed my few belongings.

"Don't go," said Lisa.

"Child, I would like nothing better than to stay, but the choice is not mine. If I depart then you are far safer, and Stuart and I shall send help."

"Will I ever see you again?"

"I do not know," I said softly, closing up my bag.

Lisa sniffed, trying very hard to hold back her own tears. "You didn't pack Florence's things."

"I was rather hoping you would look after Florence for me. She cannot come with me, for I will be taking dark roads not suitable for her."

Lisa nodded. "Okay, I'll take Florence. At least if she's here, then… you might come back to see her."

I turned to her. "Lisa, I swear, if it is at all possible, I will see you again. I wish we had met in merrier times, but we must do our best with what we have."

We embraced, saying our goodbyes. I said farewell to Florence last, smiling through my tears at the soft noises she made before returning her to her box. Ah, Florence, you have seen so much more than any guinea pig before you. What tales would you tell, had you the ability to write?

Stuart and I took his small boat back to the Bottom, stepping cautiously onto the wharf and looking carefully to see what horrors might be lying in wait for us. I looked for Valerie, but did not see her. Tanya, however, was where we had placed her, feeding the ravens and worms. That, at least, was one small mercy. I did not wish to think what evil she might have wrought as the undead. Stuart paused to gaze at her body.

"You just left her here on the lake shore?"

"You would have done the same had you known her."

We stood by the lake shore, listening, trying to ascertain whether there was anything close at hand of which we needed to be wary.

"It seems safe enough," I said. "I hear no moaning."

"Nor do I," said Stuart. "Does that not strike you as strange?"

"I confess as to knowing so little in regards to shroud eaters that I cannot say whether it is strange or not. I will say that the few days since we left hardly seems time enough for these creatures to have departed. What they lack in wit they more than make up for in persistence."

Stuart nodded. "So why would they have left?"

"Valerie said they were rising forth to breed. Perhaps they left because they had devoured all the humans here."

"Let us explore the area," said Stuart. "Perhaps it is safe for Lisa and her father to return. They would be more comfortable here."

Together we explored the area, but found nothing, no shroud eaters of any kind. The night was silent. We heard no moaning, smelled no stink of walking undeath, saw no movement. At first, we were silent and cautious in our search, but after a time we cast off our caution. We shouted. We threw things. We even lit a bonfire upon the beach, but nothing came out of the darkness. The monsters, it seemed, had moved on.

"I do not understand this," I said. "Did we not hear moaning last night? Did I not chase away a nightmare?"

"They may have been stragglers," said Stuart. "Come, let us find a cabin with a television. I would like to know if anything has changed elsewhere."

"Peter's house has one."

We entered Peter's cedar house and sat down to watch the news. Much had changed in the brief time that had lapsed since Stuart was in Nanaimo; those who had been quarantined and were awaiting transport now lay dead and rotting in the streets, slathered in their own fouled blood, their bodies covered with the stinking black buboes that gave name to this foul ailment. A few of the unfortunate stood moaning, their dead flesh bloated and grey, their eyes turned white. Amidst the strewn corpses wandered black horses, their coats rough and covered in sores, their ribs showing through their festering hides. With heads like skulls covered in old leather, they searched the dead, pawing at the fallen as they searched for something only their foul minds understood. Carrion birds gathered in great force, and filled the very air as does ash when stirred from the hearth by a strong wind.

"Hell has burst forth," I whispered. "Look at the sheer number of these creatures! See how many of the shroud eaters! I would have not thought there were so many in all the world!"

"They seem to have all travelled south in search of meat," said Stuart.

I held my hands to my mouth. "From whence have they all come? They are multitude!"

"So we have good news and bad news," said Stuart. "The good news is your friends are safe from the shroud eaters. The bad news is they are no longer safe from you and I."

"What do you mean?" I asked.

"We cannot leave the island now."

"There are still people in Victoria," I said. "And ferries! We may travel there!"

"And reach it before those monsters? Deirdre, the lower portion of the island is under strict quarantine. Any that come now will be denied access, assuming there are any alive to grant or deny!

"Are you saying we have no means by which we may bypass a simple roadblock?"

"I am saying that between the legions of the undead and those who are alive to fear them, we would be most foolish to try!"

I shook my head, rising to my feet and pacing. "No. No, Stuart, I cannot sit here and discuss eating those children. There must be another way."

"Deirdre, I am not insisting we do them harm. I am saying we are in a very dire situation. What now shall we do?"

"I shall tell you what we shall do. There are no undead here. They have gone south like the birds to find greener pastures. We will forsake all plans of going there and take a car to Royston, find a boat, and cross the Georgia Strait there."

"Deirdre," said Stuart with quiet intensity, "Royston is no more. Union Bay is no more. Any tiny coastal town you may name is *no more.* We are trapped."

"Do not force me to become more of a monster than I have already become!" I cried.

I began to weep into my hands. Stuart came to my side, pulling me close in his efforts to lend comfort.

"I am sorry, dear lady. Please forgive me. You are fond of these children, and none should seek to harm those they love."

"I have made a fool of myself. I have broken my own law; that one does not make pets of cattle. They are no longer cattle to me, nor indeed are they pets. They are my children. And I cannot harm them. I cannot. I will starve first."

"Then let us find a car and drive to Royston. Let us see if we can find even a small boat. Perhaps if we are very fortunate, we shall find a means to save your babies as well as ourselves."

"You are a good man, Stuart. Thank you. Your kindness means a great deal to me."

He kissed my brow, then rose to his feet. "I am not kind. I am a knave and an opportunist. If a pretty maid weeps, I seek to soothe her tears that she may reward me."

I smiled. "Stuart, permit me to use the vernacular of the day, though I have no doubt it shall cause my dear mother in Heaven to raise hand to brow and faint: Bullshit."

"Of course it is bullshit. But do not spread rumours, lest my reputation suffer."

* * *

We found a station wagon, and within it we placed such things as we may need should sunlight find us. I glued black cloth found in one of the cabins over the back windows, while Stuart loaded in blankets and a heavy tarp, which he stapled to the roof inside the vehicle to form a drape behind the front seat. We now had a means of transport suitable for two creatures who shun daylight. Doubtless the police would not have approved, but they had concerns far more grave than this strange ship. Stuart finished the task of preparing the vehicle by finding a pot of red paint and a brush, and wrote about the fender of the old car—"Demeter."

"Your sense of humour is truly wanting, my lord," I said.

"I'll have you know I was the funniest man in the cemetery," he informed me archly. "Come my lady, your ship awaits."

I settled myself in the opulent nest we had made in the back, rolling up the tarp so that I could see as Stuart drove, and we set out slowly, moving cautiously so we might avoid anything that may be on the road. Our caution was rewarded as we came upon a police car lying on its side like a wounded animal. One police officer stood beside it, his body bloated and grey, moaning out the single-note dirge that was the song of his miserable kind. The other police officer was clearly dead.

"Let that be a warning to us," said Stuart. "They have not all departed."

"But what drew them in such numbers to the southern points of the island?" I asked.

"There may be no great mystery here," said Stuart. "They hunger as do we, and at the risk of being disgusting... that is where the food is."

I shuddered. "We are no better."

"I beg to differ, my lady. We are much better. How many lives have you taken since you became the walking dead?"

"I slew those who murdered me," I said. "But in the centuries since, I have taken only one, and had I been better fed that would not have happened. I do not count the charlatans slain to feed myself in the time of the plague."

"Then treat yourself more gently. We are not wanton killers."

I drew myself up as I saw a form by the side of the road — a mighty boar, its bristles blacker than night, eyes burning with Hellfire. About its neck were the few remaining scraps of a floral bed sheet, used as a burial shroud. It turned and fled into the woods, and any remorse I may have felt over Tanya's end vanished. Tanya was dead. Valerie was not so fortunate.

"Did I just glimpse a wild boar? I thought those did not live here," said Stuart.

"That was no boar. It was a night pig. Once it was a little girl named Valerie. I shall tell you her story sometime, when the grief is less near."

We took the old Island Highway through Cumberland as it led past the graveyard, as we wished to see if all was as it should be there. The cemetery was dark and silent, covered with a layer of fog, and seemed for the most part to be undisturbed. A handful of graves were torn open, though most slept easy. We stopped the car and left it to see if we could find any like ourselves, but if such beings had been there, they had long departed.

I stood in the silent darkness and looked around. This place pleased me in a way few cemeteries do. The ground was flat and even, though the grass was beginning to grow long. It was oval, with a fence along one side and the remaining three sides guarded by trees. It brought to mind gardens of my youth, though different flowers had grown there, ones less stony and cold. I ran my fingertips over the headstone of one whose name I did not recognize, but the cleanness of the painted stone, despite its age, spoke to me of one who was loved.

"Ginger Goodwin, a miner's friend," I read aloud.

"Miners may be glad he still rests easy. Others in this place do not," said Stuart. "Something over yon gnaws upon itself in the grave, and I for one care not to be near when it grows weary of devouring its own meat."

"I would like to call this cemetery home when at last my cursed life is over," I said.

"That may come sooner than you would like if you do not make haste. There are more things stirring here than first we suspected. Let us be gone."

"No," I said softly. "I desire answers. The dead who lie here may have some. I shall take a grave that has been opened and lie within, that I may hear what they have to say."

"Very well. I shall keep watch."

I found a grave that suited my purpose and stepped into it, disliking the soured smell of the earth. I laid myself down upon the ground and closed my eyes, and attended to the whispering of the dead, their voices all around me like a strange cloud.

"Let me out."

"Stay silent. The time for wandering is past. Rest now."

"Let me out."

"I wish to rise! It is our time now. Here, too, the foxes shall die, as once they did in the English gardens."

"No. Sleep now. My work is done."

"Let me out."

"We must rise with the others."

"Why do you wish to rise?" I asked quietly.

"Let me out."

"We must walk. We are too few. Too few! The world of the infernal commands balance as does the world of nature. It is our time to kill and raise our numbers. The living grow arrogant with unbelief."

"Let me out."

"Oh, bloody hell, shut up already. I'm dead. I want to sleep."

I stifled an involuntary giggle at the last voice and its vexed tone. "So, is this what is causing this rising and gathering of undead?"

"It is time to walk. There can be no balance without the creatures of nightmares as well as the creatures of

dreams. There can be no peace without a time for vengeance."

I thanked the whispering voices and rose from the grave to see Stuart seated upon the hood of the old car.

"Have you learned anything?" he inquired.

"It is as Valerie said. The fell things that dwell in the night have become too few in number. They have risen up to cause plague and death, and to seek vengeance that they might find peace. There is no great mystery to unfold here, though doubtless the living shall not learn why the dead walk until they are well past caring."

My attention was drawn by a horrid green light at the far end of the cemetery, past the well-tended edges of this garden of dead flowers to the cemetery of the Chinese workers. Their garden had been left untended to rot, their grave markers jutting out of the tangled underbrush like strange and monstrous plants. Nearby lurked three hideous forms, shrouded in a strange green light, their fingernails grown into talons. Their teeth were enormous, serrated along the edges like a woodsman's saw, and their faces were rotted and hideous. They approached, but were cautious and seemed more curious than violent, at least for the moment. I rose to my feet and greeted them cautiously.

"I am Deirdre of Leeds."

They growled and sniffed as do beasts, and then one slowly took on the visage of a young and, so I thought, rather lovely Chinese man.

"I do not remember my name, or I would give it to you. I had no family to bury me, and so I, like my companions, were laid upon the ground and left to decay. And so we have become as you see us. We are *chiang-shih*. We are travelling south in search of meat."

I was delighted to hear this, for the further they travelled south, the further they were away from my children. I had heard of these creatures through my research with Lisa on the computer. Like the Nosferatu, they preyed not only upon the blood of young women, but their bodies, and I would not have Lisa flayed alive to have her flesh devoured whilst she was violated.

"Then you had best make haste. The shroud eaters are laying waste to more prey than they have need."

"Is that where you are heading?"

"Where else?" I said. "There is naught here but old bones. I require hot blood, not cold meat."

"Then I wish you good fortune on your hunt. Perhaps we shall meet again."

Once more he took on the appearance of a hideous monster, uttering a piercing scream of hate, pain, and violence. He became enveloped in a flaming green light, and his body became covered in filthy white hair like that of a very old man who no longer has sense enough to bathe. His eyes became the colour of blood, and together the three rose into the air, heading away from the cemetery and south to where they would find victims to rape and to rend. I watched them depart with no small measure of relief and prayed they would not return. I hoped especially they did not have companions who walked the shore of the lake.

Chapter Seven

We resumed our sojourn to Royston, but ere we even reached the beach, we knew our quest was futile. Someone, I assumed the military, had razed all buildings to the ground and burned them, seeking to destroy whatever it was that may be causing this strange illness that so mimicked the Black Plague. Any ships that may have remained had been removed or carried their owners across the strait. I stood among the still-smoking ruins, looking around, my heart breaking.

"I did try to tell you," said Stuart gently.

"Yes," I said quietly. "You did. But how did you reach these shores?"

"I stowed away on a ferry bound for Nanaimo. The soldiers were already burning the houses and leading away those who were not ill. Some had escaped in crafts of their own. Already a great exodus was underway, and already the lake had been struck. I thought there was still a chance, but it seems I was wrong. By the time they knew what was happening, it was already too late."

We stood in silence, lost in our thoughts. Sadness gripped my heart that all these pretty little towns were now little more than ruins.

"Shall we set out for Victoria?" Stuart asked quietly.

"Is there nothing farther north?"

"Nay, it seems to have begun there and swept downwards. If there *is* salvation, it lies south, though I doubt very much we shall find succour."

"Yet Vancouver seems untouched," I said.

"For now.

"Yes, for now," I said.

Stuart gazed at me as I slowly took in the desolation that had once been a pretty little town.

"Shall we try for Victoria?" he asked.

"Let us try. But not now. The morning draws near. Let us rest and make the journey tomorrow."

We slept in the station wagon, our alterations proving an effective barrier against the sun, though my hand missed Florence's furry warmth. I hoped she was faring well and wondered if she missed me, or if she knew I was gone at all. I confess I know little about the minds of guinea pigs, though they seem not to have much mind at all. But she was dear to me, and I found it comforting to imagine she would sometimes pause and wonder where I was.

Evening came, and I knew upon awaking that I had not left Lisa, Peter, and Melissa too soon. I was starving, and my ghastly hunger would need sating quickly, or my actions would be that of a ravening beast. We drove down the shore-side highway, the beauty of it marred by burning as frightened men and women sought to remove the source of the plague. They would likely have relied upon scientific knowledge of how the Black Death is spread, and with this being such a virulent strain, they had taken no chances in routing out every flea, louse, and tick, as well as their hosts. Alas for them, in this instance the lowly parasites were guiltless. This plague came not from them, but the walking dead. I noticed also that the few remaining shroud eaters we spied in our travels had bullet wounds to the head. I know not if a bullet to the brain would truly fell a zombie, but it worked not upon a shroud eater, and the sight of them droning their dirges with the better part of their heads missing was enough to turn even my undead stomach.

Just outside of Nanaimo, we came upon a barricade of great military vehicles, barbed wire, and enormous steel devices like great metal crosses. Milling about were soldiers, moaning, their eyes white, black ichors leaking from their mouths. More soldiers lay on the ground, broken, partially devoured, and rotting. As we gazed upon this horrid scene, Stuart and I knew there was no sanctuary farther south.

"I suggest we turn back to whence we came," said Stuart.

"I concur," I said. "But not to the lake. We cannot be trusted among the children until we have fed."

We slowly reversed away from the hideous barricade, drawing as little attention to our selves as possible. We managed to turn the vehicle around and drove away. As we left Nanaimo in the distance, Stuart guided the car to in inland Island Highway, leaving the older, scenic highway that wound its way past the beaches.

"Why are you going here?" I asked.

"I mean to turn into Parksville and see if we may find any alive. If it has not been levelled in its entirety yet there may be a few alive in a church or motel."

We drove into Parksville, finding portions of the town untouched. The soldiers had far more to contend with here, it being larger than the tiny towns along the coast, and little time to clear the dead. There were indications that an orderly evacuation had begun, but something had interrupted it. Slowly we prowled the silent streets.

"There," said Stuart. "A church.

I peered out the window at the building, a sign before it proclaiming the name to be Arbutus Grove Church. It seemed peaceful and untouched, and a light was burning within.

"Stuart, I confess, the idea of dining upon those seeking sanctuary within a church sits ill with me."

"Shall we pray for looters?"

"I would rather dine upon those *blaspheming* within a church than *praying* within it, yes."

"Then we shall pray for looters. Let us also pray for restraint," said Stuart as an elderly woman and a boy of about twelve years of age raced across the grass towards us. They reached the car, and beat upon the window, weeping and pleading for help. Stuart rolled down the window.

"What vexes you, good lady?"

She pointed a trembling hand to the church just as three forms emerged.

"Please," she said. "You must help us. They're feeding us to those things."

Stuart opened the door. "Hide within the car. We shall deal with them."

We stepped out to face the trio of men racing toward us. The elderly woman and boy got into the car and closed the door. Then, as we stood in utter amazement, she drove away. The men approached.

"Why did you let her go?!" one demanded. "She's been looting food from the survivors and threw our pastor to the monsters!"

I raised a hand to my brow, sighing. "Chivalry is highly over-rated."

"I am sorry for our mistake, but we had no way of knowing that," said Stuart. "Truly if we had, we would have stopped her, but now we are without a car and without means of—"

The man punched Stuart, with considerable force, enraged that we would dare make such an error. Stuart's head rocked back, but that was all the reaction the man's blow received. Stuart blinked at him, shocked.

"I'm sorry, but did you just punch me in the face?

The men seemed rather daunted by the lack of pain inflicted. Stuart simply seemed astounded that any man would react thusly to what was a simple mistake. We had no means of determining whether this elderly woman was as she seemed, and no reasonable person would refuse aid to an old woman and her grandchild. But these men were of no mind to be reasonable; they were hungry and frightened, and trapped in a most unreasonable situation. It was likely we were not seeing them at their best. However Stuart and I were not at our best, either. We were starving, and bloodlust does not make for quiet discussions with vampires. I felt my mind begin to cloud with the rage of starvation, and Stuart and I began to silently stalk them. The men began to back away.

"Look, I'm sorry," said Stuart's assailant. "I was just... I mean I—"

"Had no idea what you were dealing with?" Stuart asked, his eyes burning with a golden-red light. "Permit me to introduce ourselves. This Is Deirdre of Leeds. She died in 1663. I am Stuart Cooper; I died a scant twenty years later. We are the walking undead, dear fellow! Surely you must have assumed as much; you are up to your ears in corpses seeking the flesh and blood of the living! But no! You are such fools, so full of your own self-righteous indignation that you lash out at strangers who have done you no wrong!"

"You cannot touch us! This is a house of the Lord!"

"No, I must correct you, dear fellow. This is the *lawn* of the Lord. That quaint structure over *there* is the *house* of the Lord. And we are about to offer up nourishment to His most sacred worms."

They turned and fled, and we gave chase. Stuart caught his first, felling the man like a lion and lunging for his throat. I caught mine next, catching hold of his jacket collar and yanking him off his feet. I threw him to the ground, taking care to stun him so I might feed in peace. Stuart, it seemed, had chosen more lively prey, and I could hear his meal screaming as he fed.

We glutted ourselves on the hot blood, feasting until we could take in not one more drop. We were streaked with blood, and it was smeared across the grass as if some child had tried to paint the sod red. Overcome with passion, brought on by the hunt and inflamed by blood, we consummated our friendship on the red-tainted grass with animal joy. We laughed as our bodies joined, kissing and biting, howling unholy ardour to the moon above. I was delighted to find I could still enjoy such things, and can only assume that the glut of hot life-fluid was what enabled Stuart to perform as does a stallion. Only Stuart's eventual exhaustion and the literal cooling of his blood ended our joy. We lay together on the grass amidst the clots and corpses, gazing at the stars, panting.

"Well, that was an unexpected delight," he said.

"My mother would be appalled," I stated.

"Well, if we meet the lady we shan't tell her. Still I cannot imagine you make a habit of such things."

"Certainly not! I cannot think, for one moment, why I did it now, though the handsomeness of my companion may be partly to blame."

Stuart sat up, red smears adorning his naked body. "I do believe it was catharsis. We have all been under a great strain. Odd things are bound to happen."

"Catharsis and nothing more?" I chided.

"Making love to a beautiful lady is perfectly understandable. Coupling on a church lawn surrounded by one's dinner remainders is an expression of stress."

I giggled. He reached out to pick up the remains of his cotton sweater to find it was now merely a collection of unravelled strings. He sighed and tossed it aside.

"Well we can go no further in our present shape. Let us find a house in which to hide from the daylight, and to bathe and seek clothing."

"That one!" I said, indicating a great house of white and pale tan. It was the finest house in the area and had the look of having been hastily abandoned. "Let us try that one."

We entered the house cautiously, checking to see if it was at all inhabited, either by the living or the dead. It seemed those who had dwelled here had indeed fled hastily; pictures were gone from the walls, odd bits taken from rooms and closets, food removed from the fridge, and a stain on the kitchen floor spoke of a pet food bowl that had long occupied that place. Naked and bloodied, I ascended the stairs to find the master bath, and filled the tub with hot water and bubbles.

"I've found some wine!" Stuart called from the kitchen. "Shall we have a drink before bed?"

"See to the doors first! And do not turn on the lights! We do not wish to give any indication of our presence. I do not fancy a stake to the heart."

I regarded my torn and stained gown sadly, then placed it in the only suitable receptacle – the dust bin. A thorough investigation of the house revealed only clothes either far too small or entirely too large. At one point I stood nude within the bedroom of whom I assumed to be the owners of the house and held aloft a garment of such singular size and hideousness that I truly wondered if the purchaser was in command of all her faculties. Stuart, upon passing the room, was brought to a halt, and not because he noticed my state of undress.

"Dear God above, did someone actually pay good coin for that thing?"

"It is more terrible than you know," I said dryly. "It is hand-made. And polyester."

"Bring it along, it may ward off evil."

"Nay, I think not. A garment this shockingly hideous would cause evil to rejoice, and the Archangel Michael to flee shrieking."

"Well, if we meet him, we will not make him wear it, then."

I finally located some acceptable clothing in the room of what seemed to be a teenaged girl. I confess that black jeans, boots, and a 'Mastodon' T-shirt are hardly my style, but they would have to do until I found something more suitable.

Stuart locked the doors and windows, then came upstairs with the wine and two glasses. We bathed together in the decadently large tub, then found our way to the master bedroom. We drew the drapes closed, then tacked up a heavy blanket over them to fully block the sun's rays. At last we shut the bedroom door and blocked it with a heavy dresser, then settled together in the large, soft bed, sleeping away the cursed day.

* * *

We awoke to the sound of the evening rain. All was silent, and cautious exploration told us that we had not been discovered. There was no sign of our home having been entered, so we were safe for now. I made coffee, there being no tea, and we settled together in the bedroom to watch the news. It seemed those left on the island could expect no further aid in light of the swift infection of troops helping with the evacuation, and of refugees seeking to flee this place of death. Thousands had been killed or infected with the plague, and it was simply too dangerous to lend any more assistance.

"So there is no help for my babies," I said quietly.

"Nonsense," said Stuart. "They have us! And we are well fed and of no danger to them for the moment! We shall help ourselves to a vehicle and fill it with supplies."

He suddenly ceased speaking, and I wondered if something had just now occurred to him. I watched as he raised one eyebrow, and I giggled despite myself.

"Have you an idea, my lord?"

"I have, my lady! And it is really rather a good one. What is the one thing we lack that we most need?"

"A boat."

"Quite. So why do we not take one?"

I crossed my arms. "I do believe we have already tried and failed to find a boat, my lord. And Peter's tiny lake-craft will hardly take us across the strait."

"You're right. It will not. But why have we not thought to see if there are any dealers? If we take a large enough truck, and then search out any boat dealers in the area, we may find something!"

I had my doubts about this plan, but I could think of no reason not to try. Surely, we had more to lose by doing nothing. And so we went out into the night and sought out a truck, eventually finding one at the side of the road, its owner standing but a few yards away, moaning. We took the vehicle and sought out what dealers there may be, finally locating one. We saw no boats in the yard, which was to be expected. But there was a great concrete building with enormous grey doors, locked firmly against intruders. Therein lay hope.

We drove into the yard, cautious and fearful. Mortals who may have laid claim to any vessels within the locked building would be loathe to part with them, and desperate people are dangerous. There was also a chance the place could be infested with shroud eaters, but as we stopped the truck and stepped outside, we heard nothing. Cautiously we approached the building. Stuart took hold of the great iron latch and padlock holding the door closed and yanked it out of the concrete with a loud 'bang!' that seemed to echo across the yard. We listened closely to determine if anything was approaching, but again we heard nothing. Stuart raised the door, and we looked inside. We could scarcely believe our eyes as we spied a boat resting on a trailer within.

"This cannot be real," said Stuart. "Check it for holes in the hull."

The boat itself was intact. However, the motor was not. Our attempts to start it resulted only in a great deal of smoke and a lot of grinding noises. But at least we had a boat.

"Peter has a motor," I said.

"It is far too small."

"It is better than nothing. Let us tow it to the lake and fetch Peter and the children, and dear Florence. I miss her mindless devotion to the pagan vegetable gods."

"Deirdre, if we are seen towing a boat, any people who are left alive will make it their life's work to track us to the ends of the earth."

"What do you propose?"

"I will stay with the boat and guard it. You fetch your children."

I shook my head. "I like not the sound of that."

He smiled. "Do you not trust me?"

"I trust not the idea of you here alone. Too many things could happen. What if others have had the same idea as we?"

"You will be gone but a few hours, a day at most. Drive to the lake, get them and the motor, and hurry back. I will be here. I swear. I shall not run away and leave you again."

"You had best not, for I shall not mourn this time. I will hunt you down like the knave you are."

We kissed, and then I hurried off to make the drive back to Comox Lake, hoping Stuart would be all right as he closed the door and bolted it from within.

I drove to the lake with all speed. The highway was never busy at the best of times, but now it was as empty as the corridors of the houses it wound past. I arrived at the lake with hours of darkness to spare and ran down the darkened paths to the wharf, stopping short as I realized that the small boat in which I had crossed was not there.

A cold thrill ran through my body, and I stared at the place where the boat should be, trying to understand why it would not be where we had left it. Had Peter taken his own boat over and fetched it? It seemed odd to me but perhaps they had determined they had need for a second craft. Indeed it was possible some desperate soul also seeking to flee this island of death had come upon it and taken it away, though I had my doubts a boat so small could cross the strait. But desperation does not make for sane thought.

I studied the lake, noting the low rolling mist moving across the water. I dislike using my infernal powers, but in this case, it was simply necessary. I could not walk upon the water; such a thing as done by our Lord is forbidden to the damned. But mist and fog belong to the grave, and the dead. They are our cloak against prying eyes. I had no boat with which to cross the water, but I needed one not, for I had a road before me.

I leapt from the wharf and ran in perfect silence over a path of mist and darkness.

I reached the small cabin, stepping onto the wharf and pausing, listening. I heard no sound. I heard not the TV, or the sound of voices, or movement. I heard not even the small sounds of the sleeping. Had they left? Had something come upon them from the dark and driven them away? Or worse? Did they lie now dead upon the floor? I scented the air, but did not detect the odour of death or blood.

Cautiously I approached the cabin, reaching my hand out to place it upon the door. It swung open, and the noise of hinges elicited a response: a high-pitched whistling, not unlike an exceptionally tiny car alarm. I hastened my way to Florence, picking her up and holding her furry warmth close to my breast. Her box held no food or water, and her bedding had not been cleaned.

I could not see Lisa leaving Florence in such a state willingly and began to fear the worst. Had the *chiang-shih* learned of her whereabouts? Had a shroud eater found the cabin? What horror had taken away the only family I had known in centuries? I gave Florence some food and water, and then left her to feed whilst I sought what had become of those who should have been here.

I found a creature on the upper floor. It was not a nightmare, but it *was* a horse-creature. It had the body of a man, and the head of a horse. A long flowing white tail was tucked down his leg and into his boot. The creature's face had been shattered by a blow, likely from the heavy sledgehammer that lay on the floor beside it. I knew it at once, though the tales regarding such horrors were rare, and sightings more so. In its home of Romania it would have been called St. Toader's Horse—a creature that sought "immoral" young women behaving "improperly." I could see how such a creature could be drawn to a strong-willed young lady like Lisa; in my day she would have been seen as most improper.

But times change, and none know this better than the vampire. "Improper" behaviour has long since become "they will grow out of it." But creatures such as this do not mark the change of time. And now with the liminals between the world of the living and the fantastic down, it would be but a matter of time before a creature such as this came to teach young ladies "a lesson." It never fails to confuse and infuriate me that a creature that holds itself the keeper of feminine purity and morality seeks to perform its duties through rape and murder. A locked door is enough to keep one out, but Lisa had either not locked the door quickly enough, or as was likely was drawn by its shining whiteness. It was possible she had seen it as a holy creature, and indeed it is considered as such. So she would have approached, and it would have tried to draw her into a "dance." That I believe would be when Peter went for his hammer.

I suspected Lisa's "improper" virtue was still fully intact.

I cut off the being's long silky tail and kept it, though I am not certain what compelled me to do so, other than the rarity of the creature. I tucked it into a bag, then went to see what else I may learn of the fates of my friends. They had taken nothing with them, not even their coats. They had either fled in great haste, or been taken forcefully. Fear clutched my cold heart.

"Lisa? Peter! Melissa! Where are you?"

"They're not here, are they?" said a voice, seething sweetly with hate.

I turned, and found myself staring at the same little old woman who had stolen our truck.

"Explain yourself, hag!"

"I owe you no explanations! I owe you nothing! It is you who owe me!"

"I owe you nothing! I know you not!"

"Oh, but you do," she hissed. "You know me. You wronged me. But like all of your class, you thought nothing of the poor and unfortunate. You strode over us and saw us not. But I saw you." She pointed a long bony finger at me. "I saw you that night in 1663, when you arose from the crypt to tear the throat from your husband, painting the room in red."

I was utterly stopped in more than my tracks. My mind went blank, my jaw fell, and I stared at the aged crone for a very long time.

"You were the trollop!" I exclaimed. "You were too drunk to move, and so I left you."

"Oh, you left me, all right," she hissed. "You left me in a haze to awaken to a nightmare. I arose slathered in dried blood, with men standing all around, accusing me of murder. They would have killed me, but I told them it was you! I saw you in your burial clothes, and I was not the only one! The doctor whose tongue you tore out nodded that I spoke true. And so they went to your crypt and saw you were gone. But I was far from cleared. Why had this abomination attacked her former husband, and not me? There was only one obvious conclusion—I was in league with you."

"You were in league, of that I have no doubt," I said. "But not with me."

"No, not with you. With your husband. It was I who told him to throw you down the stairs. Then I could have taken my rightful place at his side."

I laughed. "Marry *you*? A *whore*? He would have no more married you than he would have wed a goat. You were a warm tunnel for his rabbit and nothing more. No matter what sweet things he said to you, when I was cold and buried you would have still been a whore."

My words struck hard, and I saw the rage fill her eyes. "He loved me!"

"He *fucked* you," I spat scornfully. "Are all sluts as dense as you?"

"Do not mock me! I have tracked you through the centuries seeking my revenge!"

"The revenge is not yours to take. It is mine!" I bent down to lift the great sledgehammer. "You are the last survivor of the murder plot. It is your fault I walk the night!"

"And it is your fault that I do as well! It was your foul deed that cast a darkness over my life! The courts did not judge me, but all others did! I was cast out! I could find no home, no sanctuary, no comfort! I struggled to live in a shack in the woods, where I dared not emerge for food lest the whispers and the pointing fingers and cruel stares find me."

"You deserved them! All of them, and worse! You murdered my babies! You killed even my son in the womb!"

"I rid the world of a simpering, mindless, little nothing!" she hissed. "And was cursed for my trouble. It was the blood of your deed on my hands that condemned me to walking the night!

"It was your own deed, far darker than mine, that set you here! How very like a whore to blame those she has wronged for her punishment. How died you, hag? Clearly not repenting before a church or we would not now be speaking."

She pointed to the creature whose tail I had claimed. "The horses came for me in the night. I left England and made my way as an aging woman to far and dark lands, where I might spend my final days in peace, but was caught outside my hovel at night. And as they took my body, I offered my wretched soul to the darkness, that if one of them would serve me in death, I would find it more deserving victims. So for years we rode the whole of Europe, the hag on her nightmare. But times change, and now it suits me better to be a little old lady with her grandson. The horse cared not, so long as I found him careless tarts to mount, and we could each take our fill in our own way."

"Where are Lisa and Melissa?" I asked, my fist tightening upon the handle of the hammer.

"I know not and nor do I care! My fight is with you!"

I did not think about what I must do. I struck her full force with the hammer, snapping bones beneath its weight and throwing her into the wall. I struck again and again, splintering every bone she had, crushing her skull. I had no time to bandy words with trash. I had to seek my children. I crippled the hag, not knowing if she could be killed by a hammer's blow, then ran downstairs to find a fireplace poker. I ran back upstairs, and before she could heal herself to rise up against me, I pinned her to the floor with the poker. She screamed and swore, clutching the thing and trying to draw it forth as she raged.

"I shall see you dead!" she screamed.

"You already have done so, and were your heart not made of demon's waste then we would not be here. But I must find my children, and that I cannot do that if you are dead, for that shall spell my own end."

The hag laughed. "You think so? You think that I am the only one tracking you through the ages?"

I gave her a look of confusion. "There cannot possibly be any more than you. That is just well beyond what one would call the law of averages."

"Yet in your case it is true. Do you not believe me? Then kill me and see for yourself! You will have had your vengeance, yet you will still live!"

I bound her broken limbs to the iron poker driven through her body and into the floor. "Oh, no. I shall do no such thing. I will not kill myself and leave my children to die alone."

"You call me a liar?"

I gazed down at her as she lay broken on the floor. "Well, you are a covetous whore and a conspirer., I fail to see how calling you a liar as well is a greater slight."

"You will see. You may do to me what you like, but I claim more accomplices than the one whose tail you claimed. And what shall you do with it, thief?"

I finished binding her arms. "I thought I would entwine the strands with yarn and knit it into a shawl."

* * *

I ran into the darkness. The night was icy cold and damp. I could tell by the scent of the air that dawn was not far away, and I had no time to think on the hag's words. I ran into the silent woods, just as the first few flakes of snow began to fall. I called for my children, using all my senses to their utmost, desperately searching for the scent of warm living beings and finding it not. At last I was forced to retreat to the cabin, finding the hag struggling against her bonds. I tightened them, then returned to my room to sleep away the day, leaving the hag in the hall where she could see the light of day and lie in fear that a single beam should touch her, burning her like a judgement.

I awoke at sundown and, after checking to see the hag was still bound and cursing, apparently unscathed by sunlight, once more ran into the night, bearing a lantern and travelling through the woods. I walked far, calling loudly, my caution forgotten. There were fewer monsters in the area, but there were still monsters aplenty, though I chose to ignore them for now in favour of finding those who had taken me in and named me friend. I drew to a halt as a veritable giant of a man appeared before me, dressed in a manner that had not been seen in Russia for centuries. He stared at me with blank white eyes, and I saw that his lower jaw was made of cracked and rusted iron. His jagged teeth were broken and worn from centuries of use but still more than wicked enough for the prey he sought: infants and toddlers, asleep in their beds. I was of no interest to him, and so he went on, striding purposely through the woods, his mighty woodsman's axe over one shoulder, leaving me to quake at his passing.

It seemed the dead of all the world had arisen to increase their numbers.

I searched until I very nearly despaired and knew there was no way I could reach the cabin before the sun caught me. I could only hope for storm clouds, or all would end in misery. The only place I could think was the Nosferatu's cavern, but I knew not where it was, and it was entirely too great a distance away. Then, just as I seated myself on a frozen log, resigned to my fate, I caught the sound of a small whimper. I raised my head as does the dog who hears her mistress' tread upon the stair.

"Lisa?"

My heart soared as I heard a response.

"Deirdre?"

"Lisa!" I ran to the sound and found her alone in a pit, filthy, wet, and weeping. She embraced me without hesitation as soon as she saw me, and we held one another.

"I was scared you wouldn't come."

"Where are Melissa and Peter?" I asked.

"I don't know. I think they might be dead. I'm so cold…"

The pit was small. I do not know what its function was, or if indeed it ever had one. Perhaps it was simply a natural drop in the earth. I knew it would be easier to warm her here than it would be in a larger area. However not even a vampire can make fire with sodden wood.

"I have to get you back to the cabin."

"But it's getting close to daylight."

Indeed it was. I searched the sky. It was cloudy, but I did not know if it was overcast enough to be safe.

"I have no choice. We cannot make a fire here—you will freeze to death. Pray for thunderclouds, that I may live long enough to assist you. How did you come to be in this pit?"

"I don't know. I was in my own bed, and when I woke up, I was dressed and in this hole. I tried to get out, but the ground's too soft, it kept crumbling."

I pushed her out of the pit, landing her on the edge of it, then leapt out after her. "Have you heard either Peter or Lisa?"

"No. But we're not alone out here. I kept hearing footsteps and noises all night. Once I saw a huge black pig, but it just stared and then left. And once I saw an ugly old woman, or thought I did. I don't remember. It's all jumbled up in my head, I just… need time to sort it. I think I dreamed I heard Melissa screaming, and then I heard Peter… Deirdre, what's going on?

"Sins of the past are rising," I said. "One of those who had wronged me when I was alive hath discovered me."

"Is that who put me in that hole?"
"I believe so. Can you walk?"
"No. I'm so cold. I hurt…"

I scooped her up and hurried back to the cabin. The sky grew dark and cold as we walked, and there was snow falling as we made it back to the house. I carried Lisa to the bathroom, setting her down as I prepared her a bath. She was shivering uncontrollably, and I feared for her as I poured the bath, taking care not to make it too hot. I helped her to undress and climb into the water.

"You're not asleep," she said.

"The day is dark enough that I may walk about," I said. "You warm up. I'll prepare you some hot tea and something for breakfast.

I sighed as I heard the hag in the corridor shriek.

"You will all die! Sluts! Bitches!"

Lisa's eyes grew large. "What's she still doing here?"

"Do not concern yourself. She is bound to an iron spike driven into the floor. She cannot escape."

"But what if she does? What if she hurts us? Who is she?"

"A remnant of past misdeeds," I said softly. "Warm yourself and pay no heed to her screechings. She is naught but a chained dog."

"But why don't you kill her?" Lisa asked. "I don't want her here!"

"Because if I slay her, then my life, too, shall end. I will have had vengeance on all who wronged me and at last be laid to rest. I cannot do so when we have yet to find Melissa and Peter. Now warm yourself and gather your strength. Stuart and I have found a boat. It should be large enough to take us to the mainland."

I hurried downstairs to prepare breakfast for Lisa, knowing too well the pain of hunger. My cooking skills are sadly limited, as it was never a chore I was called upon to perform when I was alive, and certainly nothing I ever had need of after I became undead. Still, I managed to prepare eggs and toast with reasonable competence, though I do think Lisa was ravenous enough to eat mud. She arrived in the kitchen just as I was placing it upon the table.

"I want to come out with you. I want to help you find them."

"That is admirable but foolhardy. You are tired and would simply be putting yourself in harm's way. Besides, I need you here in the event Melissa and Peter find their way home. They will need you here to help them."

"But it's daytime! What if the skies clear? You'll die!"

"It is nearly October. There is far greater chance of foul weather than fair."

"But—"

"Lisa, you cannot go back out there so soon after your rescue, and I know you realize that. I need you here."

"But what if the hag breaks loose?"

"She cannot. The poker is made of iron and is holding her to the floor. She is quite trapped, I assure you. And do not listen to anything she says. She is like Tanya. She will spew venom and hate for her own pleasure. And not one word is true."

Lisa nodded. "Okay. I'll just hide here and be quiet. But what about the horse-boy? Is he...?'

"Dead."

"Good. He... he scared me."

"He will trouble you no more. Peter, it seems, ended his days of troubling young women."

Lisa sniffed. "Oh, that wasn't Dad. That was Melissa."

I smiled. "Good for her," I said softly.

I left the cabin and made my way back into the woods once more, wishing I had at my side my father's good hunting dogs. They would have found Melissa and Peter in less time than my brothers could find a tavern. I feared that when I located them, it would be too late.

* * *

I searched all the day and well into the night. Stuart would be wondering where I was, assuredly, as would poor Lisa. Then as the night grew old and pale, I was forced to hide beneath some rotted logs and leafy debris. I awoke but a few hours later to a veritable maelstrom. The sky was dark enough for my needs, but I was soaked and filthy, and I feared for Lisa. Hoping that Peter and Melissa would have found their way back to the cabin, I returned to the little shingled house.

I returned to a nightmare.

I stepped out of the woods to hear the single-note dirge of a shroud eater's moan. I crept cautiously around the cabin so that I might see where the fiend stood and heard myself draw a loud gasp of horror as I saw the beast.

"Peter…" I whispered. "Oh, Peter, what monster did this to you?"

He stood on the wharf, moaning, his eyes filmed white, his body bloated and covered in black slime and burst buboes. Flakes of snow settled upon his shoulders and hair, rotting ichors running from his mouth. What dark and vile punishment was this, that this kind man should have been taken from the child who needed him so and met such a hideous end?

I entered the cabin through a window near the back, out of sight of Peter, and was immediately pounced upon by Lisa, who was in tears.

"It's all my fault, Deirdre, it's all my fault!"

"Hush, child, what are you speaking of?"

She drew back, weeping openly. "It was the hag! She kept taunting me, saying things to me. Then Peter came back just a few hours after you left. I told him… I told him not to kill her, but she was so hateful! He shoved a coin in her mouth and cut off her head, but before he killed her, she spit something black into his face. At first, we thought he was fine, but… but then he… walked onto the wharf… and began to moan…"

I held Lisa close, trying to comfort her. "I am so very sorry, child. So very, very sorry. I know how dear he was to thee."

"I told him not to kill her! But she wouldn't shut up."

I held her tightly against my cold bosom, but my mind was not on her grief. Rather it was on the news that the hag was dead. How could this be true? Unless the hag had spoken truly, and she was not the last of those who had wronged me. That would mean there was indeed one more, but who that may be, I had not the slightest idea.

"Has there been any word of Melissa?" I asked.

Lisa pulled back. "Yes! She came home with Peter. But there's something not right with her. I'm scared for her."

"Take me to her, child."

"Are we leaving now? Please, I want to go."

"We are leaving just as soon as we may. But first let us look in on Melissa."

Lisa led me to the room wherein her friend lay. Melissa did not look well to me. She was bruised and battered, and it was clear some creature had torn at her flesh. Her eyes held a fevered glare, and she gave no sign that she was aware of either Lisa or myself, or if she *was* aware, she did not care.

"I shall carry her," I said. "Are you packed?"

"Yes. But what about Peter?"

Yes, that was a very good question. I would have to destroy him if we were to have even a small chance at escape. In his present condition, he would follow us until we were either caught and devoured, or he was killed.

"I shall tend to him, child. Make yourself ready."

Lisa burst into tears anew. "You're going to kill him."

I touched her little face. "He is dead already, Lisa. All that stands outside is a body. He was a dear man, and we loved him. It would bring him no joy to harm us, and we must keep that in mind."

Lisa began hurrying with the task of packing what things she thought she and Melissa might need and of putting poor indignant Florence in yet a smaller box. ~~She~~ Florence, more than any of us, I believe, wished to see this trial end. As Lisa packed, I searched for anything that would serve as a harpoon. I had no desire to stand too close to Peter in his present condition. Nor do I believe I would have the heart to destroy him, for though he was now but a monster,

168

once he had been a kind man. Though I wonder if destruction would not have been kinder?

I found a crowbar and a length of chain, and invented a plan of childish simplicity. The first thing done was to place such things as we required near the door, as well as poor, ill Melissa and dear, vexed Florence. I then fastened one end of the chain to a support beam in the center of the room, fashioned out of a great log, and, upon my command, Lisa flung open the door.

"Peter!" I called.

He made for me with the horrible speed of his kind, rushing heedlessly toward his meal. I thrust the crowbar deep into his breast, then forced him against the beam. As I held him, Lisa wrapped the chain about him and closed it with a small padlock. It would not hold him long, but it would contain him until we were away.

"Let us make haste," I said. "I will gather Melissa. You take Florence. Let us be on our way."

Lisa nodded, slinging the one bag she was taking over her shoulder and scooping up the box which contained Florence. As we were about to depart this place of death, the thing that was Peter spoke.

"Lisssssaaaaa... stay..."

She whirled to face the monster, her mind knowing he was dead but her heart unwilling to believe.

"Daddy...?" she whimpered.

"Lisssssaaaaa... stay..."

"Do not listen to him, child," I said quietly.

She gazed at him, her eyes filling with tears. "Daddy?" she questioned once more.

"Lisssssaaaaa... stay..."

"Lisa, we must go," I said gently.

"But... he—"

"Come along."

Slowly, reluctantly, she did, weeping silently as we hurried to the boat, his droning voice sounding in our ears as we started the boat motor and departed.

"Lisssssaaaaa... stay..."

"Are you sure he's dead?" she asked, tears spilling from her eyes.

"Yes," I said quietly. "I am very sorry. There is naught we may do for him. What happened after I left?, Do you remember?"

She shook her head, wiping impatiently at her eyes with her sleeve as she did so. "It was like a dream. I was asleep, or thought I was. I got out of bed and... followed this sound... like someone whispering my name. When I awoke, I was in that hole and couldn't get out. I... I just don't know!"

"Try to remember," I urged gently.

"I'll try, but... it's not easy. It all seems kinda dream-like, almost like I was under a spell.

"Try," I gently urged, her words reminding me of the strange, leaden weariness I had felt in my flat before I was attacked.

"Well, you and Stuart left, and we settled in to watch the news, and see if things were improving. Then we heard the boat pull up and I jumped up to see if it was you. But it wasn't. It was that old woman and the boy. And... we let them in. We had no reason not to! But then…" She stifled a giggle of what may have been hysteria. "Then Melissa says, 'Hey kid, you got a ponytail!' And I laughed because… he *did*. And I asked him where he got it because it looked so real and I thought it would be fun to have one of my own, and then… and then he turned… and… the old woman turned into this disgusting hag, and she attacked Dad and the horse-boy came for me, and… and it was just this huge fight and… And Melissa beat the boy to death with a mallet, but when we went downstairs, Peter and the hag were gone. Melissa and I tried to find them, but we saw a huge man striding along with a gigantic axe over his shoulder, so… so we stayed in the cabin. Then, somehow, we fell asleep, and I woke up in the pit."

"How long were you there before I found you?"

"I don't know. A day, I think. Maybe longer. It's so hard to think." She paused for a long moment, straining to recall as our small vessel bore us across the lake. Then she resumed speaking.

"You had left just a few hours before, then Peter showed up with Melissa. He was carrying her, and she was all bitten and clawed. And the hag began to scream how he should have left her to the dance, until the horses were done with her. And I told Peter not to kill the hag, but…" She drew a steadying breath, gathering herself admirably. "But he did."

"Yes, I saw his work. I cannot fault his actions, though it gives me much pause to wonder as to why I am still alive. I can only assume she spoke the truth when she said there were others upon which I need to take vengeance. But I cannot see how I could ever..."

A thought came to me—a terrible, terrible thought that I did not wish to have. Lisa seemed to note something was amiss.

"Deirdre?"

"It's nothing, child. Let us make haste."

We reached the wharf and tied up the little boat, then made our way past the cedar cabin and up the path to the parking area. There I found the Demeter, parked and awaiting myself and my charges. It was parked well within the shadows, and I had not spied it when I arrived. Even if I had, the knowledge that the hag had arrived before me would have served me no purpose. Still it would make better transport than the truck. I placed Melissa in the back, that she may lay upon the bed Stuart and I had made, and then I slipped behind the steering wheel and turned the engine on.

The fuel gauge revealed that the tank was very nearly empty. I sighed heavily.

"What next?" I snapped, shutting down the engine.

"What's wrong?" asked Lisa.

"Our steed is in need of fodder."

"Huh?"

"We are out of gas."

"Oh. I can fix that."

Lisa got out of the car and walked over to one of the three vehicles left in the small lot, vehicles whose owners would never again have need of them. One was the truck in which I arrived, but she ignored it in favour of the other two cars, one of which was a well-used compact. She opened the back with the practiced ease of one who is familiar with a vehicle, and drew out a gas can and siphoning hose. I watched as she drained the little car of its lifeblood, using it to fuel the station wagon. She next drew out a spare gas can and loaded it into our car before carefully closing up the small compact and getting into the station wagon.

"How did you know that would be there?" I inquired.

Lisa put on her seatbelt, not looking at me. "It was Valerie's car," she said quietly.

I said nothing further. I started the car and then drove with all the haste I dared back to Parksville, to where Stuart still waited with the boat. He was absolutely frantic by the time we pulled up.

"Where were you?!" he demanded, seemingly torn between delight at seeing us once more and rage that we had made him worry so. "I was on the verge of coming to find you!"

"I will tell you all, but not now," I said wearily. "The night is very old. We need a place to rest. Melissa is ill, Lisa is exhausted, and we are all in need of a bath and a bed. But I am sorry to have worried you."

Stuart appeared to be calming down, enough so that it he noticed our party was a member short.

"Where's Peter?" he asked.

No one answered. There was no need, for he gleaned the answer on his own.

"Come," he said softly. "Let us find sanctuary for the night."

Chapter Eight

Sanctuary was a small motel near the boat dealership. After careful inspection by Stuart and myself, we found nothing more dangerous than a single pathetic looter. Ensuring we were well out of sight of Lisa and Melissa, we felled the miserable thief and drained him, then hid his remains in a dumpster before returning to the wagon.

"Is it safe?" Lisa asked, her dark eyes large.

"Yes, it is safe," assured her.

"I thought I heard a scream."

Stuart and I exchanged glances, then he cleared his throat.

"That was just me. I... tripped."

One need not be a psychic to discern that Lisa did not believe him. "You tripped," she said flatly.

"Yes."

She just stared at him, blinking. "And is that your *official* lie, or just the one you're using now until you think of a better one?"

I sighed. "It was just a looter and no one for you to be concerned with."

Lisa became angry. "But what if he rises?!"

"He will not rise," I assured her.

"Bullshit! *You* did! You don't think we have *enough* problems without you creating *more*?!"

My temper grew short. "And what *precisely* would you have us do? Starve until madness takes us and we devour you?"

"Maybe it would be better if you did!" she screamed. "My whole fucking *family* is dead, and my only living friend is probably getting ready to turn into one of those fucking *things*! So what the hell do I care if you kill me?! It's not like anyone *else* gives a fuck if I live or die!"

"That is not true, and you know it," I said quietly. "Peter cared a great deal, as did Valerie. And so do Stuart and I. Do not let despair take you. Not when you have come so very far and risen above all who have done you wrong.

She lowered her head, weeping once again. I suspected that she would weep many more times ere this trial ended.

"So what if he does rise? And why was he looting? Maybe he has a family hidden around here. What was he taking?"

"If he rises then Stuart and I shall deal with him," I said. "And if he was stealing to feed his family then they must feast upon jewelry and televisions."

She smiled faintly. "I just was worried, y'know… that maybe he had someone depending on him."

"He was taking naught but things he may sell," I said. "If indeed he had been taking bread, we would have left him. Now come. Let us get you inside."

She sniffed, but left the safety of the old car. "I'm hungry," she said quietly.

"I shall find you some fare, m'lady," said Stuart. "What would you care for?"

"A hamburger and some nice greasy oversalted fries, but since I'm not gonna get those, let's go into that little convenience store and grab some stuff."

Stuart offered her his arm. "Your escort awaits."

She managed a second smile as she took his arm. "I'm sorry I yelled."

"Think no more upon it," I said quietly. "If this is not a time for anger and high emotions, then never shall the time come. I will put Melissa in the cabin and make her comfortable."

"Is she gonna be okay? I don't know what happened to her. She hasn't spoken."

"We will care for her as well as we are able and pray for her recovery."

I moved Melissa and our belongings into one of the motel rooms. There were two large beds, as well as a television. I was finding myself developing very mixed feelings toward the foul things; on the one hand it was useful for keeping our little group abreast of how things fared in the outside world, but on the other it seemed to bring us naught but despair. Still, I turned it on, only to find myself confronted with one of those dreary and poorly-written evening melodramas. I was about to turn to another channel, when I heard a small voice emanating from the bed upon which Melissa lay.

"No, don't change it, I really like this show."

I was delighted to hear her speak and set aside the remote, though not without voicing my derision of her choice of viewing. "It is utter dreck."

"I know, that's kinda why I like it."

I rolled my eyes. "Oh, dear God in Heaven."

"Well it's fun if you just… take it for what it is."

I walked over to the bed upon which she lay and seated myself beside her. "And how are you feeling?"

"Sick."

"Do you know what happened to you?"

"Nuh-uh. I was attacked by some kind of animal. I think it was a dog."

"A dog? Not a wolf?" I asked cautiously.

"Wolves don't have a curly coat. This was a huge, huge, huge dog, with like… long legs and curly-shaggy hair. And it had a collar. It wasn't a wolf. I know what a wolf looks like. I have pictures of them all over my bedroom. I like wolves. I think they're cool."

I began inspecting her scratches and cuts. Some of them had clearly been inflicted by a great hound. In my time, such wounds would have been treated by having strands of the dog's hair stitched into the injury to ward off rabies, hence the term 'hair of the dog that bit you.' I cannot vouch for its usefulness at curing rabies, but it assuredly resulted in some very severe infections. In this case I felt the first aid kit would work better than dog hair.

"What made the dog cease his attack?" I rummaged through our belongings for anything that may be of use, and finally located a small bag full of antiseptics and bandages.

"I think someone called him. He froze, like dogs do when they hear something. Then he just ran off and left me on the ground. Do you think he was, like, a vampire, or werewolf?"

"It is hard to say. It seems the gates of Hell are wide open, and all manner of horrors are unleashed. However, I find it more likely it was merely a starving and forsaken pet."

"Hope so. I don't wanna be a werewolf. Werewolves are like the lamest monsters in movies. Totally." She rubbed at one eye with the heel of her hand. "I don't feel good. I feel... like I'm... stuck in a dream. Like I'm not really awake."

I placed my hand to her brow. "You do seem rather warm. Just rest and watch your show. Lisa and Stuart shall return shortly."

"And Peter?" she asked hopefully.

"No," I said softly. "Not Peter."

"No," she said quietly. "I didn't think so. I saw him kill the hag, but she vomited up like this... cloud... or something. Like really oily smoke, so oily it was almost like liquid. He breathed it in, and then in a few hours he began to change. I think I breathed in a bit of it, too."

"You will be fine," I assured her, though now I feared I did not speak the truth. Many vampires spat forth unholy vapours that spread the plague, and certainly 'twas the plague that had claimed Peter. "Just let me have a look at you."

I felt her neck and under her arms, and checked her for any other signs of plague. Assuredly she had chills and a fever, but those are harbingers of many ailments, and certainly an unpleasant night in a ditch after being bitten by a dog would see them manifest. But I saw none of the other symptoms I knew too well, and the strain spread by the undead worked with ghastly swiftness. Melissa was not well, but she did not appear to have the plague.

"I think some rest will see you well," I assured her.

"It's not the plague?"

"No. The vampire-plague moves so swiftly that I think we would have seen it take you by now."

"But I breathed the smoke. Or thought I did."

"Let us not make mountains of mole hills, nor raised blisters of a simple ant-bite. There may be something at play here of a common and easily mended variety, and I feel no tell-tale lumps. Now enjoy your dreck. Lisa and Stuart shall return soon enough with something pretending to be food."

Indeed what they returned with could *claim* to be food, though I had my doubts as to its nutritional value. Still it seemed to cheer Melissa up to be greeted with ice cream, gummy worms, and pickles. It was not what I would have wished for a feast, but it has been very long indeed ere I was a fifteen-year-old girl. Then Lisa stopped in her tracks and stared at me.

"I just realized you're not wearing a dress!"

"Yes, well, I could hardly roam about nude, could I?"

"I don't know about that," said Stuart. "It might lend some charm to the area."

"I will not be roaming about nude," I said firmly.

"It is kinda funny to see you ~~in the t-shirt of a death metal band~~ in a Mastodon t-shirt," Lisa said. "I didn't think you liked death metal."

"My options were limited between the death-metal band and pink kitties printed in balloon-paint. And I will not be caught undead in pink." I checked the time. It was late, but not so late that I could not risk a quick chat outside with Stuart. I had questions that very much required answers.

"Stuart, would you accompany me outside for a moment?"

"If you insist, but if my father catches us, you'll have to marry me."

"Attend me, knave. Do not force me to call the dogs."

I led Stuart outside and closed the door, then turned to him. His eyes were bright and merry, and it broke my heart to challenge him thusly.

"Who are you?" I asked.

He blinked, puzzled by my question. "I told you. I am Stuart Cooper of—"

"And what was your name before you changed it?"

His smile lessened, and his eyes began to dart nervously. "Truly my lady, I have no—"

"Stuart. Please. Do not lie to me, and do not insult my intellect. I knew it was too great a gift to find a companion from my country and my century. There is a tale to tell here, and I would have it."

He sighed and leaned against the wall of the motel, slowly shaking his head.

"I had no desire to tell you of any of this."

"Who were you?" I asked. "How came you to be in this mess?"

He sighed once more and stood in thought for a long time.

"Our fates are intertwined, by my own hand. For two long and bitter years before my death I cursed you, and two hundred more after my death. I damned myself in rage and hate, and tracked you as well as I was able across the planet, sometimes losing sight of you for decades until some whisper would alert me to your presence. Then I would begin tracking you anew."

"Well, who were you?" I asked.

"I was one of the healers you slew during the time of the plague. I also made for your husband a number of potions, but for what use I do not know. He swore to me they were for his dogs, but I do not know."

"You poisoned my babies," I whispered.

"I did no such thing, I swear to you! I sold him no poisons! I gave him potions to rid a bitch-dog of unwanted whelps."

"To rid a dog of…?" I paused in confusion. "Do you think he meant the potions for his round-heels?"

"What round-heels?" he queried.

"The slut he died in bed with, his stinking harlot."

Stuart drew himself up, his eyes becoming large. "I heard of no slut!"

I laughed, despite the horror of the situation. "Stuart, why do you care if he died in bed with some…?" I blinked as the answer to my own question struck me. "Stuart… were you fucking my husband?"

"Well… no… *he* was fucking *me*."

I reacted not at all as I was taught by my mother to receive shocking news. I did not faint. I did not weep. I did not flee. I punched him with every ounce of strength with my infernal body possessed, sending him staggering back. His nose leaked a few cold and listless drops of half-congealed blood.

"Ow!"

"You… you… you… sodomite! Am I to understand you were lying with my husband?"

"Yes! But he assured me that I was his only love!"

"Well I have terrible news for you — he assured *me* of the same thing!

Stuart carefully wiped at his pained nose. "Well had I known the potions were for his whore I would have refused him. And had I known he had a wife *and* a whore, I would have warmed his bed not at all!"

"Well he *did* have a wife. And he *did* have a whore. And he had *you*. Who else, I wonder, was in that most singularly crowded bed? So what wrong did I do unto you, other than tear out your throat for inflicting pain upon the damned?"

"You killed the man I loved. The man I had risked my very soul to be with. Had you any idea what cruelty would have befallen me had I been caught?"

"Yes," I said. "They would have burned you alive, unless they were feeling particularly creative. In which case you may well have had flaming pokers inserted into your nether reaches *before* they burned you alive, assuming they did not just smear you with honey and leave you for the rats to devour. Or perhaps they simply would have poured boiling lead down your gullet, if they did not reach for the pear! It is a fate you may yet endure!"

"I loved him," said Stuart quietly. "Though I was young and believed his lies. I do not claim innocence. I claim willful ignorance. I had skill with herb-lore and craft, and many times my potions served his needs. What I thought was love was him using me for his own ends, but I cared not. When you killed him, I was so distraught I thought my very heart would cease from grief. However, my mourning raised eyebrows within the town, and I departed Leeds for London, and used my knowledge of potions to earn a meagre living. When the plague descended, I took such knowledge I had into the houses of the afflicted, and there met you." He sniffed, wiping at his broken nose once more. "You killed my lover, and then you killed me. And it was sheer hate raised me up out of the pits of unblessed dead and set me on your trail."

"And what changed your hate?" I asked softly. "Or is what we shared a lie?"

"It was no lie. My feelings toward you did not change quickly, make no mistake. Long I gazed upon you as I mused on the words 'of woman came the beginning of sin, and thanks to her, we all must die.' In my case it was true."

I crossed my arms. "I did not kill you because I am a woman, I killed you because you were shoving flaming pokers into the armpits of a twelve-year-old girl."

He gave me a cold look of anger. "Believe it or not, I really was trying to help, which sounds utterly mad in this day and age of reason and science, I know, but what knowledge did we have? How many women were put to death for adultery because she bore twins, ~~and as such~~ clearly proving she had relations with two men at the same time and conceived by both? Healers drank the urine of their patients to check for maladies! Food was inserted into the rectums of the bedridden in the belief it would be easier to consume! We were uneducated fools in search of reason, and yes, back then it seemed perfectly logical to me to shove a flaming poker into the buboes of a twelve-year-old girl in order to cure her. That doesn't mean I would try it today!"

"So you really were there to help," I said. "Not to cheat the dying."

"I swear to you I was doing my best to aid them. I did not know I was simply doing more harm than good. But then you appeared, drenched in blood and mire, and my last thought was wondering why this emanation of the damned wore a gold cross adorned with pearls."

I smiled weakly. "Because it was my mother's gift. And she was very dear to me. But still you have not answered my question."

"I have no answer. For centuries I travelled with the hag and her steed, our goals the same. But my intent was only to bring harm unto you, whilst hers were to bring harm to any who crossed her path. So I parted company with her and her strange beast. When at last you and I met, quite by accident I swear, I thought I had been given a gift – a chance to take my vengeance. But you know as well as I how gruelling it is to dwell in solitude. So the vow to kill the vampire who slew my lover and me was shadowed by the need for companionship. I thought I could kill you just as easily the next night. But... by then I found I did not wish to. And so friendship slowly flowers in what was once barren."

"Did you know it was she who stole our car?" I asked. "The old woman and her grandson?"

"No," he said quietly. "It was the same woman? You are certain of this?"

"I am indeed. The boy was the horse, and the old woman was the slut who lay a-bed with my husband the night I tore out his miserable throat. I would quite happily wager she told you none of that.

"Nay," he said quietly. "She did not. What became of her?"

"She was waiting at the cabin when I returned to claim Peter and the children. It was she who killed Peter and used some foul magic to lure Lisa and Melissa into the woods to be prey for what creatures may find them. Peter slew the hag, but not before she infected him with plague-breath, and Melissa dispatched the horse. Which leaves me with the question of who else has escaped my vengeance, for surely it is not you. It is clearly I who wronged you in this case. And for that I am sorry, Stuart."

"The wrong was not yours. It was your husband's. His lies and treachery condemned all three of us to this overly-long Shakespearian tragedy. Would any of us be here were it not for him? Nay, the threads of this unravelled tapestry all lead back to his bed, and where once his name made my heart leap, it now makes my stomach roll."

"Thomas was indeed a man who inspired emotion," I said. "We both loved him once, Stuart. And he played us both false. Now he leaves us here with yet another tragedy to unfurl."

Stuart gave me a puzzled look. "What tragedy is that?"

"It is I who dealt you the wrong. You can have no peace unless you kill me."

"I will not kill you," he said quietly. "I will raise no hand against she who has become my dearest friend, even though the path to that friendship was circuitous indeed. I try not to kill at all if I can avoid doing so, sharing a looter betwixt us notwithstanding. But if I needs must kill you to find peace, then who yet walks that calls for your ire? Was it not the whore who wronged you?"

"I do not know," I said. "I would have thought yes, but she is dead and here I stand. And she, like you and I, has her thread in this tale tied to Thomas as well. Are we so certain Thomas himself is not still roaming the earth?"

"Nay, Thomas lives not. I held vigil beside his bed myself. He does not walk."

"And what of the lying physician, whose tongue I tore free and gave to the dogs?" I asked.

"Dead also. The wound festered, and he sickened and died." He sighed quietly, looking up at the darkened sky. We had little time left to pursue this conversation. "Perhaps there are none left after all."

"Nay, there must be one," I said. "The hag swore there was."

"Well we shall not learn the answer to this riddle tonight, if indeed we ever do," he said. "I am sorry, Deirdre. I feared if you learned who I truly was, you would turn your back on me. And as you said—it is a rare gift to find a friend from one's own land and time."

I stepped forward to take his hand and place a kiss upon his lips. "I am sorry as well that it was my hand who dealt you this fate. You did not deserve it."

"Neither of us did, but we must endure and carry on." He looked up to the sky. "But we shall not do so if the sun catches us. Let us go inside."

We went back into the motel room, and there found new drama. Melissa and Lisa were weeping openly. As Stuart seated himself upon the unoccupied bed, at a loss as all men are when confronted with weeping females, I walked to the girls and seated myself near them.

"What is the matter?" I asked.

"We can't go to the mainland," said Lisa. "They're setting up barricades to keep everyone from the island out. They're trying to prevent a pandemic. The virus spreads so fast and they have no idea how to control it, so they're just... locking the island up. Anyone caught trying to leave will be arrested and contained. They have military patrols up and down the strait. We can't leave. We can't even go to the little islands between here and the mainland. They'll send us back because we might have the plague."

"Is there any hope of slipping in at a seldom-used location?" Stuart asked.

"No!" said Lisa. "People are really freaked about this! They have the whole coast blocked off, from Alaska straight down to Mexico! And it's just a matter of time before Mexico does it, too. People have seen the news reports. Everyone knows what's going on here! They know there is a very rapid and fatal strain of bubonic plague that kills within hours, and that it doesn't seem to respond to known treatments, and that those who don't die go into sort of a zombie-like trance, decomposing visibly but... violent and fast. They're calling it the zombie-plague."

"Appropriate if not entirely correct," Stuart mused.

"People are losing their minds over this," said Melissa, remote in one hand, gummy worm in the other. "They're forming all sorts of ethics committees about how to deal with the survivors and how to get medicine and doctors in and all kinds of stuff."

"Fat lot of good it does us," said Lisa. "They're not stuck in a motel room with monsters running around *out*side and two vampires *in*side."

"No one is eating anyone," I declared.

Three sets of eyes turned toward me. Had I still possessed a functioning circulatory system, I would have blushed.

"Within this room," I added.

Florence suddenly set up a shrill complaint. I placated her with carrots and slices of apple, musing that at least someone's problems were easily mended.

* * *

It was our second night within the motel, as we were still making up our minds as to where best take ourselves next. Lisa and Melissa were asleep in their own bed, while Stuart and I lay together and waited for sleep to claim us. Florence complained quietly within her box, managing to do so with a mouthful of lettuce. She is a lady of many talents, my Florence.

It was exceedingly dark within the room, and I felt as if my very body was turning to lead. It was difficult to so much as open my eyes, though I was aware of my surroundings with exceptional clarity. I could hear the children breathing in their bed as they slept, Melissa's breath slightly more ragged due to her cold. I could hear Florence cluck and chatter and munch, and Stuart made no sound at all, as is customary when one is dead. All around the air seemed to gather close and fall darker, as if thickening into a dense smoke. Then from the direction of Lisa and Melissa's bed, I heard the first low, creaking sound of a shroud eater's moan…

I sat up abruptly and looked around. It was still dark, though dawn was very close. Had it been a dream? It could not have been; the dead do not dream. Still, it had that same strange feel to it.

I heard the creaking moan once more, and rose from the bed to check Lisa and Melissa. They were asleep and well, if one did not count the cold. Stuart too was fine, and sleeping as only a corpse can. I chanced a glance into Florence's box, and she froze as I did so, greens poking out of her mouth. Moments later she resumed chewing. It seemed all was well with her also.

I went to the door and peered out through the small peephole, and spied the source of the noise. It was an exceptionally rotted shroud eater, his maggot infestation well-established. He would not exist much longer. I wondered how many of these fell creatures would be destroyed by maggots and beetles.

"Deirdre?"

I turned to see Lisa seated upright in bed.

"Go to sleep. It is nothing."

"I thought I heard one of them."

"He is in no shape to do us harm. If we are quiet, he will have no cause to try."

"Is he really gross?"

"Well I do not believe he would care to have his picture taken in his present condition."

I walked back to the bed and seated myself beside Stuart's sleeping form, pulling the covers up. No, I could never return to the grave. I am too accustomed to soft, clean bedding.

"Deirdre? Where are we gonna go from here? I mean, you and Stuart are gonna need to… eat… soon."

"I do not know, child. I have no answers. We will have to discuss the matter this evening when all are awake." I pushed at Stuart's inert form. "A bigger bed may be in order as well."

"I'm just… y'know… kinda scared."

"I know," I said softly. "As are we all. But we shall stay together through this, regardless of what the future holds. I for one shall not leave you."

"I'm glad. It's… nice to have a mom again."

I gazed at her in shock as she spoke that one singularly small word—*Mom*. Three simple letters and nothing more, yet they brought a joy to my heart that had long been cold in a tomb beside three tiny caskets.

"It is good to be one again," I said softly. "And I shall be yours for as long as you have need of me or wish for me to be such."

Stuart rolled onto his back, effectively taking over most of the bed. With a great deal of difficulty I managed to move his inert carcass to his own side of the bed once more. Lisa giggled quietly.

"It's kinda funny to see you in bed with him. I mean, I didn't think ladies from your time did things like… sleep beside guys you weren't married to."

I sighed. "Well there is naught to be done about the matter. It is a small room with but two beds, and I am not making him sleep on the floor, nor am I tolerating him lying in bed with one of you. Besides, given all the things that I have done in my life, laying with a man who is not my husband hardly seems worthy of any note at all."

Lisa smiled. "Makes me think of a joke I heard once. This woman goes to her priest and says, 'Father, I am getting married., What colour should my dress be?' And he says, 'Well, if you are pure, your dress should be white. If you are not pure, you should wear blue.' And the woman thinks for a while and says, 'Then my dress shall be white… with little blue spots'.'"

I laughed. I am not entirely certain why; it was a terrible joke.

"Go to sleep, child. We have much to ponder on the morrow."

* * *

It was early evening when next I opened my eyes. Stuart was already seated upright on the bed, and Lisa was kneeling on the floor, peering outside through the smallest opening in the curtains. All around was the droning sound of shroud eaters, like some foul siren of Hades.

"Lisa, what do you see?" I asked in a whisper.

"They're everywhere," she whispered in return. "Oh, God, Deirdre they're *everywhere*! Do you think they know we're here?"

"No," said Stuart. "If they knew we were here we would have been torn asunder and devoured by now. But we must be very silent. I suggest we place Florence in the bathroom with some food and close the door. She is most vocal when hungry."

"I'll do it," said Lisa.

She slipped away from the window and took up Florence's box and hurried her into the bathroom, heaping her bowl with vegetables before slipping out and closing the door behind herself. We sat and stood in silence, listening to the droning.

"What are they doing?" asked Lisa.

I rose to my feet and walked to the door, gazing out of the peephole. The parking lot that lay beyond the door was full of bloated, dead, and milling figures, dripping maggots and bits of flesh. A heavy rain was falling, and the wind was gusting hard, which did nothing to improve the appearance of the creatures outside our sanctuary. As I watched, a gigantic hound prowled by, or perhaps it was a wolf. I could not tell in the nature of the beast as it roamed the darkness, and was of no mind to ask. It was larger than a horse, and as I watched it bit a shroud eater in half with casual violence before continuing on its way.

"Travelling, I believe," I said very softly. "There are very few living people here, if indeed any. They are seeking prey. If we are very quiet, we may yet remain unnoticed."

"Gonna be a long boring wait," said Lisa. "But don't get me wrong, boring is a definitely improvement on ripped apart and eaten."

"So glad we agree," said Stuart. "However, we had best hope they move along soon. The young ladies are set for dinner, but thee and me are not.

"Oh, way to go, Stuart, I really wanted to be reminded I'm stuck in a room with a couple of hungry vampires," said Lisa.

He smiled. "You're welcome."

"No one is eating anyone," I said firmly. I turned my gaze toward Melissa. "How are you feeling, child?"

"Sorry I woke up," she mumbled.

"Excellent vital sign," said Stuart.

I chose to ignore him. "How else are you feeling?

"I'm fine, Deirdre, really. Just sore and crappy."

I went to her side to examine her bites. They did not seem infected, but I worried nonetheless. She had been mauled by a hound that may not be of earthly origin, and had possibly breathed the plague-breath of the hag. No matter how she seemed, I feared for her, and for our own well-being should she become one of the moaning damned.

I tucked her in, then examined the groceries. There was nothing of any food value that I could see, no fruit, no meat, no bread, and any vegetables that had been taken had been given to Florence. I took out a bag of sour candy and gazed at them with disapproval.

"They're grapefruit flavoured," said Lisa. "Grapefruit is food."

"It is before it is ground into mash, blended with tree gum, and filled with sugar," I said dryly. "I think I shall handle the shopping from now on, as Stuart clearly cannot be trusted."

He sighed with great drama. "It is so difficult being misunderstood."

I smiled, then after replacing the bag of candy, rose and walked to the door, gazing once more through the peephole at the slow parade of the infernal.

"They do indeed appear to be moving on," I said. "The shroud eaters and other vile things. I fear this charming little island shall never again be home to the living, save what beasts and birds may survive."

"Are all those creatures vampires?" asked Lisa.

"I do not believe so," I said. "I believe they are creatures that, like the shroud eaters themselves, have fallen too few in number. Regardless, they are all moving away together, so let us hope that we may soon be able to leave. I am thinking it may be wise to seek out a hospital."

"Hospital?" asked Lisa.

"Melissa is ill. She was bitten by a dog. Some antiseptics and antibiotics would be welcome."

"And how, pray tell, would we have the first idea what drugs to look for?" inquired Stuart.

"My doctor has a gigantic book that lists all the drugs in his office," said Lisa. "The hospital probably would, too. It would be a good idea to pack up like… a sort of super-duper first aid kit. Especially since we're like… never gonna get off this island."

"We may," I said. "Let us not give in to despair just yet."

* * *

The passing of the vile horde was long and slow. It drew into the next morning and continued throughout the day. When next I awoke, the sun was set, the parking lot was silent, and Melissa was clearly far more ill than we had previously thought. She was burning with fever, and though I felt no lumps and could find no red spots, I was not reassured.

"I suspect pneumonia," said Stuart quietly.

"That is my belief as well," I said. "There is a pharmacy close at hand. I shall go there for medicine. Lisa, I would like you to stay with Melissa. Stuart, perhaps you should… have a look around."

He nodded. "And we shall meet back here in an hour. No more."

"Agreed. Lisa, lock the door behind us. Draw no attention to yourself. There may be shroud eaters about yet, and there may be looters or worse. Do not endanger yourself needlessly.

"I won't," she said softly. "Just be careful."

I was careful, and I was silent, moving in the open areas so that I may see if anything was approaching. I was drawing near to the pharmacy, when I heard a small voice pleading for help. I froze in my tracks, wondering if this was the feeble ruse of a shroud eater.

"Have you a mind with which to answer me?" I inquired.

"Please… help… please…"

"Where are you?"

"By the tree…"

The response satisfied me that this was no parroting monster. I searched for a tree, and quickly spied a small and gnarled apple tree of great age. It was growing from what had once been an irrigation ditch, and was surrounded by tall grass. I hurried to it and saw lying in the grass a young man. He was no more than twenty years of age, and I could smell the stink of burned flesh and drying blood. Because of the darkness and the depth of the grass it was difficult to see how badly he was injured, but his eyes spoke of the agony of the soldier lying lonely upon the field. I knelt by his side.

"What happened to you?" I asked.

He seized my hand, weeping in his fear and agony. "Something attacked me. I had stopped because it looked safe, y'know, I didn't see any of those monsters around. Then I saw a small fire, like… a bonfire or something. I walked up and saw… bodies. People. They looked dead but… they were moaning as they lay and… and I thought they were in pain, so I tried to help! But they grabbed me and started to bite and rip and then I fell in the fire and… and I can't feel anything below my chest…"

"Let me move you, so I may see how badly you are hurt."

He nodded, clearly more afraid of dying than of being crippled. I carefully picked him up… and gasped in horror as I felt parts of his body drop away, striking the ground like dead meat. I did not scream, but it was not without a great deal of effort on my part. I made a muffled sound of utter revulsion, my heart tearing itself asunder in grief for this poor boy. I do not know how he had managed to stay alive, but by moving him I had taken what life remained in his frame. Disgusted by myself, yet unable to refuse the scent of lifeblood, I drained such blood as he had and left him where he was. There were worse places to lie than beneath an old apple tree. I prayed he found peace. I did not try to bless him, for the blessings of the blasphemous mean nothing.

I made my way to the pharmacy and indeed located the book Lisa described. I sought out what drugs were required and gathered a few other things such as bandages, splints, antiseptic and anything else I thought may be required. I found next a radio and batteries, then, as a treat for young girls trapped in a motel, I filled a bag with makeup, perfume, hair ~~things~~ ties, and other items young ladies require that would doubtlessly never occur to Stuart. The bags were full and heavy but were not too great a weight to carry.

I ran back to the motel.

The door to our room was wide open.

I set the bags down and ran inside, and entered a nightmare. Lisa was locked in the bathroom, screaming, while Melissa and Stuart tore at each other like dogs. Blood sprayed as Stuart bit her, the red fluid having had no time to cool and thicken. Melissa had become the moaning undead, and now she was trying to devour Stuart.

We had no means to kill her, but I found a rough stone and managed to cram it into her snapping jaws. As she tore at her own face in an attempt to free herself of the object, Stuart ran to the car and started it as Lisa and I grabbed up the bags, as well as Florence who was not at all pleased with the situation, threw the bags into the station wagon, and got into the car and drove away before Melissa could pry the stone free and come for us.

I held Lisa as she wept, overwhelmed with loss and grief of the likes of which I cannot imagine. She now had naught in the world but us, and the dead are poor company for the living.

* * *

We drove back to Courtenay, and, after filling our car as full of supplies as we could, including a trip to a pet shop to find suitable housing and proper food for Florence, we returned to Peter's cabin by the lake. There was no escape from this island of death. I feared for Lisa and for the health of her mind. She had lost far too much in too short a time, and Melissa's turning seemed to have been the final blow for her. I hoped some peace and stability would bring her back to health, but she seemed to me as one who has lost the will to live.

A few days after our return to the lake house, I took the car into town, intending to raid a second pet store, and was delighted to find survivors among the bodies of creatures who had been left helpless when their human caretakers were chased off and killed. There was a tiny and weak kitten and a strange-looking, long-faced puppy of a breed I could not identify, until I realized the starved, limp thing was a dachshund. I fed both, then, with food and supplies all creatures now in our care, I drove back to the cabin. I said nothing to Lisa as I placed the sad little animals on her lap, simply leaving them there and walking away. At first, I feared they would not be enough to raise her spirits, but as weeks passed and they slowly recovered and gained strength, so did she.

Winter set in, and soon we were encased in a blanket of snow. Stuart and I were forced to roam the nighted forests for such animals as rabbits, squirrels, and the small island deer, which are poor substitutes for human blood, but I was determined Lisa should not be preyed upon, even willingly.

We were puzzled by the continued supply of electrical power, until Lisa received a phone call from an organization that had been informed by the rescuers we had called so long ago of our presence. It seemed we still had some hope of rescue, and it was they who were ensuring we were not without electricity and a phone. Lisa told them that the lake was now free of plague, and we had seen no wandering dead, apart from Stuart and me, for weeks. Our benefactors told us they would inform other survivors, and within days, the cabins surrounding Peter's were alive once more with people.

The first to arrive were John and Iris Barber; a fat, elderly couple full of humour and life, who had survived the plague by simply moving everything they required into the attic of their house and staying quiet. Following them was Megan Turner, a young woman with a large car and even larger dog. She, like the

Barbers, had chosen to hide and wait out the hours of death. She claimed the small cabin on the hill above us, while the Barbers laid claim to the cabin Valerie had once called home. Following them came Mrs. Filmore, a woman of pleasant disposition and less pleasant hygiene, and Elyse and her little son Andy, and her husband Marc and his twin brother Martin. Others, too, came, and soon our lakeshore population numbered nearly thirty. We were becoming quite the little community.

I saw the shape of a gigantic boar lurking outside the red house on many nights, but if Valerie was vexed by their presence, she gave no indication in her present swinish form. As the days passed, more people arrived, some with children, and soon there was a living community around us. However, Stuart and I did not dare look to them for blood; these people were far too wary to be prey. We would need to feed upon animals a while longer.

The holiday season came to this place that had seemed damned. Gifts were looted freely from abandoned shops, wrapped, and piled beneath trees decorated in gold and red and silver. Venison was caught in the woods and roasted, and there was again the sound of laughing children and life around this lake that had been so silent. It was all very lovely and wonderful, and Lisa seemed to regain her strength as she planned parties with her new neighbours. However, Stuart and I were under no delusions. All too soon these people would realize there were wolves among them, and no matter how tame the wolves may seem, they would not be tolerated. We made up our minds to depart.

"Will you be back?" Lisa asked. She was watching as Stuart and I packed.

"Yes," I assured her. "You are by no means rid of us! We shall return. We are merely taking ourselves out of harm's way. We shall call, and we shall visit. We are not abandoning you.

"But you can at least stay until Christmas?" she said. "It will be horrible without you. Are you sure you can't stay? I mean, you kept your promise! You haven't hurt anyone!"

"It is not that simple," said Stuart. "The first time something happens, they—"

"I know," she said. "I just don't want to be alone anymore. Please, just stay. I don't have anyone anymore. You're all the family I have. I don't want to be alone!"

I wanted to harden my heart and do what I knew was wise. But how could I abandon this child who had lost all.

"And what shall you tell them when they learn what Stuart and I are?"

"You haven't hurt anyone! And this was your home first!" She crossed her arms. "You're staying."

"Lisa, I do not know how to say this delicately, so I won't," said Stuart. "I'm really tired of biting rats and squirrels."

She curled her lip. "So bite Mrs. Filmore, she's gross."

"Oh, I quite agree," said Stuart. "Hence my reluctance to bite her."

Mrs. Filmore was the newest neighbour to have come to our tiny village. She had a lovely personality. However, her grasp of personal hygiene was tenuous at best.

"Just stay. Please," Lisa implored. "Don't leave me. I don't have anyone left."

Stuart and I exchanged glances and knew we were defeated.

"We will stay," I said. "But if I awaken on the lake shore in the middle of a sunny day I shall not be pleased."

Chapter Nine

It was Lisa's idea to have the neighbors in for dinner. I frankly could have done without the disruption, but I could not blame the child for wishing to surround herself with her fellow living beings, having lost all those whom she held dear. I viewed the gathering as little more than a bother, but it so clearly meant such a great deal to Lisa that I could not deny her.

I will not pretend that I assisted with the meal preparations in any manner. Tea and scones I can make, and, if needs must, jam. However, vampires rarely find it necessary to roast chickens or turkeys or venison. Indeed I am only adept at tea and scones because it takes my mind to happier times, when the sun was soft upon my skin, and flowers bloomed at my feet, and I need not worry why I continued to walk the night and what unattended wrong still held me to this earth.

The night of Lisa's party found Stuart and I lurking about much as we are—oddly-garbed ambulatory furniture. Long had it been since last we attended a party, and I in my gowns and he in his finery hardly blended in. More than one person declared that they had no idea this was meant to be a costume party.

"Don't mind them," said Lisa. "My aunt and uncle are a bit odd."

I glared. Stuart handled his insult in a different manner; after dinner he hid the child's phone.

However, at the moment we were trapped at the table and hardly in a position to leave without appearing rude. In an attempt to make amends, Megan turned to me.

"So, what do you do for a living?" she asked.

I confess that I find this question quite rude, although in this day and age it seems to pass for polite conversation.

"I am a violinist," I said.

"Oh, how wonderful! I've always wanted to learn to play!"

"I don't do anything," said Stuart, a glass of wine in his hand. "I'm far too pretty to work."

"Yes, well, I always was most firmly of the opinion that a man's place was in either the kitchen or the bed chamber," I said. "Sadly, in Stuart's case, he insists on escaping from both rooms, and he refuses to tell me where he has hidden his lock-picks."

"I have told you repeatedly that you may search me," he said.

"And sully my hands? You jest. As I said, I am a violinist."

"And you play the strings of my heart so beautifully."

I had been about to take a sip of wine. My glass paused halfway to my mouth.

"Well, I *am* rather lacking in catgut." I said.

He waggled his eyebrows. I chose to ignore him in favour of speaking to Megan.

"And yourself?" I inquired.

"Oh, I'm a midwife," she said and smiled.

Something about her words sparked something in my mind; some odd little thought that nibbled like a mouse, but I could not think what the term 'midwife' would ignite in my thoughts. I tried to set the niggling feeling aside.

"Really," I said. "Such an old and honoured profession. Is there much call for midwives? Do most ladies not birth in hospitals these days?"

"It's becoming more common for women to have babies at home," said Megan. "Most women would just rather be someplace comfortable and familiar."

"I would never have a baby at home," said Lisa. "What if something went wrong?"

"That's what ambulances are for," said Megan. "And if there seems to be a chance that the birth may be dangerous or compromised in any way, then it's my duty as a midwife to make sure you are either in the hospital when the time comes or at the very least fully apprised of what could go wrong.

I was filled with a morbid curiosity. "Have you ever assisted a mother who lost her child?"

"No," said Megan. "I've been lucky so far, all the women I assisted were strong and healthy and there were no complications. Why?"

"Forgive me," I said. "I find myself thinking too long at times upon how very wrong a birth can turn. I have… lost… babies."

The softness in her eyes endeared her to me. "I'm so very sorry," she said. "Was it in childbirth?"

"They… passed not long after," I said. I did not wish to say they had died at the hands of the father, so instead I told a lie. "I do not know why. I bore them all at home with the aid of a midwife and so became curious when you said you earned your livelihood thusly."

"No, as I said, I've been very lucky," said Megan. "None of the women under my care have had any problems, and I dread the day something *does* go wrong."

The distasteful Mrs. Filmore chose that moment to speak up. If ever a living being were set upon the land for the purpose of deterring a vampire from his bloodlust, it indeed was this wrinkled, seldom-bathed, snaggle-toothed crone. Stuart and I had raided a store that sold toiletries, fancy soaps, and bubble bath for her Christmas gift in the hopes she would make use of them.

"Did you hear about that case down in the States?" she said. "Terrible!"

"And what case would that be?" I inquired.

She poured herself more wine. "That case about that midwife killing the babies she helped deliver. She was like a… what do you call it? Assassin. She would be hired by people who didn't want the kid. She would deliver it, then find a way to kill it without it looking like murder. But she worked as a regular midwife, too, so it didn't look suspicious because most of the babies she delivered lived."

I heard very little after that. The nibbling mouse became a roaring lion, and I knew then whom I had overlooked in my quest for vengeance. I excused myself from the table and departed, leaving the house in order to walk down to the lake shore, feeling ill and overwhelmed.

The midwife. Only she could have been the final link in this tragedy.

It had not been difficult to overlook Mary Thatcher. Even as a very young woman, she had been a dried, disapproving, and humourless little grey thing, as if the very essence of life had been sucked from her. It seemed so very odd, for her mother was a lively, happy woman with three daughters apart from Grey Mary, all of whom were married with babes of their own. The elder three daughters were in every way like their mother—buxom and lively, their bellies like wellsprings of life. But Mary, the youngest child, had somehow been denied the waters of life and was as a dried husk. No man would draw near her, and she busied herself with such duties as were deemed proper for a woman of that time. No joy grew in Mary's heart, and I had long thought it odd that she should choose to be a midwife, as she seemed to dislike newborns and women alike. Now it seemed to me that I knew the answer to the riddle of Mary's chosen profession—she, and not my husband, would have been the one to put an end to my babies.

"Deirdre?"

I was distracted from my thoughts and turned my head to see Stuart standing beside me, his expression one of concern.

"Are you all right?" he inquired.

"No," I said. "No, I do not believe I am, nor do I think I ever shall be again. I believe I know now who it was that I missed on that dark night long ago, when I should have laid to rest all those who wronged me. The midwife, Mary Thatcher."

"Grey Mary?" said Stuart.

I could not have been more astounded had he pulled a rabbit out of his ear. "Have you heard of her?"

"Indeed. In the days after Thomas' death one could scarcely avoid her. She was like a pox, screeching about moneys owed her by Thomas. I finally paid her myself to be rid of her, but it was to no avail. She lingered still, spewing nonsense about promises unfulfilled and love lost and..."

He ceased speaking, and he and I gazed at each other.

"You don't suppose Thomas was laying with Grey Mary as well?" said Stuart.

"At this point, it would not surprise me in the least. He may have promised her my place in the marital bed in exchange for her services, the same lie he told his whore. But his infidelity is no longer my concern. I know now who I missed that night, but I have no means of finding her. I cannot even leave this cursed island and return to England so that I may search. And Leeds is not as I knew it. She may well have died elsewhere, fleeing her crimes. She may even have wed., I do not know. I doubt in my heart she lives yet as we do, and I cannot take vengeance on the dead!"

Stuart drew me close in his comforting embrace. "There is naught to be done, dear one. And if you could find her...? Nay. What I am thinking is selfish."

"No, speak your heart."

"Well, it was your wrong that raised me from the dead, and Mary's wrong that raised you. If you could take your vengeance upon her, you would be laid to rest, and as you died, perhaps so would I, if death only without vengeance is required to end our time. And Lisa would be alone."

I pulled back, anger in my heart. "Do not vex me with such thoughts, Stuart Cooper! I curse every passing night and unseen day that I walk in this cursed form! Why do you lay new guilt at my feet? Is it not bad enough I have damned you and was so weak as to be unable to keep Lisa safe and her family whole? You would burden me now with your death and her solitude?"

"But that is my very point! Why must you seek Grey Mary? Why can you not take Lisa to your heart as your daughter and raise her as your own? Why not take for yourself a family? You miss your own, I see the pain weigh upon you daily!"

"I crave redemption!" I cried. "More than anything! I despise being trapped upon this miserable earth, befouled in the eyes of God, knowing my mother awaits me in Heaven! Would you deny me this?"

"No," he said softly. "I would deny you nothing. I ask only if your redemption will come at the burning of old bones, or the realization that God has given you a family of your own, and they stand before you.

"Do not taunt me."

"I am not taunting you, dear lady! I am attempting to show you what treasure lies at your feet!"

"I am not blind to the pretty distractions that I am shown," I said.

"A distraction? After all we have endured, I am but a distraction? That is a coldness that cannot be blamed upon the grave, my lady."

"I am sorry," I said. "Truly I am. Forgive me. You are my dearest friend, and my heart knows only love for you. But you do not understand the anger that haunts me."

"No, I daresay I do not. For I have never lost a child, indeed I have never sired one, either. My life has been quite carefree, and I am fortunate. No shadows dog my step that do not belong to me. But I see the pain within you, Deirdre. You wear it as an old woman wears her winter shawl, clutching it tightly, and are loath to part with it. Even as passers-by call to you it is summer now, and the shawl may be laid aside."

"It is my shawl to wear as I may please," I said.

"I ask only that you ponder my words," he said. "Do this one thing for me. And if you will not forsake vengeance then at least lay it aside for a while. I daresay Grey Mary, wherever she is, shan't be travelling far or fast. Can we not enjoy our time among the living, before we must return to the grave?"

I could see the wisdom in his words. But my world was like a tiny tower shrouded in grey and smoke, and all I saw was the anger that burned in my heart over how this miserable creature that was Grey Mary had gone on to live her life, sparing not a thought for myself and my babies.

"I shall ponder your wisdom," I said. "I promise I shall. But more promises than that I cannot make. She had a gift that I was never granted—she held my babes in her arms. Never did I have that chance. And she used this gift to murder, not nurture. And that is a thought that brings to me such a fury that I do not know why my skull doth not split and spew forth black smoke and melted stone as doth a volcano!"

He held me close once more, as if trying to will peace into my bones. I did my best to calm myself, and slowly I felt the rage subside, waiting deep within my heart for a chance to rise up once more.

"I shall consider your words carefully," I said, returning his embrace. "I shall make no rash moves. But even if I should not seek her out now, I *shall* seek her out. If she walks as do we, then I shall smite her into the dust. If she is but bones and ash, I shall burn her remains and cast her to the wind so that she may never rest. But I shall have my revenge, Stuart."

"I do not begrudge you your chance for vengeance. I ask only that you see you have a live child before you, who needs a mother as badly as you need your children." He placed a gentle kiss upon my brow, then took my hand. "Come. Let us walk the night and see what we may find in the way of dinner.

I sighed loudly. "I do not know how you are faring but feasting upon naught but beasts sits well with me not at all! I dislike tormenting dumb brutes, and their blood satisfies my appetite poorly."

"Then let us take the car into town and hunt. There may be someone suitable about."

Stuart and I drove into the dead city that had once been Courtenay. We saw a scant handful of shroud eaters, but all were too rotted and maimed to be of any concern. They dragged their damaged remains along the sidewalks, seeking sustenance as did Stuart and I. They found no more than we did. Stuart and I searched the night until sunrise was close upon our heels, and we were forced to return to our bed unsated.

"This situation grows dangerous for the breathing," I said as we settled into our bed.

"It shall grow more dangerous for us if we dare take one of them," said Stuart.

"Mr. Barber has more than enough blood to spare. I think tomorrow night I shall give him a slight nibble."

"And who shall I bite?"

"My suggestion is Mrs. Barber. They've eaten more than their fair share. I see no reason they should not give back to the community. We will just make certain they have enjoyed their wine aforehand so that they are well asleep when we come to claim our tax.

"And if they awaken?" Stuart inquired.

"Well I do not know about you, my love, but I intend to hide under the bed and pretend to be a singularly large bedbug."

He laughed. Then the sun crept close to the sky, and he and I fell into a breathless slumber.

* * *

It was the day following the night Stuart and I went to visit the Barbers, and he and I were in our bed.

The dead do not dream. But there are times during which I wonder if perhaps we do something very similar. As the slow day passed and I lay abed, cold and still, it seemed as if my mind did roam free and my spirit walked abroad, though to which place it went, I do not know. I found myself walking through a cemetery, clad in my white burial gown. In my hands I clutched a dead bouquet of flowers, and the ground was shrouded in deep mist as the dark sky above shed listless rain drops upon me. I reached the crypt where briefly I had lain and descended the steps into it, smelling the damp and the earth that had begun to claim it. Plants grew into the stone, and many of the bricks had cracked and fallen from the wall. The place was wholly neglected and deserted, untouched for centuries, and I felt strangely cruel for having forsaken it, as one might upon coming across a house where one dwelled for a time as a child. This had been my womb from which I emerged into the eternal night, and I wondered if I would ever see it again.

I placed my dead flowers upon the broken slab where once I had lain and looked around at the desolate chamber. Why was I here? It made no sense to me. But then I became aware of a presence and glanced to the cracked and collapsing stairs. Standing there was a dried and humourless husk of a woman, wrapped in a shawl, wearing a shapeless gown of scrap fabric. It was none other than Grey Mary — a figure so utterly forgettable that she had slipped my mind for centuries.

"And so we meet," I said. "This is all your fault."

She sneered. "So like a lady to blame the poor. Being highborn makes you above wrongdoing, does it?"

"I do not feel the need to defend my virtue from the likes of you, murdering whore."

She came down the stairs, entering my crypt. Her expression was strange, as if she wished to smile but dared not.

"If it were not for me you would sleep on your cold bed in peace. You never saw me when you lived, but you see me now, do you not? Had you not slain Thomas it would have been I in the marital bed."

I laughed. "Yes, I have no doubt! And a merry warm bed it would have been! Tell me, would you, the whore, and dear Stuart have taken to his bed in turn, or would you have simply all joined at once? You were but one of three, and my guess is there were many more lovers, all told the same lie — that you were the only one, beloved above all others, sent by God to bear him a son. Well, perhaps he would not have said as such to the young *men* with whom he dallied."

She shrieked like a harpy. "You lie!"

"I do not. I have no need to lie. Thomas would lay with any lady or gentleman who would permit him, and likely a few who would not but were made to submit to his will anyway."

"You lie. You are angry he chose me over you."

"You bore me. I have grown accustomed to the idea that I was simply one of many. It would do you no ill to accept the idea as well."

I turned my back to her, and she seemed to slowly melt away, nothing more than the dull shade of an unhappy woman. Then the image of my neglected and forgotten crypt faded away, and my eyes opened. It was evening, and below me were the sounds of life. I could hear Lisa playing with her puppy and smell the scent of what she was cooking for her dinner. Beside me Stuart was a lump. I find it amusing that even as a vampire, he still prefers to sleep in.

"I think I had a dream," I said.

He did not respond. I left him to sleep and rose from the bed, dressing in a green gown I had made. Florence greeted me with whistles and clucks, letting me know that she was ready for her dinner as well. I gave her some pellets and lettuce, then left her to feast as I departed my room and went downstairs. There was a fire in the hearth, and tea and scones on a platter resting upon a small table beside a chair.

"Good evening," I said.

Lisa looked up from playing with her dog and smiled. "Hi! I thought you were gonna sleep all night!"

"Is it late?" I asked.

"It's almost ten. You're usually up hours ago.

I turned my head to look at the large grandfather clock that stood in the living room. It was indeed nearly ten p.m.

"How very odd," I said. "Especially so, since I believe I dreamed as I slept."

"Don't vampires dream?" Lisa asked.

"I cannot speak for all vampires, but certainly I do not. However it seemed to me that I did dream. I was standing in my crypt, and I saw the woman I believe killed my children."

Lisa made a face. "That's not a dream, that's a nightmare."

"I find myself in agreement." I turned on the television and found a news program, then poured myself some tea and watched to see if the monsters that had wandered south were showing signs of roaming northward once more. Victoria was a city of the walking dead, and all who could flee had done so. The creatures of death and plague wandered the streets and shops, but they did not seem to be returning to our lake, at least for now.

"I wish they would just come get us," said Lisa.

"As do I," I said. "But they must be certain we will not bring this illness with us."

She rolled her eyes and huffed. "The oldest boy here is *eight*. By the time he's old enough to notice girls I'll be an old woman."

"Positively ancient, I'm sure," I said.

"It's not nice teasing me, you know. I don't have any friends, and even if I ever do get off this stupid island, I'm gonna be known as 'plague girl' for the rest of my life!"

"Lisa," I said to her gently, "I know you will not believe this, but things do get better."

"And do you believe that?"

"I do, actually," I said. "I have you, and I have Stuart, and Florence. There were many long, cold centuries in which I had no one at all—centuries in which I would have given anything just to be clean and have a nice place to sit and drink a cup of tea. Things do get better, child. But I do not blame you for thinking this is not so."

She hung her head, looking down at her hand and playing with something upon her finger. "I saw Valerie earlier this evening. I had a muffin and she loved muffins, so I gave it to her." She made a sound of amusement. "Apparently vampire-pigs will eat muffins."

"You should be careful of her," I said quietly. "She could spread her ailment to you without intending to."

"I know. I just… didn't want her to think I was disgusted by her or hated her or something. I tied a scarf around my nose and mouth, and she didn't come close. I don't know why she's staying. But she's my friend, and I'm not gonna treat her like a freak.

"You are a very good person, Lisa," I said. "I am sure it means a great deal to her that you have not spurned her."

Lisa shrugged. She seemed unconvinced. "I just wish she wasn't an undead, plague-spreading, vampire pig.

"I am certain she wishes the same thing."

"Is there any way to like… turn her back?"

"No," I said. "At least I have never heard tell of a means.

There was a knock on the door, and Lisa went to answer it. Standing there was Mrs. Barber, looking most annoyed.

"Lisa, do you have any bug spray?"

"I don't know. I'll look."

Lisa permitted her to enter, then began rummaging through the cupboards for bug spray. I rose from my chair to greet the corpulent woman.

"Good evening, Mrs. Barber."

She cast me a disapproving glance. I do not know why she did not care for me, and I worry about it not at all. I have the distinct impression she makes her mind up about others quickly and with limited information.

"Good evening, Deirdre."

"You are having trouble with insects?" I inquired politely.

She pulled up her sleeve and displayed a pair of red spots of which I was the cause. However the area surrounding the bite marks was festooned with more spots, which I certainly did not do.

"Some bug is munching on me while I am in bed. I have no idea what kind of a bug it is, but it seems to enjoy my blood!"

"Well you know what they say," I said primly. "You're nobuggy until somebuggy loves you."

Mrs. Barber stared flaming daggers at me. Lisa groaned loudly.

"Deirdre, that was awful."

"Do not blame me, that was one of Stuart's dreadful attempts at humour. And if I must endure them, then so must you."

Lisa located a can of bug spray and passed it to Mrs. Barber, who accepted it.

"I wish those people could have found a more suitable place for us to live! These cabins are barely habitable, there are bugs all over, and there's a giant black pig roaming around. If I see it once more, I'll have my husband shoot it!"

"You will do no such thing!" I said sharply, and she gasped in surprise. Never before had I raised my voice to her. Indeed I suspect few people raised their voice to her. "You will not harm that pig., It is a family pet. It belongs to my niece Lisa, and if any harm comes to it, I shall know for whom to look!"

"Then keep it on a leash!" she snapped.

She took the can of bug spray and departed. Lisa closed the cupboards beneath the sink and straightened up.

"Thanks for sticking up for Valerie, even though I'm pretty sure she'd be really unhappy to know she ended up a pet pig."

"We will have to find a way to discourage her from staying near this place," I said. "So far as I know she will not harm anyone directly, for night pigs are said to feed only upon their kin. But she *will* spread the plague, even if that is not her intention."

"I'll talk to her," said Lisa quietly. "Maybe she'll understand."

"I hope she does. If it is discovered she is undead, then we will not be able to protect her."

"Yeah, and speaking of undead, I noticed two of those bug bites were not bug bites."

"Yes, well, I would like to see how well you controlled your impulses if after weeks of eating naught but gruel you found yourself confronted with chocolate cake and ice cream. I swear if I had to bite one more animal I would have screamed."

"Don't get caught, because I don't think I can take losing one more person."

"I will not be caught. I have not lived this long by being careless."

We looked to the door as a figure shambled into the room. Stuart looked positively ill, which is a very odd look for a man who is already dead.

"Stuart? Are you okay?" asked Lisa.

"I feel dreadful," he said.

"You look dreadful," I said.

"Thank you, I was worried I looked healthy." He seated himself in a chair, looking pallid and, dare I say, dead. "I had the worst sleep of my unlife. I was… dreaming…"

"Dreaming?" I said.

"I believe it was a dream. I was with Thomas…"

I snatched up a dish towel and struck him with it. "You are not permitted to dream about my husband."

"I'm not old enough to hear about this," said Lisa.

She left the room, leaving Stuart and I alone. I seated myself at the kitchen table and faced him.

"You are certain it was a dream?"

"It was a dream, and it was Thomas. We were… well we weren't playing chess, just let me say that. And I swear I felt my life draining from me."

"I dreamed as well last night," I said softly.

Stuart gave me a look of surprise. "You as well? You cannot tell me that is a coincidence."

"I will not attempt to. I dreamed of Grey Mary. She was baiting me with tales of being Thomas' next wife, but I turned my back on her."

"So you resist the urge to throttle her and are well. I do not resist and am feasted upon. What foul game is this?"

"I do not know," I said. "But it seems perfectly clear that you should not be having filthy dreams about my husband."

"I find it very confusing that you are bothered by the dream-infidelity of your deceased husband."

"It is not *his* infidelity that concerns me!" I swatted Stuart repeatedly with the towel.

"Point taken," he said. "I shall never more dream about pretty ladies or pretty men. And he was a bastard, but there was no denying his beauty."

"I am not denying his beauty. I wish it had been inward as well as outward. But what evil is happening here that you have had your strength drained by a dream?"

"I do not know. I have never heard tell of anything like this. We will just have to be careful until we understand this matter."

We froze as we heard a distant moan. Lisa ran into the kitchen, looking terrified.

"Is it one of them? Are they back?"

I listened. It did sound like a shroud eater, and yet...

The sound changed, and we breathed a sigh of relief. "It is only a dog," I said.

"Where would a dog come from?" asked Lisa. "The only dog here is my dog, and he's on the sofa, not out in the woods. It's not Megan's dog either, she doesn't let him roam at night."

"I do not know, but we are not going out into the night to search for it," I said. "Melissa was attacked by a great hound. That may be the dog we are hearing."

Lisa sighed loudly. "I wish this would just end! We can't even run away to someplace safe! There is no place that's safe! What if those things come back? I don't want to end up like Valerie!"

"We will do our best to survive," I said.

"Yeah, we're doing a bang-up job of *that* all right," she snapped, and left the room.

"She has a point," said Stuart.

"She does, but there is nothing we can do save be on our guard. We are being attacked from within as well as without, and unless we look after one another we shall all fall. As for you and I, the best thing to do, it seems, is be mindful that any images we see whilst in our bed are to be ignored. Clearly, they are dangerous. We know well enough that there are other monsters besides vampires about. Nightmares are said to prey upon those who are sleeping, are they not?"

"Yes, but I never heard of one preying upon the undead in daylight, or indeed of preying upon undead at all."

"And until very recently you and I would have both sworn that shroud eaters fed only upon the undead and do not trouble the living. Our lore in these matters is clearly wanting."

Somewhere in the darkness, the dog howled mournfully. I rose from my chair to busy myself making fresh tea in an attempt to block the monster from my mind.

"Have you thought any more about Grey Mary?" asked Stuart.

I set the kettle on the stove to boil. "A little. Mostly I have pondered how very difficult it would be to visit justice upon her. She will not be undead. Murderers often rise, 'tis true, but just as often they do not. Indeed more so, and I find it most unlikely that this incident produced more than three undead, being thee, me, and the whore. In fact the mind boggles that it produced even that many. Wherever Grey Mary is, she is cold within her grave, and seeking that grave to salt her bones and set fire to them is a quest that would take years. I shall find her yet, mark my words, but such a hunt is best left until after Lisa is grown."

"That I feel is the wisest choice," said Stuart.

"Yes, well, to me it is not the most pleasing choice. I would see her ground into dust for all her misdeeds."

There was a sudden commotion from one of the cabins—a great screaming and the booming of a shotgun. I heard glass shatter, and the screaming became shriller. Stuart and I raced from our own cabin and into the cold night. It was snowing, and the lake was still as glass as Stuart and I ran to the small cabin up the hill where once Hazel had lived.

The screaming was unbearable, and as Stuart and I ran onto the porch of the small cabin we were confronted with a hideous sight. Before us was one of the monsters I had seen weeks ago in the forest as I sought Lisa—a great man, clad in furs, with a wild mane of black hair. His lower face was not flesh but metal, his jaws made of rusted, flaking iron. At his side stood a gigantic hound, and I knew then what beast had attacked Melissa. The hound lowered its head and growled as its master tore the flesh from a live and shrieking child, feasting upon him as the boy's parents fought to free their baby from the monster that had reached through the window to grab him.

I do not know what came over me. I can only say I was blinded by a sudden and violent rage, and I flew at the thing holding the boy, clawing at its eyes. I felt the hound lunge and bite my leg, then heard it scream as Stuart struck it so hard that both fell from the porch and rolled down the hill, continuing their battle at the lake shore. I fought with the child's attacker, using claw and fang and all the infernal strength I possessed to force him to drop him. The boy fell to the porch with a thump, and was snatched up by his frantic mother and pulled into the house.

I am no warrior. Never have I been trained to carry a sword or pistol. But I was so enraged by this horror that it seemed I lost my mind. He struck and pummelled at me, and I felt the blows land heavy, breaking my ribs, but still I did not retreat. I thrust my fingers into his eyes as far as they could go, then, holding tightly, pulled with what power I had and ripped the bones of his face from his skull. Black rotted matter and maggots spilled out, and I was about to pull out the hideous iron jaws as well when he threw me to the floor. Before I could move, he swung at me with his axe, and I shrieked as I felt it chop through my stomach, the cold iron pinning me fast to the floorboards.

Stuart suddenly appeared, moving with a speed that was daunting even for the undead. He struck the monster, and the pair fought like hellish cats, tearing, ripping, clawing, and biting, scattering bone and ichors and maggots and brains in a disgusting rain as I tried to pull the axe from my guts. Lisa suddenly ran up and took hold of the handle, fighting to drag it free. At last it came forth, and I was on my feet again. I lunged at the monster, managing to slash my way into its throat and take hold of the neck bones, which I proceeded to bite and break until I managed to sever them completely. As the head fell to the ground, Stuart shoved the axe head into the jaws, and then fled with his hideous prize, leaving the body to flop and writhe on the porch.

"Where is the hound?" I asked as I sank to the porch.

"Dead," said Lisa. "Stuart broke its neck and then found something to jam into its jaws. I poured some gas on it and set it on fire. Deirdre, are you all right? You… you kinda… have a hole in your middle."

In truth I had absolutely no idea if I would recover or not—this was the first truly serious wound I had taken in my vampiric life. Small cuts healed, but I had no idea if a gaping axe-wound would.

"How is the child?" I asked. "Were we in time?"

Lisa went into the cabin to see if the little boy was well, as I sat on the porch in a pool of blood and pus and maggots. The others were arriving now, and it only just then occurred to me that Stuart and I had signed our death warrants. We had openly attacked a monster and revealed ourselves to be monsters as well. The mother of the child stepped out of the cabin, staring at me.

"You saved my little boy," she said softly.

I arranged my gown, too weak to flee if they should turn on me. "I did what anyone would, had they strength enough."

"But you're—"

I looked up sharply, meeting her gaze. "I am Deirdre of Leeds, and I died in 1663. Whatever else I may be, I am not one to stand aside and witness the brutal murder of a child. How is the boy?"

The child set up a loud screeching and wailing as Megan and his father tended to his injuries, binding them and stitching them. His mother, Elyse, gazed in the direction of the screams.

"We don't know. It... it bit *pieces* out of him. And its jaws..."

"Were iron, yes I know," I said softly.

She turned her gaze to me. "What was it?"

"A creature from Russia. It has jaws of iron and feeds upon babies."

"Will it turn Andy into a—?"

"No," I said. "Andy will be as he has always been—a little boy with much growing to do. And you should go to him. I feel in my heart that he needs you very much right now."

She gazed at me for a time as if I were a cat that had learned to speak. Then she hurried into the house, leaving me upon the porch, surrounded by the neighbours, just as Stuart leapt over the railing to stand beside me.

"Everything all right?" he asked.

"No, everything is not all right!" shouted Mr. Barber. "What are you two?"

"I used to be a healer; now I'm a layabout. Deirdre is a violinist.'

"That is not what I meant, and you know it!" He marched forward and showed Stuart the bite marks on his arm. "Did you do this?"

Stuart regarded his work in silence, clearly trying to think of an answer that would not gain him a stake through the heart. Lisa stepped out of the cabin just then, holding a fireplace poker as if she intended to use it.

"They just saved Andy, so why don't you all just back off? They saved me, too, and you weren't here when they tried to save my dad and my friends. They've done nothing to harm anyone!"

That was not entirely true, and Lisa knew it, but certainly we had done nothing to harm her or our neighbours, nibbling on Mr. and Mrs. Barber aside.

"Calm down, Lisa," said Mrs. Filmore. "We're just a little surprised is all. I mean we had a right to know that."

"No, you didn't," said Lisa. "You had no right to know. You would have acted just like you're acting now, only worse. It doesn't matter to you that Deirdre got chopped with an axe saving Andy, or that Stuart was chewed on by a hellhound doing the same thing, or that they're the only family I have left in the world. You don't give a shit. You just know they're big bad vampires so you want to kill them to save your own asses, and you don't even have brains enough to think that we wouldn't even have *this* place if they weren't here to keep the bad monsters away. So why don't you all just back the fuck off now, and I'll let you keep your teeth and kneecaps."

Mr. Brandon stepped forward. "Lisa, I don't think—"

I watched in surprise as she deftly broke his knee with one stroke of the poker, sending him onto his backside in a pool of disgusting mire.

"I'm *serious*, motherfucker!" she screamed.

Such a distasteful insult; I wonder if anyone ever pauses to think precisely what it implies? Mr. Brandon lay on his back, clutching his broken knee.

"What the hell did you do that for?" he shouted at Lisa.

"I told you I would," she pointed out.

"Enough," said Stuart. "I think it is time for everyone to calm down. There will be no further harm done to anyone this eve. We've wounded enough on our hands. Yes, Deirdre and I are vampires. And you have dwelled ~~nigh~~ near us for many weeks now and come to no harm, nor will you, providing you do no harm to us. I do not think that is asking too much."

"We're just a little confused," said Marjorie, our latest pilgrim to this odd little holiday camp we call home. "Don't vampires prey on living humans?"

"Yes," said Stuart. "We do. But there are many, many kinds of vampire, and their habits are not our habits. Some feast upon helpless babes, some violate young girls as they prey upon their souls, some stand moaning upon the lake shore and tear to pieces anything that crosses their paths. Deirdre and I take only what we need and nothing more. We are not murderers, whatever else we may be. Once we were living beings. And we have not forgotten that. Now if you do not mind, I would like to get my lady off the floor."

The crowd backed up slightly. Stuart bent to gather me into his arms and raise me from the porch while Lisa stood guard with her poker. Together we returned to our house, where Stuart carried me to the washroom before darting outside to tend to the burning hound. The shore of the lake was almost entirely coal, and fires cannot be permitted to burn long, lest they sink deep within the ground, and spread like burning vines to emerge unexpectedly and destroy whole forests and towns. I seated myself on the edge of the bathtub and began carefully undressing myself, hoping the crowd of neighbours did not turn into an angry mob. I was in no condition to endure a second battle.

Lisa poked her head into the room. "I don't think anyone's coming after us."

"Who would dare to do so after such a display?" I said. "Mighty Lisa, wielder of the poker, defender of vampires! I suspect you and Joan of Arc would have made a very merry pair indeed."

"I wasn't gonna let them hurt you after you got an axe in your stomach for trying to save Andy. I hope he's okay."

"As do I," I said. "But his injuries will be grave no matter where the monster bit. The rusted iron will have entered the wounds, and he will require a great deal of attention."

I removed my bodice and let it fall to the floor as I gazed upon the hole in my middle.

"That... looks like it hurt." said Lisa.

"It did, as well as ruin my gown. I grow weary indeed of mending clothes. Tomorrow I shall loot a fabric store."

There was a knock on the door. Lisa grabbed up her poker and marched determinedly to answer it, no doubt envisioning the destruction of yet more knee caps. Moments later, Andy's father, Marc, peered into the room in which I sat, along with his brother Martin.

"I just wanted to let you know, it looks like Andy will be okay. We cleaned out the bites and sedated him so he can rest and got everything bandaged and stitched. I mean, we're no doctors, but Megan has some medical training and… I think he's going to be okay. Um… thank you. I don't know what else to say but thank you. I shot the thing with both barrels, and it didn't even flinch. If you hadn't been there…"

"It is my honour to have saved your child. I hope he recovers swiftly."

Martin laughed briefly. "He went to sleep asking if this was going to delay Christmas. I told him no, Christmas would be right on time."

"Deirdre, I just can't thank you enough," said Marc "I… I don't care what you are. I'm just damned glad you were there."

"I am glad I was there as well. Now be on your way home. I have no doubt your wife will be anxious to have you near."

He nodded and was about to leave, when something gave him pause, and he turned his gaze to me once more.

"You should know that Mrs. Filmore is speaking out against your being here. You should also know she's alone in her opinions. Not even Mr. Brandon is against you, despite what Lisa did to his knee."

"If I were Mrs. Filmore, I should attempt to bathe more and complain less. But I am glad to hear she is failing in her attempts to summon a mob against us."

"There's no mob," said Marc. "I'm not gonna say we aren't all a little shaken up and surprised, but Mrs. Filmore isn't getting any support and a couple people want to know if you'd like to eat her."

"Good gracious no, I tend to avoid things that smell as she does."

"Yeah, it's a heck of a reek, isn't it? My wife said it was almost like spoiled meat."

"Very close to it," I said. Once more I felt a mouse nibble at my thoughts, but could not think what vexed me. "We shall keep an eye on her. If she is intent upon causing strife then I think it best she be encouraged to seek sanctuary elsewhere. We have a nice community here; I will not have it sullied by cowards who know not how to bathe."

"I'll pass on the word," said Martin. "And… thank you again."

"You are most welcome," I said.

Martin and Marc departed, leaving me to undress in peace. Not long after he left, Stuart peered into the room.

"How are you?"

"Injured." I removed the last of my garments and stood looking down at myself, studying the lumps caused by broken ribs and the hole through my middle. "I will be most distressed if this does not mend."

"What did Marc have to say?"

"He thanked me for saving his child and warned me that Mrs. Filmore feels you and I ought not to be permitted to remain. However, she appears to be alone in her opinions."

"If I were Mrs. Filmore I would try to balance that aroma with a sweeter disposition."

"She does have quite a stench to her, doesn't she?" I mused as I gently prodded my new opening.

"Like meat left in the sun."

"Yes, rather." I continued to examine my injury. "I wonder if she is not more than she seems?"

"She walks abroad in daylight."

"Yes, but that proves only she is no vampire, and we have already seen she is not a shroud eater. Ghouls may walk abroad by day, or so I have heard tell."

"Yes, but ghouls are merely living beings with an unholy taste for the flesh of the dead," said Stuart. "Still, it *would* explain the smell."

"I think it is in our best interest to keep an eye on her," I said. "The gates of Hell are open wide, and more than the undead have escaped."

* * *

The evening after Andy was attacked, I arrived on the porch of his parents' small cabin. Since my green gown was destroyed I was once more resplendent in my Mastodon shirt until such time I could sew a new dress. Gauze about my middle concealed my axe-wound, which was healing, albeit slowly. I was carrying a tray of hot scones, clotted cream, and jam. As I said, I do not bake, else Andy would have been given something more festive and sweet. But I have yet to meet a child who will turn down hot scones covered in sweet cream and jam.

Granted, I very rarely meet children.

To my left stood Stuart, to my right stood Lisa, and in a cotton-lined bag of velvet constructed for her travelling comfort over my shoulder was Florence. Stuart insisted that a guinea pig simply isn't smart enough to appreciate mingling in society, but I felt that was hardly an excuse to neglect her. She was bathed and brushed, and had a ribbon in her hair, and she chatted quietly as she peeked out of her satin-trimmed conveyance. I tapped upon the door, and moments later Elyse answered. She looked exhausted, but she smiled as she spied us.

"I was hoping you would come over. Come in."

We entered, and I handed the tray to Elyse. "I made scones. I thought Andy might like them. How is he?

"Scared, hurt, but he seems to be okay. Some of those bites were just so deep. If you hadn't arrived when you did… I don't like to think about it. I'll put some of these on a plate for him."

She whisked the tray into the small open kitchen, placing some scones on a plate before setting the remainder out for the few people in her living room. Marc gazed at the offering in puzzlement.

"I had no idea vampires baked."

"We don't," I said, seating myself in an antique wing chair. "We have little need of it. You are viewing the entire repertoire of my abilities on this one tray."

"Still more than I can do." He gazed at Florence. "You're not going to eat that, are you?"

"Certainly not! Why does everyone always assume poor Florence is a snack?"

Mrs. Barber chose this moment to inject her own wisdom on the matter, addressing Martin. "If she was going to eat it, why would she put a ribbon on it?"

"I don't know, why do they put little pants on lamb chops?"

Our conversation was cut short by a rank stench as Mrs. Filmore entered the room. By all the angels in Heaven, did she actually smell worse? How could that possibly be achieved? She gazed at me and Stuart in a most unfriendly manner.

"I was going to go home, but perhaps I should stay and keep an eye on you two."

Lisa made a show of opening a window. "Sure, why not? It's not like you have anything else to do, like say take a bath, maybe?"

I was scandalised. "Lisa!" I reprimanded.

Mrs. Filmore was likewise affronted. "How dare you! I don't stink!"

Stuart poured himself a glass of wine from a bottle he had brought with him. "Madam, I beg to differ, I have been dead since 1666 and even I do not smell as badly as you."

"Stuart!" I said, horrified. True as that may be, one hardly speaks of such things to the offender's face.

Mrs. Filmore stormed out of the cabin in a rage. I hid my face in my hands, shaking my head as Marc and Mrs. Barber fought to keep their amusement under control.

"Oh, come on, Deirdre," Stuart said. "Another few minutes of that stench and I would have done myself an injury if that reek hadn't done it for me."

"And it's getting worse!" said Lisa. "I mean when she first arrived she was just kinda smelly, and you could ignore it. Now she stinks like a broken fridge."

"It *is* getting worse," said Marc. "But it's not an unbathed body smell, it's a rotten meat smell. Where is she sleeping, with a dead animal? Seriously, if she doesn't start taking a bath once in a while she can't come into my house anymore."

"I think we should check *her* house," said Lisa. "Maybe she's a serial killer. That's how they caught John Wayne Gacy. They could smell the bodies rotting in his crawl space."

"I find it very unlikely she is murdering people," I said. "No one in our little community has gone missing. It seems more likely she is immune to her own foul habits."

"I do think we should find a way to check her house," said Marc. "If she is leaving garbage to rot and collect maggots and then sleeping with that filth around she could spread any number of diseases. And Andy does not need to get sick. I think he's been through enough."

"We all have," said Mrs. Barber. "I still have nightmares about watching my neighbors get sick with that disease and turn into monsters."

"We all do," said Lisa quietly. She picked up a scone and began picking at it, nibbling small bits.

"So shall we examine the esteemed and fragrant Mrs. Filmore's home?" asked Stuart.

"Why don't we wait until morning?" said Marc. "Then I can go there under some pretence and see what she has happening."

"Or I could go now," said Stuart.

"Is that a good idea?" asked Martin. "She doesn't care for you much."

Stuart set down his glass, but not before draining it. "True as that may be, I do have a few tricks up my sleeve not available to you."

"Gonna turn into a bat?" Marc inquired, grinning.

Stuart and I exchanged glances. "These people know nothing of our kind," he said.

I helped myself to some of his wine. "I blame the Victorians—most of this nonsense is their doing."

"You blame the Victorians for everything. And Cromwell."

"I have *met* Cromwell, my darling. Everything *is* all his fault. They should have hung him *before* he died, not after."

"We shall discuss Cromwell another time," said Stuart, "I have old ladies to vex."

"Well we all must do such things as we do best. Vexing ladies is indeed your greatest talent."

He kissed me then silently departed the room just as Elyse returned from Andy's room, holding an empty plate. She gave me a smile.

"The scones were a huge hit. Andy loved them. I'm just going to give him a couple more." She looked around. "Where is Stuart?"

"We sent him on a mission," said Marc. He looked up as his twin brother Martin appeared, eating a sandwich.

"Beer run?" inquired Elyse.

"To find out why Mrs. Filmore smells so bad."

"Yeah, she really needs to do something about that," said Elyse. "I wouldn't let her into Andy's room; the stink was so bad I was scared he would catch something."

"That's why we sent Stuart over to look into it," said Marc. "If she's living in mountains of garbage and waste then she can't stay here. I think we've all had our fair share of plague."

"Hear, hear," I said.

"Yeah, no kidding," mumbled Lisa.

Stuart returned within the hour, appearing with spectral silence in the doorway of the little house in which we were gathered.

"Did you find anything?" I asked.

"I found nothing strange or out of place. I saw no garbage, nor filth of any manner. The house is neat as a pin. But it does smell, though from the inhabitant or more sinister reasons, I could not say.

"So she's just a smelly old woman," said Martin.

"So it would seem," said Stuart. "But I do find it very odd the smell is that of dead meat."

"Nothing we can do about that," said Martin. "Does the cabin have a crawl space?"

"It does, and I checked it," said Stuart. "I found nothing more than Lisa's pig."

Martin looked to Lisa. "That black monster is yours?"

"Sorta," said Lisa. "I've been feeding it muffins."

"It gives me the chills. I've seen it standing on the shore a few times. It just… stares. And the eyes are red."

"She won't hurt anyone," said Lisa quietly. "Her name is Valerie. She's just a hairy, black pig., She wouldn't hurt anyone."

Martin gazed at Lisa, as if wondering if there was not more to the black pig than he knew. Mrs. Barber seemed to have no such questions as she hefted her considerable self from the couch upon which she had been seated.

"It's bedtime for me. I want to get up early to put a turkey in the oven."

"Turkey?" said Martin. "Where did you get a turkey?"

"The house we moved into had a freezer full of stuff," said Mrs. Barber. "Ducks, chickens, pork, beef, fish… there's enough food in there for months."

"My friend Valerie lived there," said Lisa. "Her parents had been laying in food for the winter."

"Oh, we'll have to thank them when we see them," said Mrs. Barber.

"You won't see them," said Lisa softly. She then added, "I… named the pig after my friend."

There was a long, uncomfortable silence. Mrs. Barber said an awkward goodnight and then departed, heading into the night.

"We should leave as well," I said. "Do let us know if we may be of any service."

Marc nodded. "We will. Thank you."

Stuart, Lisa, and I departed for home, Florence peering from her bag and sniffing at the cold winter air. We walked down the trail to the lake shore and followed it to our own home, entering gratefully. Lisa went to build up the fire, while I took Florence from her bag to place her back in her cage.

"So you truly found nothing?" I inquired of Stuart.

"No," he said. "But that does not mean there is nothing to find, and you and I both know that an old woman who smells of rancid flesh may be more than she seems. I would wager good wine she is keeping secrets. I find it most interesting that she alone chooses to despise us when the rest of our neighbours are willing to forgive us our sin of being undead."

"That may not be so strange an idea," I said. "We performed one noble act. If she has lost family to the legions of undead that walk the land now she may not be so swift to forgive. And then she is insulted on top of all."

"If she does not wish to be insulted then she should take care not to do things that warrant insult." He sighed loudly. "I am starving."

"As am I," I said. "Animals are fine for a while, but they do not satisfy the blood lust. We should feed ere we grow so hungry we commit an act that is less noble than saving a child."

"Whom shall we visit? The Barbers?"

"Nay, I think not. They have taken to growing potted garlic in their bedroom. I believe we are suspect in our misdeed."

Stuart laughed. "What about the esteemed Mr. Brandon?"

"We cannot both feed upon the same man, that will take too much out of him. You bite Mr. Brandon. I shall visit Miss Megan. How I wish for an invasion of thugs and brigands that we may drink our fill!"

"Take heart, dear one. I am certain there must be a few ne'er-do-wells roaming about the island. As for me I think I shall bite Mr. Brandon and the new fellow who lives at the top of the hill, Mr. Aster."

"Why two?" I inquired.

He kissed me. "So I have hot blood enough in my veins to fully express my appreciation of your beauty."

I laughed. "Then feed quickly. I shall be waiting."

Chapter Ten

I awoke early the next evening and knew in my heart something was not right with Stuart. It took nearly all my strength to waken him, and he looked not at all as a vampire should after having fed well the night before. He was weak and grey and shaken, and he seemed confused in his mind. He returned to sleep only a few minutes after waking, and I remained at his side, fear gnawing at my heart. Clearly something plagued him, but I could not think what that may be. Were vampires subject to illness? The strain was nearly more than I could bear, and when at last Stuart finally roused himself from sleep, he asked me that very question.

"It would seem the answer is yes," I said. "Did you dream?"

"I do not believe so, but… several times I thought I felt a weight upon my chest. A nightmare perhaps, or a hag.

"Do such things trouble the likes of us?" I asked.

"Well *something* certainly is. Honestly, Deirdre, I'm frightened to go to sleep! You turned your back on the thing you saw in your dream. I did not. That seems to be part of the riddle."

"There is no riddle here, only a monster whose name we do not yet know," I said.

"We had best learn it quickly." He raised his head as there was a knock at the kitchen door, and the sound of Lisa's voice as she greeted someone. Soon there came the sound of voices and laughter.

"I do believe Lisa is throwing a Christmas party," I said.

"How nice of her to have let us know. I suppose I shall have to attempt to be charming."

"You will do no such thing. Rest. I will go downstairs and help Lisa entertain her guests."

"And what will you say when they inquire as to my whereabouts?"

"I shall give them the awful truth and tell them you shall return."

"Such a darling you are.

I kissed him tenderly, then dressed in my finest gown — a creation found whilst looting a fabric shop after nibbling the neighbors. It was made of pink and gold satin. I do love to sew, which is fortunate because the gowns I choose to wear have not been fashionable for centuries, but it was nice to not have to labor. My vanity was stroked greatly when my appearance was met with applause. I curtseyed.

"Greetings, dear guests!"

"You look absolutely lovely," said Martin. He then proceeded to show me his arm. "By the way, did you do this?"

"Certainly not! I am a married woman., I do not go about biting *men*!"

"I am noticing the qualifier, there," he said dryly.

"Champagne?" I offered, my fan a-flutter.

"I suffer from anaemia. You and your little boyfriend are not helping."

"Where *is* Stuart?" asked Lisa.

"He is in bed," I said. "He is not well."

"Biting anaemics will have that effect on a vampire," said Martin.

"Oh, hush," said Elyse. "A spider did that."

"Big spider," Martin grumbled.

Lisa meanwhile was gazing at me with an odd expression. "He's sick? How can he be sick? He's *dead*."

"Yes, well that *is* the question we have been asking ourselves," I said.

"Don't you have any idea what could be causing it?" she asked.

"I have thoughts on the matter, but no proof."

Megan had approached, a glass of wine in her had. "What are his symptoms?"

"Weak, pale, exhausted—"

"See?" said Martin. "He was up biting anaemics."

"Martin, give it a rest," said Elyse. "Stuart hasn't bitten anyone. If he had, somebody would have turned into one by now, and vampires bite on the neck, not the arm."

I never thought I would be thankful for erroneous beliefs, but in that moment I was indeed. Stuart and I did our best not to feed upon our neighbours, and our reasons for this were many. Foremost was not wishing to have them rise up against us.

"Whatever the reason," I said, "I would like to learn the nature of his malady ere it afflicts us all."

Megan toasted me with her glass. "Hear, hear. Now let's go take a look at Mr. Tall, Dark, and Undead.

Ordinarily I would ask him if he's getting enough sunlight, but that seems in really poor taste."

"Quite," I said stiffly.

Together we ascended the stairs to the attic, where Stuart and I had made our bedroom. He was face down in the pillows when we entered, and he did not seem especially glad of company.

"One of you had better have wine and the other be naked," he grumbled.

"Megan came to have a look at you," I said.

"She's seen me."

"Stuart..."

He rolled onto his back. "Deirdre, I sincerely doubt there is anything the esteemed young lady can do for me."

"You do look anaemic," said Megan.

"Hooray, I *feel* anaemic. May I go back to sleep now?"

"Stuart don't be rude," I chastised.

"My problem, dear ladies, is not anaemia."

"Well what is it, then?" asked Megan.

"If I knew, I would put an end to it. All I know is I had a nightmare the other night, which is a *most* singular thing for a vampire to experience, and since then I have not been right. I suspect it is no malady, but a hag."

I noticed Megan did not protest the existence of such a monster. The past months of horror had made believers of all those who now called the lake home.

"Well in that case, we had best start reading up on hags," she said simply.

* * *

We did not begin reading about hags that very moment. We returned to Lisa's party, where Florence reigned supreme as mistress of the ball, resplendent in her pink gown. She was sitting in a shallow box, nibbling a variety of treats. Andy, who was not well enough at all to be attending parties but nonetheless had talked his parents into bringing him, was hand feeding her morsels of spinach. He gave me a wide smile as he saw me.

"Hi! Thank you for saving me from the bad monster."

"You are very welcome," I said, seating myself in a chair beside his. "How are you feeling?"

"Sore. And I don't like the dark anymore. I don't know if I will ever be able to sleep without the light on again."

"Well there is no need," I said. "So long as it makes you feel better."

"Yeah." He pulled up the leg of his pants to show me his bandages. "That's where he bit me. Mommy and Daddy and Megan were cleaning an' cleaning an' cleaning for ages so I wouldn't get sick. Now I have to take medicine an' I can't walk because it hurts too bad. Would he have eaten me up?"

"Yes," I said quietly. "He would have."

"I'm really glad you were there. But you looked pretty scary, too! Rar!"

He gave me his best vampire impression, complete with fangs, which he made by dangling his fingers by his mouth. I was not amused, I dare say, but since this was a child I chose to overlook my displeasure at seeing myself portrayed thusly.

"I was a little angry," I said.

"You totally kicked his ass."

Just the sort of statement my mother longed to hear regarding her daughter, I am sure.

"Would you like some scones?" I asked.

"Yes, please!"

"Then scones you shall have." I left him in his chair and made my way into the kitchen to fetch some.

* * *

The night grew long, and the party ended, leaving Lisa, Megan and I gathered at a table as Megan searched for any lore she might find on her laptop.

"I've found some information about hags," Megan said. "I can't seem to find anything really definitive, so some of this is going to be guess-work. It says here that when night comes, the hag is free to either shed her skin or leave her body. That would seem to imply they're capable of appearing as something else during the day. To reach the home of her victim, she will capture a horse and ride it hard, tangling its mane and tail into knots that can never be undone, and nearly crippling it from beating it to run so hard that it nearly dies of the strain."

"Nice," said Lisa.

"We have no horses here," I said.

"No horses that we know of," said Megan. "We should look in the daytime and see if we can find one stabled nearby. It may not even be a literal horse; in this day and age it could just as easily be a stolen car."

"We should still look," said Lisa.

Megan nodded, continuing to read from the screen of the small computer. "The hag will ride her victim night after night, sitting on his chest and smothering him, stealing his voice so he cannot cry out for help. If struck, the hag is said to have the feel of cold meat. She is also said to be invisible, although some have claimed to have seen her hideous visage."

"What does it say about killing it?" asked Lisa.

"Not much," said Megan. "Supposedly if you can catch it, you can throw it into the fire. Oh, look. This page says they can come in the day, too. There's not really a lot about how to get rid of a hag, and the only advice I can find is *"don't sleep on your back."* Not terribly helpful, especially since it says also that not sleeping on your back is no guarantee she won't come bother you anyway."

"Why bother Stuart?" I cried, frustrated. "Is not the purpose of the hag's rides to kill the sleeper? He's already dead!"

"No, he's *un*-dead," said Megan. "And not a stumbling, mumbling zombie but an intelligent form of supernatural being. This *may* be territorial. If the hag sees having a couple vampires lurking around the only humans for miles she may think it's a better idea to get rid of them than share. Personally, I would rather share space with you two than this hag, whatever it is. I suggest someone watch over you and Stuart while you sleep."

There came a sudden sound upon the roof, and we froze in fear, looking upwards as something moved quietly over the shingles.

"What in Hell is that?" asked Lisa.

"I believe the question you wish to ask is 'what *from* Hell is that?' And I do not know, but if it is on the roof then we had best tend to the fire before it decides to come down the chimney," I said.

Lisa tore out of the room and thundered downstairs, racing to the fireplace to heap wood upon the flame. Megan and I hurried after her, and were just in time to hear her cry out in horror.

"Something is looking in the window!"

Something was indeed looking in through the window — a leering green face with masses of tangled and filthy white hair. The shrivelled lips were pulled back over blackened and rotting teeth, and it scraped at the glass with fingernails grown into long, blackened talons. I recognized the creature as one of the *Chiang-shih* whom Stuart and I had met in the graveyard.

"Begone!" I screamed at the unholy wretch. "There is nothing here for you!"

"You are wrong," it said, grinning at Megan. "There is much here to appease the hungry dead! Now I know why you tried to send my brothers and me south! You wished to keep the feast for yourself!"

"There is no feast here, monster," I said. "Return from whence you came!"

"No, I do not think we will do that."

Megan uttered a sound of fear, and I turned to see she was gazing through the large living room window to the lake shore. Moving along the water's edge were two more hideous forms, their bodies stiffened and dried, their nails grown into claws. They seemed unable to move their limbs, as if death had robbed them of all suppleness. They moved in a strange hopping manner, bending as little as possible as they came towards the cabin.

"What are they?" asked Megan.

"They are *Chiang-shih*," I replied. "Chinese hopping ghosts."

"Just ghosts?" she asked hopefully.

"I do not understand what you would mean by 'just ghosts.' If they catch you, they will violate your body as they drain your blood."

Megan looked horrified. "Oh, no. Oh, no, that is *not* happening. What do we do?"

"Why are you asking me?"

"You're the vampire!"

"That hardly makes me a repository of all knowledge regarding the undead!" I called to the chamber above our heads as loudly as I was able. *"Stuart!"*

Poor, brave Stuart rose to the challenge, though I did not know of how much use he would be in this matter. He looked positively ill as he came down the stairs, clad only in his jeans and boots. He regarded the monster at the window with little humour, and snatched up the bloodied axe that had been taken from the creature that had attacked Andy.

"There is no prey for you here," he said, his tone cold and threatening.

The sight of the axe seemed to deter the thing, and it retreated quickly, hopping like some disgusting and rotting marionette. Lisa pounced on her phone and began calling the neighbours to warn them not to emerge from their homes, however, she had only just managed to contact Elyse before we heard screams. Someone had been walking in the Christmas Eve snow, and was paying dearly for the pleasure. Fools that we are, all four of us raced into the night to do battle.

The *Chiang-shih* had not gone far for their next meal. Ellen Harper and her sister Sarah were dwelling at the farthest end of the shore, the last house before the river that drew its water from the lake cut through the land. Both women were being torn and bitten as their clothes were ripped away, their bodies being cut by filthy talons as the monsters assailing them satisfied their unholy wants all at once. To be taken by force is a horror no woman should have to endure, but to have her attacker be a stiffened corpse is a nightmare from which none could recover.

Stuart used the axe to remove the head of one of the monsters as a golfer strikes a ball, one hard swung crushing and chopping the dried skull. I dragged the monster from Ellen's body, but saw, from the blood flowing from her throat and thighs, that salvation had come too late.

As a second creature continued assailing Sarah, the third rose up against us, shrieking. It lunged for Stuart, and he grappled with it as Megan and I did our best to save poor Sarah. Megan grabbed the filthy white hair and pulled, but it simply came away from the skull with a sound like tearing sod. Sarah was screaming for help as Megan and I kicked and tore at her attacker, but it was not until I snatched up Stuart's discarded axe and struck it in the head that it was slain. I pulled the monster off of her body, but again we were too late, and we could do nothing more than watch the life fade from her eyes.

Megan did her best to stop poor Ellen's bleeding, but her efforts were in vain. Sarah and Ellen were dead.

"Start a fire!" I called to Lisa, and then joined the fight between Stuart and the last *Chiang-shih*.

The thing was green, and its eyes shone with a vile, unhealthy jade light. I chopped at one of the stiff and dried legs, and it came away with ease as Stuart tried to throttle it with his bare hands. He seemed to be gaining victory, but then he drew a loud gasp, and collapsed as if struck violently from behind. He fell to the ground, and the *Chiang-shih* screeched in victory as it dove upon him, seeking to feed its hideous wants. I put an end to its passion with a violent stroke of the axe, and watched as it turned to dusty broken bits.

I could hear Megan weeping as I helped Stuart from the ground, drawing him close and holding him, letting the axe fall from my hand as I did so. He was clearly weak and in a great deal of pain, and when I turned him around to look at his back, I saw that he had been struck a brutal blow by what appeared to be two enormous fists. Something invisible had attacked him.

"Seat yourself," I said softly. "We shall tend to the dead."

Stuart seated himself on the ground, weakened and unwell. Lisa, Megan, and I started a blaze in a small fire pit that had long ago been set up for family barbecues and marshmallow roasts. Tonight it saw a roast of a very different kind, as the bodies of the *Chiang-shih* were burned to ash.

"What'll we do with Sarah and Ellen?" asked Lisa.

"Stuart and I will take them across the river to that narrow strip of land between this shore and the next," I said. "They will rest peacefully. And if they should rise, the running water will prevent them from troubling anyone else."

We put the two women into Peter's small boat, and took them to the strip of land across the little river. Once we were well out of sight of any prying eyes, Stuart and I feasted on Sarah's cooling blood. It was not an ideal meal for either of us, but it would leave us both well-sated for days. Ellen had bled to death when her assailant bit her, but Sarah appeared to have died from the sheer horror of having her body violated by the walking dead.

After we took what blood she had, we buried her and her sister in the soft black earth in a natural trench beneath some yew and pine trees. We then left them in silence in their winter grave. I hoped they were indeed at peace and would not awaken to moan in the night.

I have seen merrier Christmas Eves.

Ensuring we were free of any traces of blood, we returned to Megan and Lisa, who were finishing burning the *Chiang-shih*. We then returned to our cabin, where Stuart eased himself down upon a couch, clearly in pain.

"Something attacked me," he said. "When I was throttling the *Chiang-shih*."

"The same assailant who is haunting your dreams, no doubt," I said.

Megan seated herself upon a chair, looking lost and confused. "Poor Ellen and Sarah. They didn't deserve that."

"No," I said quietly. "They did not. No one deserves such a ghastly fate."

"Why are they coming back?" asked Lisa as she seated herself beside Megan. "The news said that the monsters were still all down near the southern part of the island. We haven't seen anything in weeks. Now suddenly we have that thing with the iron jaws biting Andy, and those... *corpses*... attacking Sarah and Ellen. Why are they coming back?"

"I do not know," I said softly. "But something is drawing them here."

"Or someone," said Megan wearily. "The website we looked at did say hags are able to shed their skin. That implies they can change their appearance."

"The site said nothing about them calling forth other creatures." I said. "And if it is attempting to rid the area of Stuart and myself, why call in other creatures? Will it then not be compelled to chase them away as well?"

"Perhaps not," said Stuart as he lay upon the couch, an arm draped over his eyes. "Perhaps what is happening is the few undead still in the area are sensing live flesh, and there are two rather daunting protectors driving off that which would feed upon hot, living blood. So they send in a hag to weaken us, and once we are unable to fight, we will be destroyed, and the other vile monsters of the dark will arrive to take what they may."

Megan and Lisa both looked terrified. "We can't let them do that!" said Lisa. "Not just because I don't wanna get eaten, but you guys are all the family I have! I don't wanna be alone! We have to stop this hag!"

"The website said that one man managed to catch a hag and throw it into the fire," said Megan. "That seemed to kill it. Maybe today, when you and Stuart are asleep, Lisa and I can keep watch."

"Then you will need to rest," I said. "It is late, and you are sad and weary. Sleep. And tomorrow I hope you catch the thing we seek."

There was a low, plaintive moaning in the distance, and without bothering to look, we all knew from whence the sound came. It was a shroud eater.

"I have to get some sleep," said Lisa. "I can't face anything else."

"It is far away," said Stuart. "We will turn off the lights and do nothing to draw its attention."

Lisa said nothing further. She rose from the chair and went upstairs to shower and go to bed. I glanced at Megan.

"You are welcome to stay here," I said quietly.

"Thanks. I don't really want to go out into the dark."

Megan showered after Lisa was done, and soon Stuart and I were the only beings awake in the house.

"We are hypocrites, you know," I said. "Posing as protectors when we are preying upon these people as much as any other night crawler."

"We are not," Stuart said. "We take a little to sustain ourselves, nothing more. We have killed no one."

"I still feel like a hypocrite. They are looking to us as saviours."

"Then let us be saviours. At least from us they will see mercy and protection. That must be worth a little blood. They would lose more than blood if we were to depart."

"You are right," I said. "But I still feel as if I am no better than those horrors that preyed upon poor Sarah and Ellen."

"We take no more than we need. And speaking of 'taking,', the ladies here are in no fear that I shall do unto them as the hopping ghosts did. Do not trouble yourself, Deirdre. We are not the monsters in this situation, and I for one do not think that leaving these people undefended will do them any favours. All it will do is save my own tattered hide."

"I happen to be rather fond of your tattered hide."

He smiled, his arm still flung across his eyes. "As am I. But there is no certainty that leaving will save me from the hag. If she is determined to see me dead, then dead I shall be. No, we are far better staying here, Deirdre."

"I would like to know the name of this hag," I said.

"As would I, but as of yet we have no idea whom it may be. Our only suspect thus far is an old woman with a terrible odour."

"That is growing steadily worse," I said. "When first she arrived, her reek was ignorable. Her stench now has reached such levels as to be an offense to God."

"And may be nothing more than an untended wound she has chosen to let fester than bother anyone for medical supplies we can hardly spare."

"If that is indeed the case then pray let her ask! I can endure her no more! But such a stink does need looking into, be it wound or something more sinister. If she sickens then our medical supplies shall be even more strained by tending to a serious illness."

"Then let us speak to her in the evening." He lowered his arm as the shroud eater moaned in the distance. "Had I strength in my body I would kill that thing. I do not like it roaming free."

"We shall tend to it in due time as well," I said. "In the meantime, I shall make tea."

"Florence and I would like scones if any are left."

"A few. Clotted cream?"

"Yes, and honey, please. Oh, and lemon for the tea."

I managed a smile, then leaned over Florence's cage. She regarded me with blank black eyes. "And would you care for a scone as well, Miss Florence?"

She clucked and squeaked. I assumed this was an affirmative.

* * *

Megan stayed by our bed as we slept, reading a book and sipping coffee. Stuart slept face down in the pillows, whilst I chose to sleep upon my side. Her presence seemed to deter the hag, and Stuart awoke in better spirits than he had yesterday. It was Christmas day, or rather the eve of Christmas day when we awoke, and despite the loss of two more members of our tiny village, the holiday was in full swing as we came downstairs. Lisa was serving a Christmas feast fit for a royal hall as Stuart and I emerged from our slumber. The adults struggled for levity for the sake of the children, though I could sense a shroud of fear looming over all. Stuart approached the table and gazed down at one dish in particular.

"What, pray tell, is that?"

"Blood pudding," said Martin.

Stuart put a hand over his mouth and turned grey. "And what unforgiveable misdeed have I visited upon you that you torment me thusly?"

Elyse seemed positively victorious. "See!? I've been telling Marin for *years* not even a vampire would eat that!"

"Yeah!" chimed in Andy.

"What are you complaining about?" said Martin. "If it was called 'chestnut pudding' then you wouldn't have a problem with it!"

"Yes, I would, because it would *still* be a black congealed mass of blood," said Elyse.

"The only thing that could possibly make blood pudding more offensive is to serve it with…" Stuart blanched visibly. "Head cheese."

Stuart and Elyse indulged in a profound shudder of distaste.

"Well, Merry Christmas to you, too," said Martin. "All the more for me."

Mrs. Barber seemed to be enjoying Martin's pudding as well. "Where is Mrs. Filmore? Has anyone seen her?"

"Not since I told her she smelled," said Lisa.

"I'll call her," said Mrs. Barber. "At least to see if she is all right."

I seated myself at the table and served myself tiny amounts of the feast—turkey with cranberries, yams, stuffing, and some of Martin's blood pudding. I picked and nibbled my way through it as Mrs. Barber managed to contact the pungent Mrs. Filmore.

"Hello dear, we were just sitting down to Christmas dinner and wondering where you were!"

"And worried you might show up before we're done eating," said Marc very quietly. Elyse punched his shoulder.

Mrs. Barber finished her call and closed her phone, putting it away. "She says she's not feeling well and is going to bed early. You know, despite the fact that she does have an odour problem, she has been quite nice to all of us. We should try to be more supportive."

"No one is debating her kindness," said Stuart. He was not eating, but he was having a little wine.

"I'm not so certain about that," said Martin. "She's taken quite a serious dislike to Deirdre and Stuart."

"In part no doubt due to certain remarks voiced by the latter," I said.

Marc and Elyse exchanged glances, then Elyse cleared her throat.

"I would not be so certain about that. The night you saved Andy, she was talking about staking the both of you."

I coughed in surprise. "I beg your pardon?! *Staking* us? For *what*, precisely? I do not pretend to be blameless and without sin, but in this case I must say I fail to see how saving a child is a crime worthy of execution."

"That's pretty much what I said, though not as well," said Elyse. "Look, no one is going to let her hurt you. But frankly, I don't care if she smells or not, she's got a lot of nerve trying to rouse a lynch mob to go after you and Stuart. Andy wouldn't be alive if you hadn't shown up. Martin and I certainly were not strong enough to chase that thing off."

"What kind of a monster was it?" Andy asked.

"The kind that bites," said Stuart.

Andy rolled his eyes and dropped the subject. "I wish adults would just *tell* you when they don't know something," he muttered.

"If it's a choice between who stays and who goes, I vote for Mrs. Filmore to leave," said Mr. Barber.

"We're not making anyone leave," said Megan. "She's just an angry old woman who has probably lost as much as we have. No one wanted this to happen. We're all just doing the best we can. She has every right to be scared. We just won't let her do anything to hurt anyone else. And if she does, *then* we toss her out on her wrinkled old ass."

"That's it," said Stuart. "I'm done. Bad enough my evening begins with thoughts of blood pudding and head cheese, I now have it combined with an image of Mrs. Filmore's hindquarters. If anybody wants me, I shall be looking for something pleasant on the television in the next room. Perhaps a nice autopsy show."

"I brought a copy of *'Scrooge'* with Alistair Sims!" said Elyse.

"Wonderful! I love that movie."

We paused as we heard the distant moan of a shroud eater.

"He's still out there," said Elyse.

"Have you seen it?" asked Mrs. Barber.

"No. I think it's still pretty far away. Sound really carries around here at night, I've noticed."

"Wonder if it's my dad?" Lisa mused softly.

There was a long, uncomfortable silence. At last I could stand it no more and rose to my feet.

"Since Lisa was so good as to prepare for us this wondrous feast, then I shall show my appreciation by serving desert. Who would like pie?"

"Me!" said Andy.

"Shocking," I said, "I would never have thought a small boy would care for pie."

* * *

The day promised to be black and stormy as Stuart and I readied for bed. Megan took up her post in our room, and soon he and I were deep in unholy rest, still and cold and silent as we lay in our bed.

I was awakened well before evening by the sound of screaming, and a battle ensuing in the room. I sat up and spied Megan grappling with a vague, shadowy form. She was crying out for help, and I rose from the bed to assist her, and we fought with it.

Though it could not be seen, it smelled and felt like a slab of cold meat. We had nearly managed to fling it into the fire, but at the last moment it escaped, and shot from the room, slamming doors in its wake. I pulled the door open and ran after it and into the dark, icy day, only to be confronted with yet another horror. It was none other than poor Peter, standing in the rain and moaning. He and I spied another in the same instant, and he was upon me in a moment. I screamed for assistance as he caught me, biting a great lump of flesh and cloth from my shoulder.

    It was Lisa who arrived first, and she wept openly as she struck at the beast that had once been her guardian. Megan and Martin arrived soon after, and the battle raged as Peter continued to do his very best to kill me.

    "Someone look after Stuart!" I cried, as I saw the same shadow that had fled the house return, dashing inside as we struggled with the shroud eater.

    Megan ran to defend Stuart whilst Martin jammed a brick into Peter's jaws with an audible breaking of teeth and bone. Lisa looked around for anything that might be used as a stake, dashing off to a small gardening shed and returning with all haste, holding a hoe. As Martin and I managed to fling the monster to the ground, she drove the hoe into its chest, pinning it to the earth. She and Martin then held it fast as I rushed for the axe, returning with it and severing the head from the gruesome being. I then left them to the task of burying it as I ran into the house, making my way up the stairs to the attic bedroom.

I entered and heard myself utter a strange, shrill cry as I saw a horrible sight—Megan lay upon the floor, blood rushing from an injury upon her head, while Stuart lay helpless on the bed, the shadow upon his chest as it sucked the life from his cold flesh. I leapt upon the shadow and tackled it to the ground, enraged that this creature of Hell and filth would dare harm my friends. We rolled and scratched and bit like cheap harlots fighting over a coin, and at last I managed to strike the thing in the face with all my might. It screamed in pain, and in that one moment I knew indeed the identity of the hag. It was indeed none other than the old woman we knew as Mrs. Filmore.

I was flung aside, and the monster fled the room once more. I gave chase, determined to not let it out of my sight. There would be no further opportunities to do harm to those I held dear. I was as the she-wolf when she chases the hind to feed her whelps. There would be no escape for this horror that had begged shelter from us—only destruction.

It ran far and fast, knowing that I would not cease my hunt. The day was dark as night, and the hours ticking toward evening meant I had time enough to continue for many hours. The shadow darted and dodged, and at last shot into a place that looked very familiar to me. Indeed, it was the same cave in which I had met Lisa. I ran into the cave, then seized furnishings, stones, rusting machinery, and anything else at hand which might be used to plug the door. The hag was trapped, and I with her. She had crept into the hole in which I had hidden with Florence months ago, perhaps hoping that I would not know of its existence.

I climbed into the hole and stood, raging at the sight of this disgusting and cowardly creature of nightmares and death. It gazed back at me, clad once more in the form of Mrs. Filmore.

"Prepare to meet your god of lies and filth," I said.

She smiled sweetly. "Do you not know who I am?"

"I neither know nor care. I will see you dead for all you have done."

"You should," she said. "You have met me before."

"I am hardly in the mood for tricks," I said.

"You know nothing of hags. What would you think of me if I were to look like this?"

As I watched she abruptly changed form, turning into the whore who had lain with my husband the night I killed him. Astounded, I could do little more than watch as she transformed next into Grey Mary, and then the old woman I had killed in Peter's cabin who had claimed to be the whore as well. I stared as she went through her guises, then turned into Mrs. Filmore once again and laughed.

"You killed the body I wore, but you did not kill me. I was all of those women. Seldom do my kind haunt the steps of the living dead, but *you*, my dear, are very special indeed! You are like a great ox in a field of mice! Every time I turn my head, you have stepped on me yet again! You killed poor Thomas, just when I was getting ready to take his body and his lands! Think of the souls I could have harvested with his wealth and power! And if that was not bad enough, you ensured the poor consort would be thrown into jail. Oh, she had a very hard life in there. When at last she managed to escape, she found me waiting, and I sucked the life from her breast and took her body. Before her, I wore the body of poor Grey Mary. How vexed and confused her poor mother was, when one night her precious daughter went to sleep merry and gay, and awoke drained of all her prettiness and charm. I do so love the souls of babes. They are by far the sweetest treat to devour. And the best part of all, I was paid good coin by the father to do it!"

I snarled very softly as she continued to smile sweetly, clearly enjoying her game.

"You killed the body I wore that night, months ago, and though I can cast illusions, I cannot cast them so well that it masks the smell of rot. I was desperate to find a new body. Yet there you were again, in my way, fancying yourself something other than the parasite you are. How dare you keep all that sweet meat to yourself? So I sought out what fair and kind folk were left in the area and called them to the feast. I had hoped to wear Sarah's body—I did so envy her full bosom and flowing hair. She would have been a lovely suit for a while, but when I found her, I saw I had been cheated, for you and your man-whore had taken all her blood. How am I to pass for a mortal woman with a suit of cold, reeking flesh?"

I did not say as much, but I felt Sarah would perhaps have rather given her blood to Stuart and myself than been worn by a hag.

"And so this play all began with you," I said. "You took the body of Grey Mary and made her a murderer, allowing my husband to follow his foul whims. And when night came, you dressed poor Mary up as a trollop and lay with him to take his body, and so his lands and the folk living there, so that you might feed upon their souls for years."

"It really was a very clever game, was it not?" said the hag. "Until you ruined it all by having the bad manners to leave your crypt. And I was kind enough to permit you to go on your way. Out of the goodness of my heart, I pursued you not. And when the time of the Great Rising came, I followed the other damned souls and Hell-kin to this island, and this very lake. I thought I had found a great prize when I happened upon the cabin with two young ladies and a strong man. Certainly, my horse was delighted. Ah, was there ever a more perfect mount for a hag than a Horse of St. Toader? No, I think not." Her expression soured. "And then who, of all the undead haunting this sick world, should arise to trouble me once again?" She pointed an accusing finger. "YOU."

"You cannot blame me for that; I believe it was Lisa who killed you." I smiled. "My, my, you do have the worst of luck, do you not? Slain by a little girl."

"I was not slain. As you can see, I lived. I can only be slain by fire, though my host body is not so fortunate. And now that you have caught me, I suppose you will start a great pyre and put an end to me."

I caught her and dragged her into the chamber of the Nosferatu, where he had, among other things, his coffin. I threw the hag into it, then, using old iron spikes and chisels left behind years ago by those who had been making tracks for the miners to set their coal carts upon, I nailed her firmly into the coffin, which I then closed and nailed the lid tight. Once this was done, I took up a pick and began the hack at the soft earth floor. The hag tapped against the casket.

"What are you doing?"

I shook my head. "You have taken enough, hag. You have taken my life, my babes, my home, and all the things I held dear. It took me many centuries to find another family, and you shall have it not. There will be no death for you. There will be no long and blessed sleep. There will only be a millennium of pain and loneliness. And if when at last you free yourself, if I still walk this land, I shall kill you then."

She began beating her fists upon the coffin lid. "You cannot do this to me! You cannot! How can you be so cruel?"

I laughed. "It is easy to be cruel! I daresay there are times it is even fun! How well I shall sleep, knowing at long last the bitter years of torment are over, and the murderer of my babies is at last imprisoned! And when I deem it time for my passing, I need only drown you in lamp-oil and set you aflame!"

She screamed and thrashed, but the iron spikes driven through her body and into the casket held fast as I dug the hole that would serve as her grave. When at last I deemed it deep enough, I dragged the coffin into it, taking care not to break the wood. Then I began to fill the hole with stones and dirt as the hag shrieked and pounded and pleaded for mercy. Gradually, the sound of her cries grew muffled, and I set aside the shovel. Then, as a final act to ensure she would trouble us no further, I pulled out several stout timbers that supported the roof of the cave, throwing them atop the grave before I left. The roof did not collapse immediately, and so I found a seat to watch the mound, until at last the weight of the stone above brought the entire thing down with a great rumbling boom I am certain could be heard for miles.

She lived yet, but imprisoned. I would feed her appetite for grief no more. Stuart had been right. I had lived long enough to see redemption, and I would not leave Lisa alone in this world. I still hold to the belief that the dead and the living are unsuitable company for one another, but if God chooses to make the cursed undead the guardians of the blessed living, who am I to question His will? I had time enough to mull the situation now. After all, I would need a new question with which to amuse myself, now that I at last had the old one answered. I know why I live yet, and am content.

I walked back to the cabin, filthy, exhausted, and weary to the bone. There awaiting me were Stuart and Lisa, and they greeted me tearfully.

"Where is Megan?" I asked.

"She's okay, she's resting," said Lisa. "Is it over? Are we safe?"

"The hag will trouble us no more," I said. "And now that she is no longer here to lure evil things to our little village, we are safe enough. For now I deem the worst is over, and my questions as to why I live yet are answered. I did not have many foes. I had but one, clad in the dead flesh of folk I knew. Now that she is safely entombed, the foul things shall leave the lake, or be destroyed."

"But we are still trapped here on the island," said Lisa.

"That we are," I said. "And the gates of Hell still swing free. Our adventure hath not ended. It has merely reached a peaceful lull that we may sleep easy in our beds. It is as fine a Christmas gift as we may hope for. Stuart shall recover and regain strength enough to torment us—"

"My lady I assure you I am quite capable of tormenting those around me, be I ill or well."

"—and I shall live to be tormented by him. And now I desire nothing more than tea and a bath."

We entered the house, and I paused as I spied a monstrous black boar standing within the kitchen, eating muffins from a plate. Clearly it had not placed them there on its own.

"Lisa," I said, "about Valerie—"

"Well, she *is* supposed to be a pet!"

"Lisa, she is a beast of plague and darkness."

"Please, Deirdre? She's my friend."

Oh, what joke is it of Satan that saddles us with emotional teen girls and denies us the heart with which to properly chastise them? I sighed with great weariness of spirit.

"If it pleases you, child, then she may stay."

Lisa squealed with delight and pounced on me, covering me with kisses, then sped away to perform some deed or other, likely pig-related. I stared at the Horror of the Bavarian Night as it gazed at me in return with eyes the colour of hellfire.

"Mark my words, if any break out with the Black Death, we will know whom to blame."

Valerie tossed her head and grunted, and finished her muffins. I sighed heavily.

"This is hardly a proper setting for a young lady," I said.

Stuart eased himself into a chair. "And which young lady might that be, Lisa or Valerie?"

I looked down at the pig. The pig looked up at me. I sighed once more.

"I swear on silent nights I can hear the distant sound of my mother whirling in her casket and rending her hair by the handful."

ABOUT THE AUTHOR

Alyx Jae Shaw is a writer of sci-fi, fantasy, and horror for a primarily LGBTQT+ audience. Her current (and in her own opinion, BEST work), is Gryphons, which can be found on Amazon, and was attacked by a right wing hate group for reasons that cannot be determined, as they had clearly never read it. She lives in Abbotsford British Columbia with her two pet chickens. It is believed the chickens write the novels themselves using Alyx as a mind-controlled meat-bag. Alyx is fond of cooking, mead-making, drawing and painting, and talks a lot of smack for someone who once lost an entire unopened can of paint in a small apartment.

https://www.facebook.com/alyx.j.shaw